THE SCARAB MURDER CASE

THE SCARAB
MURDER CASE

S. S. Van Dine

FELONY & MAYHEM PRESS • NEW YORK

All the characters and events in this work are fictitious.

THE SCARAB MURDER CASE

A Felony & Mayhem mystery

PRINTING HISTORY
First edition (Scribner's): 1930

Felony & Mayhem edition: 2019

Copyright © 1930 by Charles Scribner's Sons
Copyright renewed 1954 by Claire R. Wright

ISBN: 978-1-63194-200-6

Manufactured in the United States of America

Library of Congress Cataloging-in-Publication Data

Names: Van Dine, S. S., author. | Van Dine, S. S. Philo Vance.
Title: The scarab murder case / S.S. Van Dine.
Description: New York : Felony & Mayhem Press, 2019. | Series: Philo Vance
   | Summary: "In the 1920s, the world went Egypt-crazy, and even Philo Vance,
   that eminent scholar-sleuth, has some sympathy for the fad-though of course he
   knows lots more about the topic than anyone else. When a wealthy Egyptologist
   is murdered, with mysterious inscriptions and artifacts dotted round,
   it's only natural that John FS Markham calls Philo for help.
   After all, Markham is merely the New York District Attorney, whereas
   Philo Vance is...well, Philo Vance"-- Provided by publisher.
   Identifiers: LCCN 2019030893 | ISBN 9781631942006 (trade paperback) | ISBN
   9781631942082 (ebook)
Subjects: LCSH: Vance, Philo (Fictitious character)--Fiction. |
   Egyptologists--Fiction.
Classification: LCC PS3545.R846 S33 2019 | DDC 813/.52--dc23
LC record available at https://lccn.loc.gov/2019030893

Dedicated with appreciation to Ambrose Lansing, Ludlow Bull and Henry A. Carey of the Egyptian Department of the Metropolitan Museum of Art

La véritê n'a point cet air impétueux.

—*Boileau*

(HARA(TER) OF THE BOOK

PHILO VANCE

JOHN F.-X. MARKHAM   *District Attorney*
                                       of New York County

ERNEST HEATH   *Sergeant of the Homicide Bureau*

DR. MINDRUM W.C. BLISS   *Egyptologist; head*
                                      of the Bliss Museum
                                   of Egyptian Antiquities

BENJAMIN H. KYLE   *Philanthropist and art patron*

MERYT-AMEN   *Wife of Dr. Bliss*

ROBERT SALVETER   *Assistant Curator*
                            of the Bliss Museum; nephew
                                   of Benjamin H. Kyle

DONALD SCARLETT   *Technical Expert of the*
                             Bliss Expeditions in Egypt

ANÛPU HANI   *Family retainer of the Blisses*

BRUSH	*The Bliss butler*
DINGLE	*The Bliss cook*
HENNESSEY	*Detective of the Homicide Bureau*
SNITKIN	*Detective of the Homicide Bureau*
EMERY	*Detective of the Homicide Bureau*
GUILFOYLE	*Detective of the Homicide Bureau*
CAPTAIN DUBOIS	*Finger-print expert*
DETECTIVE BELLAMY	*Finger-print expert*
DR. EMANUEL DOREMUS	*Medical Examiner*
CURRIE	*Vance's valet*

The icon above says you're holding a copy of a book in the Felony & Mayhem "Vintage" category. These books were originally published prior to about 1965, and feature the kind of twisty, ingenious puzzles beloved by fans of Agatha Christie and John Dickson Carr. If you enjoy this book, you may well like other "Vintage" titles from Felony & Mayhem Press.

ELIZABETH DALY
   Unexpected Night
   Deadly Nightshade
   Murders in Volume 2
   The House without the Door
   Evidence of Things Seen
   Nothing Can Rescue Me
   Arrow Pointing Nowhere
   The Book of the Dead
   Any Shape or Form
   Somewhere in the House
   The Wrong Way Down
   Night Walk
   The Book of the Lion
   And Dangerous to Know
   Death and Letters
   The Book of the Crime

NGAIO MARSH
   A Man Lay Dead
   Enter a Murderer
   The Nursing Home Murder
   Death in Ecstasy
   Vintage Murder
   Artists in Crime
   Death in a White Tie
   Overture to Death
   Death at the Bar
   Surfeit of Lampreys
   Death and the Dancing Footman
   Colour Scheme
   Died in the Wool
   Final Curtain
   Swing, Brother, Swing
   Night at the Vulcan
   Spinsters in Jeopardy
   Scales of Justice
   Death of a Fool
   Singing in the Shrouds

NGAIO MARSH *(con't)*
False Scent
Hand in Glove
Dead Water
Killer Dolphin
Clutch of Constables
When in Rome
Tied Up in Tinsel
Black as He's Painted
Last Ditch
A Grave Mistake
Photo Finish
Light Thickens
Collected Short Mysteries

PATRICIA MOYES
Dead Men Don't Ski
The Sunken Sailor
Death on the Agenda
Murder à la Mode
Falling Star
Johnny Under Ground
Murder Fantastical

Death and the Dutch Uncle
Who Saw Her Die?
Season of Snows and Sins
The Curious Affair of the Third Dog
Black Widower
The Coconut Killings

LENORE GLEN OFFORD
Skeleton Key
The Glass Mask
The Smiling Tiger
My True Love Lies
The 9 Dark Hours

S. S. VAN DINE
The Benson Murder Case
The Canary Murder Case
The Greene Murder Case
The Bishop Murder Case

For more about these books, and other Felony & Mayhem titles, or to place an order, please visit our website at:

www.FelonyAndMayhem.com

THE SCARAB MURDER CASE

CHAPTER ONE

Murder!
(Friday, July 13; 11 a.m.)

PHILO VANCE WAS drawn into the Scarab murder case by sheer coincidence, although there is little doubt that John F.-X. Markham—New York's District Attorney—would sooner or later have enlisted his services. But it is problematic if even Vance, with his fine analytic mind and his remarkable flair for the subtleties of human psychology, could have solved that bizarre and astounding murder if he had not been the first observer on the scene; for, in the end, he was able to put his finger on the guilty person only because of the topsy-turvy clews that had met his eye during his initial inspection.

Those clews—highly misleading from the materialistic point of view—eventually gave him the key to the murderer's mentality and thus enabled him to elucidate one of the most complicated and incredible criminal problems in modern police history.

1

The brutal and fantastic murder of that old philanthropist and art patron, Benjamin H. Kyle, became known as the Scarab murder case almost immediately, as a result of the fact that it had taken place in a famous Egyptologist's private museum and had centred about a rare blue scarabæus that had been found beside the mutilated body of the victim.

This ancient and valuable seal, inscribed with the names of one of the early Pharaohs (whose mummy had, by the way, not been found at the time), constituted the basis on which Vance reared his astonishing structure of evidence. The scarab, from the police point of view, was merely an incidental piece of evidence that pointed somewhat obviously toward its owner; but this easy and specious explanation did not appeal to Vance.

"Murderers," he remarked to Sergeant Ernest Heath, "do not ordinarily insert their visitin' cards in the shirt bosoms of their victims. And while the discovery of the lapis-lazuli beetle is most interestin' from both the psychological and evidential standpoints, we must not be too optimistic and jump to conclusions. The most important question in this pseudo-mystical murder is why—and how—the murderer left that archæological specimen beside the defunct body. Once we find the reason for that amazin' action, we'll hit upon the secret of the crime itself."

The doughty Sergeant had sniffed at Vance's suggestion and had ridiculed his scepticism; but before another day had passed he generously admitted that Vance had been right, and that the murder had not been so simple as it had appeared at first view.

As I have said, a coincidence brought Vance into the case before the police were notified. An acquaintance of his had discovered the slain body of old Mr. Kyle, and had immediately come to him with the gruesome news.

It happened on the morning of Friday, July 13th. Vance had just finished a late breakfast in the roof-garden of his apartment in East Thirty-eighth Street, and had returned to the library to continue his translation of the Menander fragments found in the Egyptian papyri during the early years of the present century, when Currie—his valet and major-domo—shuffled into the room and announced with an air of discreet apology:

"Mr. Donald Scarlett has just arrived, sir, in a state of distressing excitement, and asks that you hasten to receive him."

Vance looked up from his work with an expression of boredom.

"Scarlett, eh? Very annoyin'... And why should he call on me when excited? I infinitely prefer calm people... Did you offer him a brandy-and-soda—or some triple bromides?"

"I took the liberty of placing a service of Courvoisier brandy before him," explained Currie. "I recall that Mr. Scarlett has a weakness for Napoleon's cognac."

"Ah, yes—so he has... Quite right, Currie." Vance leisurely lit one of his *Régie* cigarettes and puffed a moment in silence. "Suppose you show him in when you deem his nerves sufficiently calm."

Currie bowed and departed.

"Interestin' johnny, Scarlett," Vance commented to me. (I had been with Vance all morning arranging and filing his notes.) "You remember him, Van—eh, what?"

I had met Scarlett twice, but I must admit I had not thought of him for a month or more. The impression of him, however, came back to me now with considerable vividness. He had been, I knew, a college mate of Vance's at Oxford, and Vance had run across him during his sojourn in Egypt two years before.

Scarlett was a student of Egyptology and archæology, having specialized in these subjects at Oxford under Professor F. Ll. Griffith. Later he had taken up chemistry and photography in order that he might join some Egyptological expedition in a technical capacity. He was a well-to-do Englishman, an amateur and dilettante, and had made of Egyptology a sort of fad.

When Vance had gone to Alexandria Scarlett had been working in the Museum laboratory at Cairo. The two had met again and renewed their old acquaintance. Recently Scarlett had come to America as a member of the staff of Doctor Mindrum W.C. Bliss, the famous Egyptologist, who maintained a private museum of Egyptian antiquities in an old house in East Twentieth Street, facing Gramercy Park. He had called on Vance several times since his arrival in this country, and it was at Vance's apartment that I had met him. He had, however, never called without an invitation, and I was at a loss to understand his unexpected appearance this morning, for he possessed all of the well-bred Englishman's punctiliousness about social matters.

Vance, too, was somewhat puzzled, despite his attitude of lackadaisical indifference.

"Scarlett's a clever lad," he drawled musingly. "And most proper. Why should he call on me at this indecent hour? And why should he be excited? I hope nothing untoward has befallen his erudite employer... Bliss is an astonishin' man, Van—one of the world's great Egyptologists."*

I recalled that during the winter which Vance had spent in Egypt he had become greatly interested in the work of Doctor Bliss, who was then endeavoring to locate the tomb of Pharaoh Intef V who ruled over Upper Egypt at Thebes during the Hyksos domination. In fact, Vance had accompanied Bliss on an exploration in the Valley of the Tombs of the Kings. At that time he had just become attracted by the Menander fragments, and he had been in the midst of a uniform translation of them when the Bishop murder case interrupted his labors.

Vance had also been interested in the variations of chronology of the Old and the Middle Kingdoms of Egypt—not from the historical standpoint but from the standpoint of the evolution of Egyptian art. His researches led him to side with

---

* *Doctor Mindrum W.C. Bliss, M.A., A.O.S.S., F.S.A., F.R.S., Hon. Mem. R.A.S., was the author of "The Stele of Intefoe at Koptos"; a "History of Egypt during the Hyksos Invasion"; "The Seventeenth Dynasty"; and a monograph on the Amenhotep III Colossi.*

the Bliss-Weigall, or short, chronology* (based on the Turin Papyrus), as opposed to the long chronology of Hall and Petrie, who set back the Twelfth Dynasty and all preceding history one full Sothic cycle, or 1,460 years. After inspecting the art works of the pre-Hyksos and the post-Hyksos eras, Vance was inclined to postulate an interval of not more than 300 years between the Twelfth and Eighteenth Dynasties, in accordance with the shorter chronology. In comparing certain statues made during the reign of Amen-em-hêt III with others made during the reign of Thut-mosè I—thus bridging the Hyksos invasion, with its barbaric Asiatic influence and its annihilation of indigenous Egyptian culture—he arrived at the conclusion that the maintenance of the principles of Twelfth-Dynasty æsthetic attainment could not have been possible with a wider lacuna than 300 years. In brief, he concluded that, had the interregnum been longer, the evidences of decadence in Eighteenth-Dynasty art would have been even more pronounced.

These researches of Vance's ran through my head that sultry July morning as we waited for Currie to usher in the visitor. The announcement of Scarlett's call had brought back memories of many wearying weeks of typing and tabulating Vance's notes on the subject. Perhaps I had a feeling—what we loosely call a premonition—that Scarlett's surprising visit was in some way connected with Vance's æsthetico-Egyptological researches. Perhaps I was even then arranging in my mind, unconsciously, the facts of that winter two years before, so that I might cope more understandingly with the object of Scarlett's present call.

---

* According to the Bliss-Weigall chronology the period between the death of Sebk-nefru-Rê and the overthrow of the Shepherd Kings at Memphis was from 1898 to 1577 B.C.—to wit: 321 years—as against the 1800 years claimed by the upholders of the longer chronology. This short chronology is even shorter according to Breasted and the German school. Breasted and Meyer dated the same period as from 1788 to 1580. These 208 years, by the way, Vance considered too short for the observable cultural changes.

But surely I could have had not the slightest idea or suspicion of what was actually about to befall us. It was far too appalling and too bizarre for the casual imagination. It lifted us out of the ordinary routine of daily experience and dashed us into a frowsty, miasmic atmosphere of things at once incredible and horrifying—things fraught with the seemingly supernatural black magic of a Witches' Sabbat. Only, in this instance it was the mystic and fantastic lore of ancient Egypt—with its confused mythology and its grotesque pantheon of beast-headed gods—that furnished the background.

Scarlett almost dashed through the portières of the library when Currie had pulled back the sliding door for him to enter. Either the Courvoisier had added to his excitement or else Currie had woefully underrated the man's nervous state.

"Kyle has been murdered!" the newcomer blurted, leaning against the library table and staring at Vance with gaping eyes.

"Really, now! That's very distressin'." Vance held out his cigarette-case. "Do have one of my *Régies*... And you'll find that chair beside you most comfortable. A Charles chair: I picked it up in London... Beastly mess, people getting murdered, what? But it really can't be helped, don't y'know. The human race is so deuced blood-thirsty."

His indifference had a salutary effect on Scarlett, who sank limply into the chair and began lighting his cigarette with trembling hands.

Vance waited a moment and then asked:

"By the by, how do you know Kyle has been murdered?"

Scarlett gave a start.

"I saw him lying there—his head bashed in. A frightful sight. No doubt about it." (I could not help feeling that the man had suddenly assumed a defensive attitude.)

Vance lay back in his chair languidly and pyramided his long tapering hands.

"Bashed in with what? And lying where? And how did you happen to discover the corpse?... Buck up, Scarlett, and make an effort at coherence."

Scarlett frowned and took several deep inhalations on his cigarette. He was a man of about forty, tall and slender, with a head more Alpine than Nordic—a Dinaric type. His forehead bulged slightly, and his chin was round and recessive. He had the look of a scholar, though not that of a sedentary bookworm, for there was strength and ruggedness in his body; and his face was deeply tanned like that of a man who has lived for years in the sun and wind. There was a trace of fanaticism in his intense eyes—an expression that was somehow enhanced by an almost completely bald head. Yet he gave me the impression of honesty and straightforwardness—in this, at least, his British institutionalism was strongly manifest.

"Right you are, Vance," he said after a brief pause, with a more or less successful effort at calmness. "As you know, I came to New York with Doctor Bliss in May as a member of his staff; and I've been doing all the technical work for him. I have my diggings round the corner from the museum, in Irving Place. This morning I had a batch of photographs to classify, and reached the museum shortly before half past ten…"

"Your usual hour?" Vance put the question negligently.

"Oh, no. I was a bit latish this morning. We'd been working last night on a financial report of the last expedition."

"And then?"

"Funny thing," continued Scarlett. "The front door was slightly ajar—I generally have to ring. But I saw no reason to disturb Brush—"

"Brush?"

"The Bliss butler… So I merely pushed the door open and entered the hallway. The steel entrance door to the museum, which is on the right of the hallway, is rarely locked, and I opened it. Just as I started to descend the stairs into the museum I saw some one lying in the opposite corner of the room. At first I thought it might be one of the mummy cases we'd unpacked yesterday—the light wasn't very good—and then, as my eyes got adjusted, I realized it was Kyle. He was crumpled up, with his arms extended over his head… Even then I thought he had only fallen in a faint; and I started down the steps toward him."

He paused and passed his handkerchief—which he drew from his cuff—across his shining head.

"By Jove, Vance!—it was a hideous sight. He'd been hit over the head with one of the new statues we placed in the museum yesterday, and his skull had been crushed in like an egg-shell. The statue still lay across his head."

"Did you touch anything?"

"Good heavens, no!" Scarlett spoke with the emphasis of horror. "I was too ill—the thing was ghastly. And it didn't take half an eye to see that the poor beggar was dead."

Vance studied the man closely.

"I say, what was the first thing you did?"

"I called out for Doctor Bliss—he has his study at the top of the little spiral stairs at the rear of the museum…"

"And got no answer?"

"No—no answer… Then—I admit—I got frightened. Didn't like the idea of being found alone with a murdered man, and toddled back toward the front door. Had a notion I'd sneak out and not say I'd been there…"

"Ah!" Vance leaned forward and carefully selected another cigarette. "And then, when you were again in the street, you fell to worryin'."

"That's it precisely! It didn't seem cricket to leave the poor devil there—and still I didn't want to become involved… I was now walking up Fourth Avenue threshing the thing out with myself and bumping against people without seeing 'em. And I happened to think of you. I knew you were acquainted with Doctor Bliss and the outfit, and could give me good advice. And another thing, I felt a little strange in a new country— I wasn't just sure how to go about reporting the matter… So I hurried along to your flat here." He stopped abruptly and watched Vance eagerly. "What's the procedure?"

Vance stretched his long legs before him and lazily contemplated the end of his cigarette.

"I'll take over the procedure," he replied at length. "It's not so dashed complicated, and it varies according to circumstances. One may call the police station, or stick one's head out of the window and scream, or confide in a traffic officer, or simply ignore the corpse and wait for some one else to stumble on it. It amounts to the same thing in the end—the murderer is almost sure to get safely away… However, in the present case I'll vary the system a bit by telephoning to the Criminal Courts Building."

He turned to the mother-of-pearl French telephone on the Venetian tabouret at his side, and asked for a number. A few moments later he was speaking to the District Attorney.

"Greetings, Markham old dear. Beastly weather, what?" His voice was too indolent to be entirely convincing. "By the by, Benjamin H. Kyle has passed to his Maker by foul means. He's at present lying on the floor of the Bliss Museum with a badly fractured skull… Oh, yes—quite dead, I understand. Are you interested, by any chance? Thought I'd be unfriendly and notify you… Sad—sad… I'm about to make a few observations *in situ criminis*… Tut, tut! This is no time for reproaches. Don't be so deuced serious… Really, I think you'd better come along… Right-o! I'll await you here."

He replaced the receiver on the bracket and again settled back in his chair.

"The District Attorney will be along anon," he announced, "and we'll probably have time for a few observations before the police arrive."

His eyes shifted dreamily to Scarlett.

"Yes…as you say…I'm acquainted with the Bliss outfit. Fascinatin' possibilities in the affair: it may prove most entertainin'…" (I knew by his expression that his mind was contemplating—not without a certain degree of anticipatory interest—a new criminal problem.) "So, the front door was ajar, eh? And when you called out no one answered?"

Scarlett nodded but made no audible reply. He was obviously puzzled by Vance's casual reception of his appalling recital.

"Where were the servants? Couldn't they have heard you call?"

"Not likely. They're in the other side of the house—downstairs. The only person who could have heard me was Doctor Bliss—provided he'd been in his study."

"You could have rung the front door-bell, or summoned some one from the main hall," Vance suggested.

Scarlett shifted in his chair uneasily.

"Quite true," he admitted. "But—dash it all, old man!—I was in a funk…"

"Yes, yes—of course. Most natural. *Prima-facie* evidence and all that. Very suspicious, eh what? Still, you had no reason for wanting the old codger out of the way, had you?"

"Oh, my God, no!" Scarlett went pale. "He footed the bills. Without his support the Bliss excavations and the museum itself would go by the board."

Vance nodded.

"Bliss told me of the situation when I was in Egypt… Didn't Kyle own the property in which the museum is situated?"

"Yes—both houses. You see, there are two of 'em. Bliss and his family and young Salveter—Kyle's nephew—live in one, and the museum occupies the other. Two doors have been cut through, and the museum-house entrance has been bricked up. So it's practically one establishment."

"And where did Kyle live?"

"In the brownstone house next to the museum. He owned a block of six or seven adjoining houses along the street."

Vance rose and walked meditatively to the window.

"Do you know how Kyle became interested in Egyptology? It was rather out of his line. His weakness was for hospitals and those unspeakable English portraits of the Gainsborough school. He was one of the bidders for the *Blue Boy*. Luckily for him, he didn't get it."

"It was young Salveter who wangled his uncle into financing Bliss. The lad was a pupil of Bliss's when the latter

was instructor of Egyptology at Harvard. When he was gradu-
ated he was at a loose end, and old Kyle financed the expedition
to give the lad something to do. Very fond of his nephew, was
old Kyle."

"And Salveter's been with Bliss ever since?"

"Very much so. To the extent of living in the same house
with him. Hasn't left his side since their first visit to Egypt
three years ago. Bliss made him Assistant Curator of the
Museum. He deserved the post, too. A bright boy—lives and
eats Egyptology."

Vance returned to the table and rang for Currie.

"The situation has possibilities," he remarked, in his
habitual drawl… "By the by, what other members of the Bliss
ménage are there?"

"There's Mrs. Bliss—you met her in Cairo—a strange
girl, half Egyptian, much younger than Bliss. And then there's
Hani, an Egyptian, whom Bliss brought back with him—or,
rather, whom *Mrs.* Bliss brought back with *her.* Hani was an
old dependent of Meryt's father…"

"Meryt?"

Scarlett blinked and looked ill at ease.

"I meant Mrs. Bliss," he explained. "Her given name is
Meryt-Amen. In Egypt, you see, it's customary to think of a
lady by her native name."

"Oh, quite." A slight smile flickered at the corner of
Vance's mouth. "And what position does this Hani occupy in
the household?"

Scarlett pursed his lips.

"A somewhat anomalous one, if you ask me. Fellahîn
stock—a Coptic Christian of sorts. He accompanied old
Abercrombie—Meryt's father—on his various tours of exploration. When Abercrombie died, he acted as a kind of
foster-father to Meryt. He was attached to the Bliss expedition
this spring in some minor capacity as a representative of the
Egyptian Government. He's a sort of high-class handy-man
about the museum. Knows a lot of Egyptology, too."

"Does he hold any official post with the Egyptian Government now?"

"That I don't know…though I wouldn't be surprised if he's doing a bit of patriotic spying. You never can tell about these chaps."

"And do these persons complete the household?"

"There are two American servants—Brush, the butler, and Dingle, the cook."

Currie entered the room at this moment.

"Oh, I say, Currie," Vance addressed him; "an eminent gentleman has just been murdered in the neighborhood, and I am going to view the body. Lay out a dark gray suit and my Bangkok. A sombre tie, of course… And, Currie—the Amontillado first."

"Yes, sir."

Currie received the news as if murders were everyday events in his life, and went out.

"Do you know any reason, Scarlett," Vance asked, "why Kyle should have been put out of the way?"

The other hesitated almost imperceptibly.

"Can't imagine," he said, knitting his brows. "He was a kindly, generous old fellow—pompous and rather vain, but eminently likable. I'm not acquainted with his private life, though. He may have had enemies…"

"Still," suggested Vance, "it's not exactly likely that an enemy would have followed him to the museum and wreaked vengeance on him in a strange place, when any one might have walked in."

Scarlett sat up abruptly.

"But you're not implying that any one in the house—"

"My dear fellow!"

Currie entered the room at this moment with the sherry, and Vance poured out three glasses. When we had drunk the wine he excused himself to dress. Scarlett paced up and down restlessly during the quarter of an hour Vance was absent. He had discarded his cigarette and lighted an old briar pipe which had a most atrocious smell.

Almost at the moment when Vance returned to the library an automobile horn sounded raucously outside. Markham was below waiting for us.

As we walked toward the door Vance asked Scarlett:

"Was it custom'ry for Kyle to be in the museum at this hour of the morning?"

"No, most unusual. But Doctor Bliss had made an appointment with him for this morning, to discuss the expenditures of the last expedition and the possibilities of continuing the excavations next season."

"You knew of this appointment?" Vance asked indifferently.

"Oh, yes. Doctor Bliss called him by phone last night during the conference, when we were assembling the report."

"Well, well." Vance passed out into the hall. "So there were others who also knew that Kyle would be at the museum this morning."

Scarlett halted and looked startled.

"Really, you're not intimating—" he began.

"Who heard the appointment made?" Vance was already descending the stairs.

Scarlett followed him with puzzled, downcast eyes.

"Well, let me see... There was Salveter, and Hani, and..."

"Pray, don't hesitate."

"And Mrs. Bliss."

"Every one in the household, then, but Brush and Dingle?"

"Yes... But see here, Vance; the appointment was for eleven o'clock; and the poor old duffer was done in before half past ten."

"That's most inveiglin'," Vance murmured.

CHAPTER TWO

The Vengeance of Sakhmet
(Friday, July 13; 11.30 a.m.)

MARKHAM GREETED VANCE with a look of sour reproach.

"What's the meaning of this?" he demanded tartly. "I was in the midst of an important committee meeting—"

"The meaning is still to be ascertained," Vance interrupted lightly, stepping into the car. "The cause of your ungracious presence, however, is a most fascinatin' murder."

Markham shot him a shrewd look, and gave orders to the chauffeur to drive with all possible haste to the Bliss Museum. He recognized the symptoms of Vance's perturbation: a frivolous outward attitude on Vance's part was always indicative of an inner seriousness.

Markham and he had been friends for fifteen years, and Vance had aided him in many of his investigations. In fact, he had come to depend on Vance's assistance in the more complicated criminal cases that came under his jurisdiction.*

It would be difficult to find two men so diametrically opposed to each other temperamentally. Markham was stern, aggressive, straightforward, grave, and a trifle ponderous. Vance was debonair, whimsical, and superficially cynical—an amateur of the arts, and with only an impersonal concern in serious social and moral problems. But this very disparateness in their natures seemed to bind them together.

On our way to the museum, a few blocks distant, Scarlett recounted briefly to the District Attorney the details of his macabre discovery.

Markham listened attentively. Then he turned to Vance.

"Of course, it may be just an act of thuggery—some one from the street..."

"Oh, my aunt!" Vance sighed and shook his head lugubriously. "Really, y'know, thugs don't enter conspicuous private houses in broad daylight and rap persons over the head with statues. They at least bring their own weapons and choose *mises-en-scène* which offer some degree of safety."

"Well, anyway," Markham grumbled, "I've notified Sergeant Heath.† He'll be along presently."

---

* As legal adviser, monetary steward and constant companion of Philo Vance, I kept a complete record of the principal criminal cases in which he participated during Markham's incumbency. Four of these cases I have already recorded in book form—"The Benson Murder Case" (Scribners, 1926); "The Canary Murder Case" (Scribners, 1927); "The Greene Murder Case" (Scribners, 1928); and "The Bishop Murder Case" (Scribners, 1929).

† Sergeant Ernest Heath, of the Homicide Bureau, had worked with Markham on most of his important cases. He was an honest, capable, but uninspired police officer, who, after the Benson and the "Canary" murder cases, had come to respect Vance highly. Vance admired the Sergeant; and the two—despite their fundamental differences in outlook and training—collaborated with admirable smoothness.

At the corner of Twentieth Street and Fourth Avenue he halted the car. A uniformed patrolman who stood before a call-box, on recognizing the District Attorney, came to attention and saluted.

"Hop in the front seat, officer," Markham ordered. "We may need you."

When we reached the museum Markham stationed the officer at the foot of the steps leading to the double front door; and we at once ascended to the vestibule.

I made a casual mental note of the two houses, which Scarlett had already briefly described to us. Each had a twenty-five-foot frontage, and was constructed of large flat blocks of brownstone. The house on the right had no entrance—it had obviously been walled up. Nor were there any windows on the areaway level. The house on the left, however, had not been altered. It was three stories high; and a broad flight of stone stairs, with high stone banisters, led to the first floor. The "basement," as was usual in such structures, was a little below the street level. The two houses had at one time been exactly alike, and now, with the alterations and the one entrance, gave the impression of being a single establishment.

As we entered the shallow vestibule—a characteristic of all the old brownstone mansions along the street—I noticed that the heavy oak entrance door, which Scarlett had said was ajar earlier in the morning, was now closed. Vance, too, remarked the fact, for he at once turned to Scarlett and asked:

"Did you close the door when you left the house?"

Scarlett looked seriously at the massive panels, as if trying to recall his actions.

"Really, old man, I can't remember," he answered. "I was devilishly upset. I may have shut the door..."

Vance tried the knob, and the door opened.

"Well, well. The latch has been set anyway. Very careless on some one's part... Is that usual?"

Scarlett looked astonished.

"Never knew it to be unlatched."

Vance held up his hand, indicating that we were to remain in the vestibule, and stepped quietly inside to the steel door on the right leading into the museum. We could see him open it gingerly but could not distinguish what was beyond. He disappeared for a moment.

"Oh, Kyle's quite dead," he announced sombrely on his return. "And apparently no one has discovered him yet." He cautiously reclosed the front door. "We sha'n't take advantage of the latch being set," he added. "We'll abide by the conventions and see who answers." Then he pressed the bell-button.

A few moments later the door was opened by a cadaverous, chlorotic man in butler's livery. He bowed perfunctorily to Scarlett, and coldly inspected the rest of us.

"Brush, I believe." It was Vance who spoke.

The man bowed slightly without taking his eyes off of us.

"Is Doctor Bliss in?" Vance asked.

Brush shifted his gaze interrogatively to Scarlett. Receiving an assuring nod, he opened the door a little wider.

"Yes, sir," he answered. "He's in his study. Who shall I say is calling?"

"You needn't disturb him, Brush."

Vance stepped into the entrance hall, and we followed him. "Has the doctor been in his study all morning?"

The butler drew himself up and attempted to reprove Vance with a look of haughty indignation.

Vance smiled, not unkindly.

"Your manner is quite correct, Brush. But we're not wanting lessons in etiquette. This is Mr. Markham, the District Attorney of New York; and we're here for information. Do you care to give it voluntarily?"

The man had caught sight of the uniformed officer at the foot of the stone steps, and his face paled.

"You'll be doing the doctor a favor by answering," Scarlett put in.

"Doctor Bliss has been in his study since nine o'clock," the butler replied, in a tone of injured dignity.

"How can you be sure of that fact?" Vance asked.

"I brought him his breakfast there; and I've been on this floor ever since."

"Doctor Bliss's study," interjected Scarlett, "is at the rear of this hall." He pointed to a curtained door at the end of the wide corridor.

"He should be able to hear us now," remarked Markham.

"No, the door is padded," Scarlett explained. "The study is his *sanctum sanctorum*; and no sounds can reach him from the house."

The butler, his eyes like two glittering pin-points, had started to move away.

"Just a moment, Brush." Vance's voice halted him. "Who else is in the house at this time?"

The man turned, and when he answered it seemed to me that his voice quavered slightly.

"Mr. Hani is up-stairs. He has been indisposed—"

"Oh, has he, now?" Vance took out his cigarette-case. "And the other members of the household?"

"Mrs. Bliss went out about nine—to do some shopping, so I understood her to say.—Mr. Salveter left the house shortly afterward."

"And Dingle?"

"She's in the kitchen below, sir."

Vance studied the butler appraisingly.

"You need a tonic, Brush. A combination of iron, arsenic and strychnine would build you up."

"Yes, sir. I've been thinking of consulting a doctor... It's lack of fresh air, sir."

"Just so." Vance had selected one of his beloved *Régies*, and was lighting it with meticulous care. "By the by, Brush; what about Mr. Kyle? He called here this morning, I understand."

"He's in the museum now... I'd forgotten, sir. Doctor Bliss may be with him."

"Indeed! And what time did Mr. Kyle arrive?"

"About ten o'clock."

"Did you admit him?"

"Yes, sir."

"And did you notify Doctor Bliss of his arrival?"

"No, sir. Mr. Kyle told me not to disturb the doctor. He explained that he was early for his appointment, and wished to look over some curios in the museum for an hour or so. He said he'd knock on the doctor's study door later."

"And he went direct into the museum?"

"Yes, sir—in fact, I opened the door for him."

Vance drew luxuriously on his cigarette for a moment.

"One more thing, Brush. I note that the latch on the front door has been set, so that any one from the outside could enter the house without ringing..."

The man gave a slight start and, going quickly to the door, bent over and inspected the lock.

"So it is, sir... Very strange."

Vance watched him closely.

"Why strange?"

"Well, sir, it wasn't unlatched when Mr. Kyle came at ten o'clock. I looked at it specially when I let him in. He said he wished to be left alone in the museum, and as members of the house sometimes leave the door on the latch when they go out for a short time, I made sure that no one had done so this morning. Otherwise they might have come in and disturbed Mr. Kyle without my warning them."

"But, Brush," interjected Scarlett excitedly; "when I got here at half past ten the door was open—"

Vance made an admonitory gesture.

"That's all right, Scarlett." Then he turned back to the butler. "Where did you go after admitting Mr. Kyle?"

"Into the drawing-room." The man pointed to a large sliding door half-way down the hall on the left, at the foot of the stairs.

"And remained there till when?"

"Till ten minutes ago."

"Did you hear Mr. Scarlett come in and go out of the front door?"

"No, sir... But then, I was using the vacuum cleaner. The noise of the motor—"

"Quite so. But if the vacuum cleaner's motor was hummin', how do you know that Doctor Bliss did not leave his study?"

"The drawing-room door was open, sir. I'd have seen him if he came out."

"But he might have gone into the museum and left the house by the front door without your hearing him. Y'know, you didn't hear Mr. Scarlett enter."

"That would have been out of the question, sir. Doctor Bliss wore only a light dressing-gown over his pyjamas. His clothes are all up-stairs."

"Very good, Brush... And now, one more question. Has the front door-bell rung since Mr. Kyle's arrival?"

"No, sir."

"Maybe it rang and Dingle answered it... That motor hum, don't y'know."

"She would have come up and told me, sir. She never answers the door in the morning. She's not in presentable habiliments till afternoon."

"Quite characteristically feminine," Vance murmured... "That will be all for the present, Brush. You may go down-stairs and wait for our call. An accident has happened to Mr. Kyle, and we are going to look into it. You are to say nothing...understand?" His voice had suddenly become stern and ominous.

Brush drew himself up with a quick intake of breath: he appeared positively ill, and I almost expected him to faint. His face was like chalk.

"Certainly, sir—I understand." His words were articulated with great effort. Then he walked away unsteadily and disappeared down the rear stairs to the left of Doctor Bliss's study door.

Vance spoke in a low voice to Markham, who immediately beckoned to the officer in the street below.

"You are to stand in the vestibule here," he ordered. "When Sergeant Heath and his men come, bring them to us at once. We'll be in there." He indicated the large steel door leading into the museum. "If any one else calls, hold them and notify us. Don't let any one ring the bell."

The officer saluted and took up his post; and the rest of us, with Vance leading the way, passed through the steel door into the museum.

A flight of carpeted stairs, four feet wide, led down along the wall to the floor of the enormous room beyond, which was on the street level. The first-story floor—the one which had been even with the hallway of the house we had just quitted—had been removed so that the room of the museum was two stories high. Two huge pillars, with steel beams and diagonal joists, had been erected as supports. Moreover, the walls marking the former rooms had been demolished. The result was that the room we had entered occupied the entire width and length of the house—about twenty-five by seventy feet—and had a ceiling almost twenty feet high.

At the front was a series of tall, leaded-glass windows running across the entire width of the building; and at the rear, above a series of oak cabinets, a similar row of windows had been cut. The curtains of the front windows were drawn, but those at the rear were open. The sun had not yet found its way into the room, and the light was dingy.

As we stood for a moment at the head of the steps I noted a small circular iron stairway at the rear leading to a small steel door on the same level as the door through which we had entered.

The arrangement of the museum in relation to the house which served as living quarters for the Blisses, was to prove of considerable importance in Vance's solution of Benjamin H. Kyle's murder, and for purposes of clarity I am including in this record a plan of the two houses. The floor of the museum, as I have said, was on the street level—it had formerly been the "basement" floor. And it must be borne in mind that the rooms indicated on the left-hand half of the plan were one story above the museum floor and half-way between the museum floor and the ceiling.

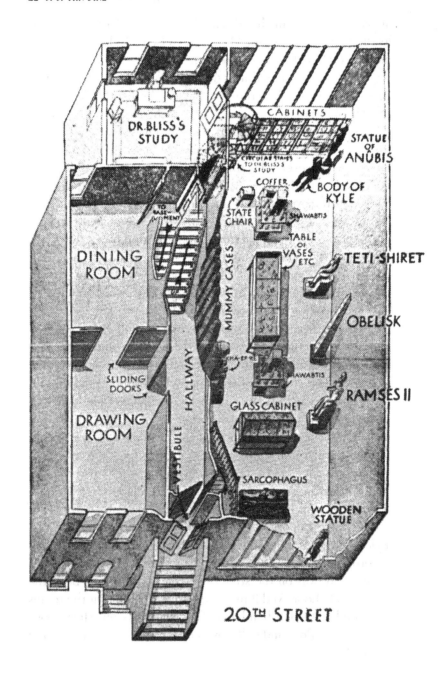

DR. BLISS'S STUDY

CABINETS

STATUE OF ANUBIS

CIRCULAR STAIRS TO DR. BLISS'S STUDY

COFFER

BODY OF KYLE

SHAWABTIS

STATE CHAIR

TO BASEMENT

TABLE OF VASES ETC.

TETI-SHIRET

DINING ROOM

MUMMY CASES

OBELISK

SHA-E-RE

SHAWABTIS

RAMSES II

SLIDING DOORS

HALLWAY

GLASS CABINET

DRAWING ROOM

VESTIBULE

SARCOPHAGUS

WOODEN STATUE

20ᵀᴴ STREET

My eyes at once searched the opposite corner of the room for the murdered man; but that part of the museum was in shadow, and all I could see was a dark mass, like a recumbent human body, in front of the farthest rear cabinet.

Vance and Markham had descended the stairs while Scarlett and I waited on the upper landing. Vance went straightway to the front of the museum and pulled the draw-cords of the curtains. Light flooded the semi-darkness; and for the first time I took in the beautiful and amazing contents of that great room.

In the centre of the opposite wall rose a ten-foot obelisk from Heliopolis, commemorating an expedition of Queen Hat-shepsut of the Eighteenth Dynasty, and bearing her cartouche. To the right and left of the obelisk stood two plaster-cast portrait statues—one of Queen Teti-shiret of the Seventeenth Dynasty, and the other a black replica of the famous Turin statue of Ramses II—considered one of the finest pieces of sculptured portraiture in antiquity.

Above and beside them hung several papyri, framed and under glass, their faded burnt-orange backgrounds—punctuated with red, yellow, green and white patches—making splashes of attractive color against the dingy gray plaster of the wall. Four large limestone bas-reliefs, taken from a Nineteenth-Dynasty tomb at Memphis and containing passages from the Book of the Dead, were aligned above the papyri.

Beneath the front windows stood a black granite Twenty-second-Dynasty sarcophagus fully ten feet long, its front and sides covered with hieroglyphic inscriptions. It was surmounted by a mummy-shaped lid, showing the soul bird, or Ba—with its falcon's form and human head. This sarcophagus was one of the rarest in America, and had been brought to this country by Doctor Bliss from the ancient necropolis at Thebes. In the corner beyond was a cedar-wood statue of an Asiatic, found in Palestine—a relic of the conquests of Thut-mosè III.

Near the foot of the stairs on which I stood loomed the majestic Kha-ef-Rê statue from the Fourth Dynasty. It was made of gray plaster of Paris, varnished and polished in imitation of the original diorite. It stood nearly eight feet high; and its dignity and power and magistral calm seemed to dominate the entire museum.*

To the right of the statue, and extending all the way to the spiral stairs at the rear, was a row of anthropoid mummy cases, gaudily decorated in gold and brilliant colors. Above them hung two enormously enlarged tinted photographs—one showing the Colossi of Amenhotep III,† the other depicting the great Amûn Temple at Karnak.

Around the two supporting columns in the centre of the museum deep shelves had been built, and on them reposed a fascinating array of *shawabtis*—beautifully carved and gaily painted wooden figures.

Extending between the two pillars was a long, low, velvet-covered table, perhaps fourteen feet in length, bearing a beautiful collection of alabaster perfumery and canopic vases, blue lotiform jars, kohl pots of polished obsidian, and several cylindrical carved cosmetic jars of semi-translucent and opaque alabaster. At the rear of the room was a squat coffer with inlays of blue glazed faience, white and red ivory and black ebony; and beside it stood a carved chair of state, decorated in gesso and gilt, and bearing a design of lotus flowers and buds.

Across the front of the room ran a long glass show-case containing pectoral collars of cloisonné, amulets in majolica, shell pendants, girdles of gold cowries, rhombic beads of carnelian and feldspar, bracelets and anklets and finger-rings, gold and ebony fans, and a collection of scarabs of most of the Pharaohs down to Ptolemaic times.

Around the walls, just below the ceiling, ran a five-foot frieze—a sectional copy of the famous Rhapsody of Pen-ta-

---

* *Kha-ef-Rê was the originator of the great Sphinx, and also of one of the three great Gîzeh pyramids—Wer Kha-ef-Rê (Kha-ef-Rê is mighty), now known as the Second Pyramid.*

† *Popularly, and incorrectly, called the Memnon Colossi.*

Weret, commemorating the victory of Ramses II over the Hittites at Kadesh in Syria.

As soon as Vance had opened the heavy curtains of the front windows he and Markham moved toward the rear of the room. Scarlett and I descended the stairs and followed them. Kyle was lying on his face, his legs slightly drawn up under him, and his arms reaching out and encircling the feet of a life-sized statue in the corner. I had seen reproductions of this statue many times, but I did not know its name.

It was Vance who enlightened me. He stood contemplating the huddled body of the dead man, and slowly his eyes shifted to the serene sculpture—a brown limestone carving of a man with a jackal's head, holding a sceptre.

"Anûbis," he murmured, his face set tensely. "The Egyptian god of the underworld. Y'know, Markham, Anûbis was the god who prowled about the tombs of the dead. He guided the dead through Amentet—the shadowy abode of Osiris. He plays an important part in the Book of the Dead—he symbolized the grave; and he weighed the souls of men, and assigned each to its abode. Without Anûbis's help the soul would never have found the Realm of Shades. He was the only friend of the dying and the dead... And here is Kyle, in an attitude of final and pious entreaty before him."

Vance's eyes rested for a moment on the benignant features of Anûbis. Then his gaze moved dreamily to the prostrate man who, but for the hideous wound in his head, might have been paying humble obeisance to the underworld god. He pointed to the smaller statue which had caused Kyle's death.

This statue was about two feet long and was black and shiny. It still lay diagonally across the back of the murdered man's skull: it seemed to have been caught and held there in the concavity made by the blow. An irregular pool of dark blood had formed beside the head, and I noted—without giving the matter any particular thought—that one point of the periphery of the pool had been smeared outward over the polished maple-wood floor.

"I don't like this, Markham," Vance was saying in a low voice. "I don't like it at all... That diorite statue, which killed Kyle, is Sakhmet, the Egyptian goddess of vengeance—the destroying element. She was the goddess who protected the good and annihilated the wicked—the goddess who slew. The Egyptians believed in her violent power; and there are many strange legend'ry tales of her dark and terrible acts of revenge..."

CHAPTER THREE

Scarabæus Sacer
(Friday, July 13; noon)

VANCE FROWNED SLIGHTLY and studied the small black figure for a moment.

"It may mean nothing—surely nothing supernatural—but the fact that this particular statue was chosen for the murder makes me wonder if there may be something diabolical and sinister and superstitious in this affair."

"Come, come, Vance!" Markham spoke with forced matter-of-factness. "This is modern New York, not legendary Egypt."

"Yes...oh, yes. But superstition is still a ruling factor in so-called human nature. Moreover, there are many more convenient weapons in this room—weapons fully as lethal and more readily wielded. Why should a cumbersome, heavy statue of Sakhmet have been chosen for the deed?... In any event, it took a strong man to swing it with such force."

He looked toward Scarlett, whose eyes had been fastened on the dead man with a stare of fascination.

"Where was this statue kept?"

Scarlett blinked.

"Why—let me see…" He was obviously trying to collect his wits. "Ah, yes. On the top of that cabinet." He pointed unsteadily to the row of wide shelves in front of Kyle's body. "It was one of the new pieces we unpacked yesterday. Hani placed it there. You see, we used that end cabinet temporarily for the new items, until we could arrange and catalogue 'em properly."

There were ten sections in the row of cabinets that extended across the rear of the museum, each one being about two and a half feet wide and a little over seven feet high. These cabinets—which in reality were but open shelves—were filled with all manner of curios: scores of examples of pottery and wooden vases, scent bottles, bows and arrows, adzes, swords, daggers, sistra, bronze and copper hand-mirrors, ivory game boards, perfume boxes, whip handles, palm-leaf sandals, wooden combs, palettes, head rests, reed baskets, carved spoons, plasterers' tools, sacrificial flint knives, funerary masks, statuettes, necklaces, and the like.

Each cabinet had a separate curtain of a material which looked like silk rep, suspended with brass rings on a small metal rod. The curtains to all the cabinets were drawn open, with the exception of the one on the end cabinet before which the dead body of Kyle lay. The curtain of this cabinet was only partly drawn.

Vance had turned round.

"And what about the Anûbis, Scarlett?" he asked. "Was it a recent acquisition?"

"That came yesterday, too. It was placed in that corner—to keep the shipment together."

Vance nodded, and walked to the partly curtained cabinet. He stood for several moments peering into the shelves.

"Very interestin'," he murmured, almost as if to himself. "I see you have a most unusual post-Hyksos bearded sphinx…

And that blue-glass vessel is very lovely...though not so lovely as yon blue-paste lion's-head... Ah! I note many evidences of old Intef's bellicose nature—that battle-ax, for instance... And—my word!—there are some scimitars and daggers which look positively Asiatic. And"—he peered closely into the top shelf—"a most fascinatin' collection of ceremonial maces."

"Things Doctor Bliss picked up on his recent expedition," explained Scarlett. "Those flint and porphyry maces came from the antechamber of Intef's tomb..."

At this moment the great metal door of the museum creaked on its hinges, and Sergeant Ernest Heath and three detectives appeared at the head of the stairs. The Sergeant immediately descended into the room, leaving his men on the little landing.

He greeted Markham with the usual ritualistic handshake.

"Howdy, sir," he rumbled. "I got here as soon as I could. Brought three of the boys from the Bureau, and sent word to Captain Dubois and Doc Doremus* to follow us up."

"It looks as if we might be in for another unpleasant scandal, Sergeant." Markham's tone was pessimistic. "That's Benjamin H. Kyle."

Heath stared aggressively at the dead man and grunted.

"A nasty job," he commented through his teeth. "What in hell is that thing he was croaked with?"

Vance, who had been leaning over the shelves of the cabinet, his back to us, now turned round with a genial smile.

"That, Sergeant, is Sakhmet, an ancient goddess of the primitive Egyptians. But she isn't in hell, so to speak. This gentleman, however,"—he touched the tall statue of Anûbis—"is from the nether regions."

"I mighta known you'd be here, Mr. Vance." Heath grinned with genuine friendliness, and held out his hand. "I've

---

*   *Captain Dubois was then the finger-print expert of the New York Police Department; and Doctor Emanuel Doremus was the Medical Examiner.*

got you down on my suspect list. Every time there's a fancy homicide, who do I find on the spot but Mr. Philo Vance!... Glad to see you, Mr. Vance. I reckon you'll get your psychological processes to working now and clean this mystery up *pronto.*"

"It'll take more than psychology to solve this case, I'm afraid." Vance had grasped the Sergeant's hand cordially. "A smatterin' of Egyptology might help, don't y'know."

"I'll leave that nifty stuff to you, Mr. Vance. What I want, first and foremost, is the finger-prints on that—that—" He bent over the small statue of Sakhmet. "That's the damnedest thing I ever saw. The guy who sculpted that was cuckoo. It's got a lion's head with a big platter on the dome."

"The lion's head of Sakhmet is undoubtedly totemistic, Sergeant," explained Vance, good-naturedly. "And that 'platter' is a representation of the solar disk. The snake peering from the forehead is a cobra—or uræus—and was the sign of royalty."

"Have it your own way, sir." The Sergeant had become impatient. "What I want is the finger-prints."

He swung about and walked toward the front of the museum.

"Hey, Snitkin!" he called belligerently to one of the men on the stair landing. "Relieve that officer outside—send him back to his beat. And bring Dubois in here as soon as he shows up." Then he returned to Markham. "Who'll give me the low-down on this, sir?"

Markham introduced him to Scarlett.

"This gentleman," he said, "found Mr. Kyle. He can tell you all we know of the case thus far."

Scarlett and Heath talked together for five minutes or so, the Sergeant maintaining throughout the conversation an attitude of undisguised suspicion. It was a basic principle with him that every one was guilty until his innocence had been completely and irrefutably established.

Vance in the meantime had been bending over Kyle's body with an intentness that puzzled me. Presently his eyes narrowed slightly and he went down on one knee, thrusting his head forward to within a foot of the floor. Then he took out his monocle, polished it carefully, and adjusted it. Markham and I both watched him in silence. After a few moments he straightened up.

"I say, Scarlett; is there a magnifyin' glass handy?"

Scarlett, who had just finished talking to Sergeant Heath, went at once to the glass case containing the scarabs and opened one of the drawers.

"What sort of museum would this be without a magnifier?" he asked, with a feeble attempt at jocularity, holding out a Coddington lens.

Vance took it and turned to Heath.

"May I borrow your flash-light, Sergeant?"

"Sure thing!" Heath handed him a push-button flash.

Vance again knelt down, and with the flash-light in one hand and the lens in the other, inspected a tiny oblong object that lay about a foot from Kyle's body.

CARAB OF INTEP V

"A scarab, huh?"

"*Nisut Biti...Intef...Si Rê... Nub-Kheper-Rê.*" His voice was low and resonant.

The Sergeant put his hands in his pockets and sniffed.

"And what language might that be, Mr. Vance?" he asked.

"It's the transliteration of a few ancient Egyptian hieroglyphs. I'm reading from this scarab..."

The Sergeant had become interested. He stepped forward and leaned over the object that Vance was inspecting.

"Yes, Sergeant. Sometimes called a scarabee, or scarabæid, or scarabæus—that is to say, beetle... This little oval bit of lapis-lazuli was a sacred symbol of the old Egyptians...

This particular one, by the by, is most fascinatin'. It is the state seal of Intef V—a Pharaoh of the Seventeenth Dynasty. About 1650 B.C.—or over 3,500 years ago—he wore it. It bears the title and throne name of Intef-o, or Intef. His Horus name was Nefer-Kheperu, if I remember correctly. He was one of the native Egyptian rulers at Thebes during the reign of the Hyksos in the Delta.* The tomb of this gentleman is the one that Doctor Bliss has been excavating for several years... And you of course note, Sergeant, that the scarab is set in a modern scarf-pin..."

Heath grunted with satisfaction. Here, at least, was a piece of tangible evidence.

"A beetle, is it? And a scarf-pin!... Well, Mr. Vance, I'd like to get my hands on the bird who wore that blue thing-umajig in his cravat."

"I can enlighten you on that point, Sergeant." Vance rose to his feet and looked toward the little metal door at the head of the circular stairway. "That scarf-pin is the property of Doctor Bliss."

---

* The daughter of this particular Pharaoh—Nefra—incidentally is the titular heroine of H. Rider Haggard's romance, "Queen of the Dawn." Haggard, following the chronology of H.R. Hall, placed Intef in the Fourteenth Dynasty instead of the Seventeenth, making him a contemporary of the great Hyksos Pharaoh, Apopi, whose son Khyan—the hero of the book—marries Nefra. The researches of Bliss and Weigall seem to have demonstrated that this relationship is an anachronism.

CHAPTER FOUR

Tracks in the Blood
(Friday, July 13; 12.15 p.m.)

SCARLETT HAD BEEN watching Vance intently, a look of horrified amazement on his round bronzed face.

"I'm afraid you're right, Vance," he said, nodding with reluctance. "Doctor Bliss found that scarab on the site of the excavation of Intef's tomb two years ago. He didn't mention it to the Egyptian authorities; and when he returned to America he had it set in a scarf-pin. But surely its presence here can have no significance..."

"Really, now!" Vance faced Scarlett with a steady gaze. "I remember quite well the episode at Dirâ Abu 'n-Nega. I was *particeps criminis*, as it were, to the theft. But since there were other scarabs of Intef, as well as a cylindrical seal, in the British Museum, I turned my eyes the other way... This is the first time I've had a close look at the scarab..."

Heath had started toward the front stairs.

"Say, you—Emery!" he bawled, addressing one of the two men on the landing. "Round up this guy Bliss, and bring 'im in here—"

"Oh, I say, Sergeant!" Vance hastened after him and put a restraining hand on his arm. "Why so precipitate? Let's be calm... This isn't the correct moment to drag Bliss in. And when we want him all we have to do is to knock on that little door—he's undoubtedly in his study, and he can't run away... And there's a bit of prelimin'ry surveying to be done first."

Heath hesitated and made a grimace. Then:

"Never mind, Emery. But go out in the back yard, and see that nobody tries to make a getaway... And you, Hennessey,"—he addressed the other man—"stand in the front hall. If any one tries to leave the house, grab 'em and bring 'em in—see?"

The two detectives disappeared with a stealth that struck me as highly ludicrous.

"Got something up your sleeve, sir?" the Sergeant asked, eying Vance hopefully. "This homicide, though, don't look very complicated to me. Kyle gets bumped off by a blow over the head, and beside him is a scarf-pin belonging to Doctor Bliss... That's simple enough, ain't it?"

"Too dashed simple, Sergeant," Vance returned quietly, contemplating the dead man. "That's the whole trouble..."

Suddenly he moved toward the statue of Anûbis, and leaning over, picked up a folded piece of paper which had lain almost hidden beneath one of Kyle's outstretched hands. Carefully unfolding it, he held it toward the light. It was a legal-sized sheet of paper, and was covered with figures.

"This document," he remarked, "must have been in Kyle's possession when he passed from this world... Know anything about it, Scarlett?"

Scarlett stepped forward eagerly and took the paper with an unsteady hand.

"Good Heavens!" he exclaimed. "It's the report of expenditures we drew up last night. Doctor Bliss was working on this tabulation—"

"Uh-huh!" Heath grinned with vicious satisfaction. "So! Our dead friend here musta seen Bliss this morning—else how could he have got that paper?"

Scarlett frowned.

"I must say it looks that way," he conceded. "This report hadn't been made out when the rest of us knocked off last night. Doctor Bliss said he was going to draw it up before Mr. Kyle got here this morning." He seemed utterly nonplussed as he handed the paper back to Vance. "But there's something wrong somewhere... You know, Vance, it's not reasonable—"

"Don't be futile, Scarlett." Vance's admonition cut him short. "If Doctor Bliss had wielded the statue of Sakhmet, why should he have left this report here to incriminate himself?... As you say, something is wrong somewhere."

"Wrong, is it!" Heath scoffed. "There's that beetle—and now we find this report. What more do you want, Mr. Vance?"

"A great deal more." Vance spoke softly. "A man doesn't ordinarily commit murder and leave such obvious bits of direct evidence strewn all about the place... It's childish."

Heath snorted.

"Panic—that's what it was. He got scared and beat it in a hurry..."

Vance's eyes rested on the little metal door of Doctor Bliss's study.

"By the by, Scarlett," he asked; "when did you last see that scarab scarf-pin?"

"Last night." The man had begun to pace restlessly up and down. "It was beastly hot in the study, and Doctor Bliss took off his collar and four-in-hand and laid 'em on the table. The scarab pin was sticking in the cravat."

"Ah!" Vance's gaze did not shift from the little door. "The pin lay on the table during the conference, eh?... And, as you told me, Hani and Mrs. Bliss and Salveter and yourself were present."

"Right."

"Any one, then, might have seen it and taken it?"

"Well—yes,…I suppose so."

Vance thought a moment.

"Still, this report…most curious!… I could bear to know how it got in Kyle's hands. You say it hadn't been completed when the conference broke up?"

"Oh, no." Scarlett seemed hesitant about answering. "We all turned in our figures, and Doctor Bliss said he was going to add 'em up and present them to Kyle to-day. Then he telephoned Kyle—in our presence—and made an appointment with him for eleven this morning."

"Is that all he said to Kyle on the phone?"

"Practically…though I believe he mentioned the new shipment that came yesterday—"

"Indeed? Very interestin'.… And what did Doctor Bliss say about the shipment?"

"As I remember—I really didn't pay much attention—he told Kyle that the crates had been unpacked, and added that he wanted Kyle to inspect their contents… You see, there was some doubt whether Kyle would finance another expedition. The Egyptian Government had been somewhat snooty, and had retained most of the choicest items for the Cairo Museum. Kyle didn't like this, and as he had already put oodles of money in the enterprise, he was inclined to back out. No *kudos* for him, you understand… In fact, Kyle's attitude was the cause of the conference. Doctor Bliss wanted to show him the exact cost of the former excavations and try to induce him to finance a continuation of the work…"

"And the old boy refused to do it," supplemented Heath; "and then the doctor got excited and cracked him over the head with that black statue."

"You *will* insist that life is so simple, Sergeant," sighed Vance.

"I'd sure hate to think it was as complex as you make it, Mr. Vance." Heath's retort came very near to an expression of dignified sarcasm.

The words were scarcely out of his mouth when the main door was opened quietly and a middle-aged, dark-complexioned man in native Egyptian costume appeared at the head of the front stairs. He surveyed us with inquisitive calm, and slowly and with great deliberation of movement, descended into the museum.

"Good-morning, Mr. Scarlett," he said, with a sardonic smile. He glanced at the murdered man. "I observe that tragedy has visited this household."

"Yes, Hani." Scarlett spoke with a certain condescension. "Mr. Kyle has been murdered. These gentlemen"—he made a slight gesture in our direction—"are investigating the crime."

Hani bowed gravely. He was of medium height, somewhat slender, and gave one the impression of contemptuous aloofness. There was a distinct glint of racial animosity in his close-set eyes. His face was relatively short—he was markedly dolichocephalic—and his straight nose had the typical rounded extremity of the true Copt. His eyes were brown—the color of his skin—and his eyebrows bushy. He wore a close-cut, semi-gray beard, and his lips were full and sensual. His head was covered by a soft dark tarbûsh bearing a pendant tassel of blue silk, and about his shoulders hung a long kaftan of red-and-white striped cotton, which fell to his ankles and barely revealed his yellow-leather babûshes.

He stood for a full minute looking down at Kyle's body, without any trace of repulsion or even regret. Then he lifted his head and contemplated the statue of Anûbis. A queer devotional expression came over his face; and presently his lips curled in a faint sardonic smile. After a moment he made a sweeping gesture with his left hand and, turning slowly, faced us. But his eyes were not on us—they were fixed on some distant point far beyond the front windows.

"There is no need for an investigation, gentlemen," he said, in a sepulchral tone. "It is the judgment of Sakhmet. For many generations the sacred tombs of our forefathers have been violated by the treasure-seeking Occidental. But the gods of old Egypt were powerful gods and protected their children. They have been patient. But the despoilers have gone too far.

It was time for the wrath of their vengeance to strike. And it has struck. The tomb of Intef-o has been saved from the vandal. Sakhmet has pronounced her judgment, just as she did when she slaughtered the rebels at Henen-ensu* to protect her father, Rê, against their treason."

He paused and drew a deep breath.

"But Anûbis will never guide a sacrilegious giaour to the Halls of Osiris—however reverently he may plead..."

Both Hani's manner and his words were impressive; and as he spoke I remembered, with an unpleasant feeling, the recent tragedy of Lord Carnarvon and the strange tales of ancient sorcery that sprang up to account for his death on supernatural grounds.

"Quite unscientific, don't y'know." Vance's voice, cynical and drawling, brought me quickly back to the world of reality. "I seriously question the ability of that piece of black igneous rock to accomplish a murder unless wielded by ordin'ry human hands... And if you *must* talk tosh, Hani, we'd be tremendously obliged if you'd do it in the privacy of your bedchamber. It's most borin'."

The Egyptian shot him a look of hatred.

"The West has much to learn from the East regarding matters of the soul," he pronounced oracularly.

"I dare say." Vance smiled blandly. "But the soul is not now under discussion. The West, which you despise, is prone to practicality; and you'd do well to forgo the metempsychosis for the nonce and answer a few questions which the District Attorney would like to put to you."

Hani bowed his acquiescence; and Markham, taking his cigar from his mouth, fixed a stern look upon him.

"Where were you all this forenoon?" he asked.

"In my room—up-stairs. I was not well."

"And you heard no sounds in the museum here?"

"It would have been impossible for me to hear any sound in this room."

---

*   The ancient Egyptian name of Heracleopolis.

"And you saw no one enter or leave the house?"

"No. My room is at the rear, and I did not leave it until a few moments ago."

Vance put the next question.

"Why did you leave it then?"

"I had work to do here in the museum," the man replied sullenly.

"But I understand you heard Doctor Bliss make an appointment with Mr. Kyle for eleven this morning." Vance was watching Hani sharply. "Did you intend to interrupt the conference?"

"I had forgotten about the appointment." The answer did not come spontaneously. "If I had found Doctor Bliss and Mr. Kyle in conference I would have returned to my room."

"To be sure." Vance's tone held a tinge of sarcasm. "I say, Hani, what's your full name?"

The Egyptian hesitated, but only for a second. Then he said:

"Anûpu Hani."*

Vance's eyebrows went up, and there was irony in the slow smile that crept to the corners of his mouth.

"'Anûpu'," he repeated. "Most allurin'. Anûpu, I believe, was the Egyptian form for Anûbis, what? You would seem to be identified with that unpleasant-lookin' gentleman in the corner, with the jackal's head."

Hani compressed his thick lips and made no response.

"It really doesn't matter, y'know," Vance remarked lightly... "By the by, wasn't it you who placed the small statue of Sakhmet atop the cabinet yonder?"

"Yes. It was unpacked yesterday."

"And was it you who drew the curtain across the end cabinet?"

"Yes—at Doctor Bliss's request. The objects in it were in great disarray. We had not yet had time to arrange them."

---

*   This unusual name, I learned later, was the result of his father's
     interest in Egyptian mythology while in Maspero's service.

Vance turned thoughtfully to Scarlett.

"Just what was said by Doctor Bliss to Mr. Kyle over the phone last night?"

"I think I've told you everything, old man." Scarlett appeared both puzzled and startled at Vance's persistent curiosity on this point. "He simply made the appointment for eleven o'clock, saying he'd have the financial report ready at that time."

"And what did he say about the new shipment?"

"Nothing, except that he was desirous of having Mr. Kyle see the items."

"And did he mention their whereabouts?"

"Yes; I recall that he said they had been placed in the end cabinet—the one with the closed curtains."

Vance nodded with a satisfaction I did not then understand.

"That accounts probably for Kyle's having come early to inspect the—what shall I say?—loot."

He faced Hani again with an engaging smile. "And is it not true that you and the others at the conference last night heard this phone call?"

"Yes—we all heard it." The Egyptian had become morose; but I noticed that he was studying Vance surreptitiously from the corner of his eye.

"And—I take it—," mused Vance, "any one who knew Kyle might have surmised that he would come early to inspect the items in that end cabinet... Eh, Scarlett?"

Scarlett shifted uneasily and looked at the great figure of the serene Kha-ef-Rê.

"Well—since you put it that way—yes... Fact is, Vance, Doctor Bliss suggested that Mr. Kyle come early and have a peep at the treasures."

These ramifications had begun to irritate Sergeant Heath.

"Pardon me, Mr. Vance," he blurted, with ill-concealed annoyance; "but do you happen to be the defense attorney for this Doctor Bliss? If you aren't working hard to alibi him, I'm the Queen of Sheba."

"You're certainly not Solomon, Sergeant," returned Vance. "Don't you care to weigh all the possibilities?"

"Weigh hell!" Heath was losing his temper. "I want a heart-to-heart talk with this guy who wore that beetle-pin and drew up that report. I know clean-cut evidence when I see it."

"I don't doubt that for a moment," Vance spoke dulcetly. "But even clean-cut evidence may have various interpretations..."

Snitkin threw open the door noisily at this point, and Doctor Doremus, the Medical Examiner, tripped jauntily down the stairs. He was a thin, nervous man, with a seamed, prematurely old face which carried a look at once crabbed and jocular.

"Good-morning, gentlemen," he greeted us breezily. He shook hands perfunctorily with Markham and Heath, and squaring off, gave Vance an exaggeratedly disgruntled look.

"Well, well!" he exclaimed, tilting his straw hat at an even more rakish angle. "Wherever there's a murder I find you, sir." He glanced at his wrist-watch. "Lunch time, by George!" His flashing gaze moved about the museum and came to rest on one of the anthropoid mummy cases. "This place don't look healthy... Where's the body, Sergeant?"

Heath had been standing before the prostrate body of Kyle. He now moved aside and pointed to the dead man.

"That's him, doc."

Doremus came forward and peered indifferently at the corpse.

"Well, he's dead," he pronounced, cocking his eye at Heath.

"Honest to Gawd?" The Sergeant was good-naturedly sarcastic.

"That's the way it strikes me—though since Carrel's experiments you never can tell... Anyway, I'll stand by my decision." He chuckled, and kneeling down, touched one of Kyle's hands. Then he moved one of the dead man's legs sidewise. "And he's been dead for about two hours—not longer, maybe less."

Heath took out a large handkerchief and, with great care, lifted the black statue of Sakhmet from Kyle's head.

"I'm saving this for finger-prints... Any signs of a struggle, doc?"

Doremus turned the body over and made a careful inspection of the face, the hands, and the clothes.

"Don't see any," he returned laconically. "Was struck from the rear, I'd say. Fell forward, arms outstretched. Didn't move after he'd hit the floor."

"Any chance, doctor, of his having been dead when the statue hit him?" asked Vance.

"Nope." Doremus rose and teetered on his toes impatiently. "Too much blood for that."

"Simple case of assault, then?"

"Looks like it... I'm no wizard, though." The doctor had become irritable. "The autopsy will settle that point."

"Can we have the *post-mortem* report immediately?" Markham made the request.

"As soon as the Sergeant gets the body to the mortuary."

"It'll be there by the time you've finished lunch, doc," said Heath. "I ordered the wagon before I left the Bureau."

"That being that, I'll run along." Again Doremus shook hands with Markham and Heath, and throwing a friendly salutation to Vance, walked briskly out of the room.

I had noticed that ever since Heath had placed the statue of Sakhmet to one side he had stood staring impatiently at the small pool of blood. As soon as Doremus had departed he knelt down and became doggedly interested in something on the floor. He took out his flash-light, which Vance had returned to him, and focussed it on the edge of the blood-pool at the point where I had noted the outward smear.

Then, after a moment, he moved a short distance away, and again shot his light on a faint smudge which stained the yellow wood floor. Once more he shifted his position—this time toward the little spiral stairs. A grunt of satisfaction escaped him now, and rising, he walked, in a wide circle, to the stairs themselves. There he again knelt down and ran the beam of his flash-light over the lower steps. On the third step the ray of light suddenly halted, and the Sergeant's face shot forward in an attitude of intense concentration.

A grin slowly overspread his broad features, and straightening up, he brought a gaze of triumph to bear on Vance.

"I've got the case tied up in a sack now, sir," he announced.

"I take it," replied Vance, "you've found the spoor of the murderer."

"I'll say!" Heath nodded with the deliberate emphasis of finality. "It's just like I told you…"

"Don't be too positive, Sergeant." Vance's face had grown sombre. "The obvious explanation is often the wrong one."

"Yeah?" Heath turned to Scarlett. "Listen, Mr. Scarlett, I got a question to ask you—and I want a straight answer." Scarlett bristled, but the Sergeant paid no attention to his resentment. "What kind of shoes does this Doctor Bliss generally wear round the house?"

Scarlett hesitated, and looked appealingly to Vance.

"Tell the Sergeant whatever you know," Vance advised him. "This is no time for reticence. You can trust me. There's no question of disloyalty now. The truth, d'ye see, is all that matters."

Scarlett cleared his throat nervously.

"Rubber tennis shoes," he said, in a low voice. "Ever since his first expedition in Egypt he has had weak feet—they troubled him abominably. He got relief by wearing white canvas sneakers with rubber soles."

"Sure he did." Heath walked back toward the body of Kyle. "Step over here a minute, Mr. Vance. I got something to show you."

Vance moved forward, and I followed him.

"Take a look at that foot-print," the Sergeant continued, pointing toward the smear at the edge of the pool of blood where Kyle's head had lain. "It don't show up much till you get close to it…but, once you spot it, you'll notice that it has marks of a rubber-soled shoe, with crossings like a checker-board on the sole and round spots on the heel."

Vance bent over and inspected the foot-print in the blood.

"Quite right, Sergeant." He had become very grave and serious.

"And now look here," Heath went on, pointing to two other smudges on the floor half-way to the iron stairs.

Vance leaned over the spots, and nodded.

"Yes," he admitted. "Those marks were probably made by the murderer..."

"And once more, sir." Heath went to the stairs and flashed his pocket-light on the third step.

Vance adjusted his monocle and looked closely. Then he rose and stood still for a moment, his chin resting in the palm of his hand.

"How about it, Mr. Vance?" the Sergeant demanded. "Is that evidence enough for you?"

Markham stepped to the foot of the circular stair-way, and placed his hand on Vance's shoulder.

"Why this stubbornness, old friend?" he asked in a kindly voice. "It begins to look like a clear case."

Vance lifted his eyes.

"A clear case—yes! But a clear case of what?... It doesn't make sense. Does a man of Bliss's mentality brutally murder a man with whom he is known to have had an appointment, and then leave his scarab-pin and a financial report, which no one else could have produced, on the scene of the crime, to involve himself? And, lest that evidence wasn't enough, is he going to leave bloody foot-prints, of a distinctive and personal design, leading from the body to his study?... Is it reasonable?"

"It may not be reasonable," Markham conceded; "but these things are nevertheless facts. And there's nothing to be done but confront Doctor Bliss with them."

"I suppose you're right." Vance's eyes again drifted toward the little metal door at the head of the spiral stairs. "Yes...the time has come to put Bliss on the carpet... But I don't like it, Markham. There's something awry... Maybe the doctor himself can enlighten us. Let me fetch him—I've known him for several years."

Vance turned and ascended the stairs, taking care not to step on the telltale foot-print the Sergeant had discovered.

CHAPTER FIVE

Meryt-Amen
(Friday, July 13; 12.45 p.m.)

VANCE KNOCKED ON the narrow door and reached into his pocket for his cigarette-case. We on the floor below watched the metal panel in silent expectancy. A feeling of dread, for some unknown reason, assailed me, and my muscles went tense. To this day I cannot explain the cause of my fear; but at that moment a chill came over my heart. All the evidence that had come to light pointed unmistakably toward the great Egyptologist in the little room beyond.

Vance alone seemed unconcerned. He casually lit his cigarette, and when he had replaced the lighter in his pocket, he knocked again at the door—this time more loudly. Still no answer.

"Very curious," I heard him murmur.

Then he raised his arm and pounded on the metal with a force that sent reverberating echoes through the great room of the museum.

At last, after several moments of ominous silence, there was a sound of a knob turning, and the heavy door swung slowly inward.

In the opening stood the tall, slender figure of a man in his middle forties. He wore a peacock-blue dressing-gown of self-figured silk, which reached to his ankles, and his sparse yellow hair was tousled as if he had just risen from bed. Indeed, his entire appearance was that of one who had suddenly been roused from a deep sleep. His eyes were hazy, and their lids drooped; and he clung to the inside knob of the door for support. He actually swayed a little as he peered dully at Vance.

Withal, he was a striking figure. His face was long and thin, rugged and deeply tanned. His forehead was high and narrow—a scholar's brow; but his nose, which was curved like an eagle's beak, was his most prominent characteristic. His mouth was straight, and surmounted a chin that was so square as to be cubic. His cheeks were sunken, and I got the distinct impression of a man who was physically ill but who overrode the ravages of disease by sheer nervous vitality.

For a moment he stared at Vance uncomprehendingly. Then—like a person coming out of an anæsthetic—he blinked several times and took a deep inspiration.

"Ah!" His voice was thick and a trifle rasping. "Mr. Vance!... A long time since I've seen you..." His eyes drifted about the museum and came to rest on the little group at the foot of the stairs. "I don't quite understand..." He passed his hand slowly over the top of his head, and ran his fingers through his rumpled hair. "My head feels so heavy...please forgive me... I—I must have been asleep... Who are these gentlemen below?... I recognize Scarlett and Hani... It's been devilishly hot in my study."

"A serious accident has happened, Doctor Bliss," Vance informed him, in a low voice. "Would you mind stepping down into the museum?...We need your help."

"An accident!" Bliss drew himself up, and for the first time since he appeared at the door his eyes opened wide. "A serious accident?... What has happened? Not burglars, I hope. I've always been worried—"

"No, there have been no burglars, doctor." Vance steadied him as he walked nervously down the circular stairs.

When he reached the floor of the museum every eye in the room, I felt sure, was focussed on his feet. Certainly my own initial instinct was to inspect them; and I noticed that Heath, who stood beside me, had concentrated his gaze on the doctor's foot-covering. But if any of us expected to find Bliss shod in rubber-soled tennis shoes, he was disappointed. The man wore a pair of soft vici-kid bedroom slippers, dyed blue to match his dressing-gown and adorned with orange trimmings.

I did note, however, that his gray-silk pyjamas, which showed through the deep V-opening of his gown, had a broad, turned-over collar in which a mauve four-in-hand had been loosely knotted.

His eyes swept the little group before him and returned to Vance.

"You say there have been no burglars?" His voice was still vague and thick. "What, then, was the accident, Mr. Vance?"

"An accident far more serious than burglars, doctor," replied Vance, who had not released his hold on the other's arm. "Mr. Kyle is dead."

"Kyle dead!" Bliss's mouth sagged open, and a look of hopeless amazement came into his eyes. "But—but...I talked to him last night. He was to come here this morning... regarding the new expedition... Dead? All my work—my life's work—ended!" He slumped into one of the small folding wooden chairs of which there were perhaps a score scattered about the museum. A look of tragic resignation settled on his face. "This is terrible news."

"I'm very sorry, doctor," Vance murmured consolingly. "I fully understand your great disappointment..."

Bliss rose to his feet. His lethargy had fallen from him, and his features became hard and resolute. He looked squarely at Vance.

"Dead?" His voice was menacing. "How did he die?"

"He was murdered." Vance pointed to the body of Kyle before which Markham and Heath and I were standing.

Bliss stepped toward Kyle's prostrate figure. For a full minute he stood staring down at the body; then his gaze shifted to the small statue of Sakhmet, and a moment later he lifted his eyes to the lupine features of Anûbis.

Suddenly he swung round and faced Hani. The Egyptian took a backward step, as though he feared violence from the doctor.

"What do you know about this?—you jackal!" Bliss threw the question at him venomously, a passionate hate in his voice. "You've spied on me for years. You've taken my money and pocketed bribes from your stupid and grasping government. You've poisoned my wife against me. You've stood in the way of all I've endeavored to accomplish. You tried to murder the old native who showed me the site of the two obelisks in front of Intef's pyramid.* You've hampered me at every turn. And because my wife believed in you and loved you, I've kept you. And now, when I've found the site of Intef's tomb and actually entered the antechamber and am about to give the fruits of my researches to the world, the one man who could make possible the success of my life's work is found murdered." Bliss's eyes were like burning coals. "What do you know about it, Anûpu Hani? Speak—you contemptible dog of a fellah!"

Hani had retreated several paces. Bliss's vitriolic tirade had pitifully cowed him. But he did not grovel: he had become

---

* *I learned from Vance that Doctor Bliss had read, in the British Museum, the Abbott Papyrus of the Twentieth Dynasty, which reported the inspection of this and other tombs. The report stated that, in early times, Intef V's tomb had been entered but not robbed: the raiders had evidently been unable to penetrate to the actual grave chamber. Bliss, therefore, had concluded that the mummy of Intef would still be found in the original tomb. An old native named Hasan had showed him where two obelisks had stood in front of the pyramid of Intef (Intef-o); and through this information he had succeeded in locating the pyramid, and had excavated at that point.*

grim and morose, and there was a snarl in his voice when he answered.

"I know nothing of the murder. It was the vengeance of Sakhmet! *She* killed the one who would have paid for the desecration of Intef's tomb..."

"Sakhmet!" Bliss's scorn was devastating. "A piece of stone belonging to a hybrid mythology! You're not among illiterate witch-doctors now—you're confronted with civilized human beings who want the truth... Who killed Kyle?"

"If it wasn't Sakhmet, I don't know, Your Presence." Despite the Egyptian's subservient attitude there was an underlying contempt in his manner and in the intonation of his voice. "I have been in my room all the morning... You, *hadretak*," he added, with a sneer, "were very close to your rich patron when he departed this world for the Land of Shades."

Two red patches of anger shone through the tan of Bliss's cheeks. His eyes blazed abnormally, and his hands plucked spasmodically at the folds of his dressing-gown. I feared he would fly at the throat of the Egyptian.

Vance, too, had some such apprehension, for he moved to the doctor's side and touched him reassuringly on the arm.

"I understand perfectly how you feel, sir," he said in a soothing voice. "But temper won't help us get at the root of this matter."

Bliss sank back into his chair without a word, and Scarlett, who had been looking on at the scene with troubled amazement, stepped quickly up to Vance.

"There's something radically wrong here," he said. "The doctor isn't himself."

"So I observe." Vance spoke dryly, but there was a puzzled frown on his face. He scrutinized Bliss for a moment. "I say, doctor; what time did you fall asleep in your study this morning?"

Bliss looked up lethargically. His wrath seemed to have left him, and his eyes were again heavy.

"What time?" he repeated, like a man attempting to collect his thoughts. "Let me see... Brush brought me my breakfast about nine, and a few minutes later I drank the coffee...some of it, at any rate—" His gaze wandered off into space. "That's all I remember until—until there was a pounding on the door... What time is it, Mr. Vance?"

"It's well past noon," Vance informed him. "You evidently fell asleep as soon as you had your coffee. Quite natural, don't y'know. Scarlett tells me you worked late last night."

Bliss nodded heavily.

"Yes—till three this morning. I wanted to have the report in order for Kyle when he arrived... And now"—he looked hopelessly toward the outstretched body of his benefactor—"I find him dead—murdered... I can't understand."

"Neither can we—for the moment," Vance returned. "But Mr. Markham—the District Attorney—and Sergeant Heath of the Homicide Bureau are here for the purpose of ascertaining the facts; and you may rest assured, sir, that justice will be done. Just now you can help us materially by answering a few questions. Do you feel equal to it?"

"Of course I'm equal to it," Bliss replied, with a slight show of nervous vitality. "But," he added, running his tongue over his dry lips, "I'm horribly thirsty. A drink of water—"

"Ah! I thought you might be wanting a drink... How about it Sergeant?"

Heath was already on his way toward the front stairs. He disappeared through the door, and we could hear his voice giving staccato orders to some one outside. A minute or two later he returned to the museum with a glass of water.

Doctor Bliss drank it like a man parched with thirst, and when he had set the glass down Vance asked him:

"When did you finish your financial report for Mr. Kyle?"

"This morning—just before Brush brought me my break-fast." Bliss's voice was stronger: there was even animation in his tone. "I had practically completed it before retiring last night—

all but about an hour's work. So I came down to the study at eight this morning."

"And where is that report now?"

"On my desk in the study. I intended to check the figures after breakfast, before Kyle arrived... I'll get it."

He started to rise, but Vance restrained him. "That won't be necess'ry, sir. I have it here... It was found in Mr. Kyle's hand."

Bliss looked at the paper, which Vance showed him, with dumbfounded eyes.

"In—Kyle's hand?" he stammered. "But...but..."

"Don't disturb yourself about it." Vance's manner was casual. "Its presence there will be explained when we've come to know the situation better. The report was no doubt taken from your study while you were asleep..."

"Maybe Kyle himself—"

"It's possible, but hardly probable." It was obvious that Vance scouted the idea of Kyle's having personally taken the report. "By the by, is it custom'ry for you to leave the door leading from your study into the museum unlocked?"

"Yes. I never lock it. No necessity to. As a matter of fact I couldn't tell you offhand where the key is."

"That bein' the case," mused Vance, "any one in the museum might have entered the study and taken the report after nine o'clock or so, when you were asleep."

"But who, in Heaven's name, Mr. Vance—?"

"We don't know yet. We're still in the conjectural stage of our investigation.—And if you'll be so good, doctor, permit me to ask the questions... Do you happen to know where Mr. Salveter is this morning?"

Bliss turned his head toward Vance with a resentful gesture.

"Certainly I know where he is," he responded, setting his jaws firmly. (I got the impression that he intended to protect Kyle's nephew from any suspicion.) "I sent him to the Metropolitan Museum—"

"You sent him? When?"

"I asked him last night to go the first thing this morning and inquire regarding a duplicate set of reproductions of the tomb furniture in the recently discovered grave of Hotpeheres, the mother of Kheuf of the Fourth Dynasty—"

"Hotpeheres? Kheuf?... Do you refer to Hetep-hir-es and Khufu?"

"Certainly!" The doctor's tone was tart. "I use the transliteration of Weigall. In his 'History of the Pharaohs'—"

"Yes, yes. Forgive me, doctor. I recall now that Weigall has altered many of the accepted transliterations from the Egyptian... But, if my memory is correct, the expedition which unearthed the tomb of Hetep-hir-es—or Hotpeheres—was sponsored by Harvard University and the Boston Museum of Fine Arts."

"Quite true. But I knew that my old friend, Albert Lythgoe, the Curator of the Egyptian department of the Metropolitan Museum, could supply me with the information I desired."

"I see," Vance paused. "Did you speak to Mr. Salveter this morning?"

"No." Bliss became indignant. "I was in my study from eight o'clock on; and the lad wouldn't think of disturbing me. He probably left the house about nine-thirty,—the Metropolitan Museum opens at ten."

Vance nodded.

"Yes; Brush said he went out about that time. But shouldn't he be back by now?"

Bliss shrugged his shoulders.

"Perhaps," he said, as if the matter was of no importance. "He may have had to wait for the Curator, however. Anyway, he'll be back as soon as he has finished his mission. He's a good conscientious lad: both my wife and I are extremely fond of him. It was he who, by interceding with his uncle, made possible the excavations of Intef's tomb."

"So Scarlett told me." Vance spoke with the off-handedness of complete uninterest, and drawing up a collapsible wooden chair sat down lazily. As he did so he gave Markham an admonitory glance—a glance which said as plainly as words could have done: "Let me do the talking for the time being." Then he leaned back and folded his hands behind his head.

"I say, doctor," he went on, with a slight yawn; "speaking of old Intef, I was present, don't y'know, when you appropriated that fascinatin' lapis-lazuli scarab..."

Bliss's hand went to his four-in-hand, and he glanced guiltily toward Hani, who had moved before the statue of Teti-shiret and now stood with his back to us in a pose of detached and absorbed adoration. Vance pretended not to have seen the doctor's movements, and, gazing dreamily out of the rear windows, he continued:

"A most interestin' scarab—unusually marked. Scarlett tells me you had it made into a scarf-pin... Have you it with you? I'd jolly well like to see it."

"Really, Mr. Vance,"—again Bliss's hand went to his cravat—"it must be up-stairs. If you'll call Brush—"

Scarlett had moved forward beside Bliss.

"It was in your study last night, doctor," he said, "—on the desk..."

"So it was!" Bliss was in perfect control of himself now. "You'll find it on my desk, stuck in the necktie I was wearing yesterday."

Vance rose and confronted Scarlett with an arctic look.

"Thanks awfully," he said coldly. "When I need your assistance I'll call on you." Then he turned to Bliss. "The truth is, doctor, I was endeavorin' to ascertain when you last remembered havin' your scarab pin... It's not in your study, d'ye see. It was lyin' beside the body of Mr. Kyle when we arrived here."

"My Intef scarab here!" Bliss leapt to his feet and gazed, with a panic-stricken stare, at the murdered man. "That's impossible!"

Vance stepped to Kyle's body and picked up the scarab.

"Not impossible, sir," he said, displaying the pin; "but very mystifyin'... It was probably taken from your study at the same time as the report."

"It's beyond me," Bliss remarked slowly, in a hoarse whisper.

"Maybe it fell outa your necktie," Heath suggested antagonistically, thrusting his jaw forward.

"What do you mean?" The doctor's tone was dull and frightened. "I didn't have it in this necktie. I left it in the study—"

"Sergeant!" Vance gave Heath a look of stern reproval. "Let's go at this thing calmly and with discretion."

"Mr. Vance,"—Heath's aggressiveness did not relax— "I'm here to find out who croaked Kyle. And the person who had every opportunity to do it is this Doctor Bliss. On top of that fact we find a financial report and a stick-pin that hooks Doctor Bliss up to the dead man. And there's those foot-prints—"

"All you say is true, Sergeant." Vance cut him short. "But ballyragging the doctor will not give us the explanation of this extr'ordin'ry situation."

Bliss had shrunk back into his chair.

"Oh, my God!" he moaned. "I see what you're getting at. You think *I* killed him!" He turned his eyes to Vance in desperate entreaty. "I tell you I've been asleep since nine o'clock. I didn't even know Kyle was here. It's terrible— terrible... Surely, Mr. Vance, you can't believe—"

There was a sound of angry voices at the main door of the museum, and we all looked in that direction. At the head of the stairs stood Hennessey, his arms wide, protesting volubly. On the door-sill was a young woman.

"This is my house," she said in a shrill, angry voice. "How dare you tell me I can't enter here?..."

Scarlett at once hurried toward the stairs.

"Meryt!"

"It's my wife," Bliss informed us. "Why is she refused admittance, Mr. Vance?"

Before Vance could answer, Heath was shouting:

"That's all right, Hennessey. Let the lady come in."

Mrs. Bliss hastened down the stairs, and almost ran to her husband.

"Oh, what is it, Mindrum? What has happened?" She dropped to her knees and put her arms about the doctor's shoulders. At that instant she caught sight of Kyle's body and, with a gasp and a shudder, turned her eyes away.

She was a striking-looking woman, whose age, I surmised, was about twenty-six or -seven. Her large eyes were dark and heavily lashed, and her skin was a deep olive. Her Egyptian blood was most marked in the sensual fullness of her lips and in her high prominent cheekbones, which gave her face a decidedly Oriental character. There was something about her that recalled to my mind the beautiful reconstructed painting made of Queen Nefret-îti by Winifred Brunton.* She wore a powder-blue toque hat not unlike the headdress of Nefret-îti herself; and her gown of cinnamon-brown georgette crepe clung closely to her slender, well-rounded body, bringing out and emphasizing its sensuous curves. There were both strength and beauty in her supple figure, which followed the lines of the old Oriental ideal such as we find in Ingres' *Bain Turc.*

Despite her youth she possessed a distinct air of maturity and poise: there were undeniable depths to her nature; and I could easily imagine, as I watched her kneeling beside Bliss, that she might be capable of powerful emotions and equally powerful deeds.†

---

*   *This colored portrait (with the Queen's name spelled Nefertiti) appears in "Kings and Queens of Ancient Egypt" (Charles Scribner's Sons).*

†   *I learned subsequently from Scarlett that Mrs. Bliss's mother had been a Coptic lady of noble descent who traced her lineage from the last Saïte Pharaohs, and who, despite her Christian faith, had retained her traditional veneration for the native gods of her country. Her only child, Meryt-Amen ("Beloved of Amûn"), had been named in honor of the great Ramses II, whose full title as Son of the Sun-God was Ra-mosê-su Mery-Amûn. (The more correct English spelling of Mrs. Bliss's name would have been Meryet-Amûn, but the*

Bliss patted her shoulder in an affectionately paternal manner. His eyes, though, were abstracted.

"Kyle is dead, my dear," he told her in a hollow voice. "He's been killed...and these gentlemen are accusing me of having done it."

"You!" Mrs. Bliss was instantly on her feet. For a moment her great eyes stared uncomprehendingly at her husband; then she turned on us in a flashing rage. But before she could speak Vance stepped toward her.

"The doctor is not quite accurate, Mrs. Bliss," he said in a low, even tone. "We have not accused him. We are merely making an investigation of this tragic affair; and it happens that the doctor's scarab-pin was found near Mr. Kyle's body..."

"What of it?" She had become strangely calm. "Any one might have dropped it there."

"Exactly, madam," Vance returned, with friendly assurance. "Our main object in this investigation is to ascertain who that person was."

The woman's eyes were half-closed, and she stood rigid, as if transfixed by a sudden devastating thought.

"Yes...yes," she breathed. "Some one placed the scarab-pin there...some one..." Her voice died out, and a cloud, as of pain, came over her face. But quickly she drew herself together and, taking a deep breath, looked resolutely into Vance's eyes.

---

form chosen was no doubt based on the transliterations of Flinders Petrie, Maspero, and Abercrombie.) Meryet-Amûn was not an uncommon name among the queens and princesses of ancient Egypt. Three queens of that name have already been found—one (of the family of Ah-mosè I) whose mummy is in the Cairo Museum; another (of the family of Ramses II) whose tomb and sarcophagus are in the Valley of the Queens; and a third, whose burial chamber and mummy were recently found by the Egyptian Expedition of the Metropolitan Museum of Art on the hillside near the temple of Deir el Bahri at Thebes. This last Queen Meryet-Amûn was the daughter of Thut-mosè III and Meryet-Rê, and the wife of Amenhotep II. The story of the finding of her tomb is told in Section II of the Bulletin of the Metropolitan Museum of Art for November, 1929.

"Whoever it was that did this terrible thing, I want you to find him." Her expression became set and hard. "And I will help you. Do you understand?—*I* will help you."

Vance studied her briefly before replying.

"I believe you will, Mrs. Bliss. And I shall call on you for that help." He bowed slightly. "But there is nothing you can do at this moment. A few prelimin'ry routine things must be done first. In the meantime, I would appreciate your waiting for us in the drawing-room—there will be several questions we shall want to ask you presently... Hani may accompany you."

I had been watching the Egyptian with one eye during this little scene. When Mrs. Bliss had entered the museum he had barely turned in her direction, but when she had begun speaking to Vance he had moved silently toward them. He now stood, his arms folded, just behind the inlaid coffer, with his eyes fixed upon the woman, in an attitude of protective devotion.

"Come, Meryt-Amen," he said. "I will remain with you till these gentlemen wish to consult you. There is nothing to fear. Sakhmet has had her just revenge, and she is beyond the mundane power of Occidental law."

The woman hesitated a moment. Then, going to Bliss, she kissed him lightly on the forehead, and walked toward the front stairway, Hani servilely following her.

CHAPTER SIX

A Four-Hour Errand
(Friday, July 13; 1.15 p.m.)

SCARLETT'S EYES FOLLOWED her with a troubled, sympathetic look.

"Poor girl!" he commented, with a sigh. "You know, Vance, she was devoted to Kyle—her father and Kyle were great cronies. When old Abercrombie died Kyle cared for her as though she'd been his daughter... This affair is a terrible blow to her."

"One can well understand that," Vance murmured perfunctorily. "But she has Hani to console her... By the by, doctor, your Egyptian servant appears to be quite *en rapport* with Mrs. Bliss."

"What's that—what's that?" Bliss lifted his head and made an effort at concentration. "Ah, yes... Hani. A faithful dog—where my wife's concerned. He practically brought her up, after her father's death. He's never forgiven me for marrying her." He smiled grimly and lapsed into a state of brooding despondency.

Heath's cigar had gone out, but he still chewed viciously on it.

He was standing beside Kyle's body, his legs apart, his hands in his pockets, glaring with frustrated animosity at the doctor.

"What's all this palaver about, anyhow?" he asked sullenly. He faced Markham. "Listen, Chief: haven't you got enough evidence for an indictment?"

Markham was sorely troubled. His instinct was to order Bliss's arrest, but his faith in Vance halted him. He knew that Vance was not satisfied with the situation, and he no doubt felt, as a result of Vance's attitude, that there were certain things connected with Kyle's murder which did not show on the surface. Moreover, there was perhaps an uncertainty in his own mind as to the authenticity of the evidence that pointed to the Egyptologist.

He was on the point of answering Heath when Hennessey put his head in the door and called out:

"Hey, Sergeant; the buggy from the Department of Public Welfare is here."

"Well, it's about time." Heath was in a vicious mood. He turned to Markham. "Any reason, sir, why we shouldn't get the body outa the way?"

Markham glanced toward Vance, who nodded.

"No, Sergeant," he answered. "The sooner it reaches the mortuary, the sooner we'll have the *post-mortem* report."

"Right!" Heath cupped his hands to his mouth and bawled to Hennessey: "Send 'em in."

A moment later two men—one the driver of the car, the other an unkempt "pick-up"—came down the stairs carrying a large wicker basket shaped like a coffin. Without a word they callously lifted Kyle's body into it, and started toward the front door with their gruesome burden, the "pick-up" at the rear end of the basket doing a playful dance step as he moved across the hardwood floor.

"Sweet sympathetic laddie," grinned Vance.

With the removal of Kyle's body a pall seemed to lift from the museum. But there was still that pool of blood and the recumbent statue of Sakhmet to tell the terrible story of the tragedy.

Heath stood eyeing the huddled, silent figure of Doctor Bliss.

"Where do we go from here?" His question contained both disgust and resignation.

Markham was growing restless and, beckoning Vance to one side, spoke to him in low tones. I could not hear what was said; but Vance talked earnestly to the District Attorney for several minutes. Markham listened attentively and then shrugged his shoulders.

"Very well," he answered, as they strolled back toward us. "But unless you reach some conclusion pretty soon we'll have to take action…"

"Action—oh, my aunt!" Vance sighed deeply. "Always action—always pyrotechnics. The Rotarian ideal! Get busy—stir things up. Efficiency!… Why do the powers of justice have to emulate the whirling dervish? The human brain, after all, has certain functions."

He paced slowly back and forth in front of the cabinets, his eyes on the floor, while the rest of us watched him. Even Doctor Bliss roused himself and gazed at him with a curious and hopeful expression.

"None of these clews ring true, Markham," Vance said. "There's something here that doesn't meet the eye. It's like a cypher that says one thing and means another. I tell you the obvious explanation is the wrong one… There's a key to this affair—somewhere. And it's staring us in the face…yet we can't see it."

He was deeply perplexed and dissatisfied, and he walked to and fro with that quiet, disguised alertness which I had long since come to recognize.

Suddenly he halted in front of the pool of blood before the end cabinet, and bent over. He studied it for a moment, and then his eyes moved to the cabinet. Slowly his gaze ascended the partly drawn curtain and came to rest on the beaded wooden ledge above the curtain rod. After a while his eyes drifted back to the pool of blood, and I got the impression that he was measuring distances and trying to determine the exact relationship between the blood, the cabinet, the curtain, and the moulding along the top of the shelves.

Presently he straightened up and stood very close to the curtain, his back to us.

"Really, now, that's most interestin'," he murmured. "I wonder..."

He turned, and, drawing up one of the folding wooden chairs, placed it directly in front of the cabinet on the exact spot where Kyle's head had lain. Then he mounted the chair, and stood for a considerable time inspecting the top of the cabinet.

"My word! Extr'ordin'ry!" His voice was barely audible.

Taking out his monocle, he placed it in his eye. Then his hand reached out over the edge of the cabinet, and he picked up something very near to where Hani said he had placed the small statue of Sakhmet. Just what it was none of us could see; but presently he slipped the object into his coat pocket. A moment later he descended from the chair and faced Markham with a grim, satisfied look.

"This murder has amazin' possibilities," he observed.

Before he could explain his cryptic remark Hennessey again appeared at the head of the stairs and called out to Sergeant Heath:

"There's a guy here named Salveter who says he wants to see Doc Bliss."

"Ah—*bon*!" Vance, for some reason, seemed highly pleased. "Suppose we have him in, Sergeant."

"Oh, sure!" Heath made an elaborate grimace of boredom. "O.K., Hennessey. Show in the gent. The more the merrier... What is this, anyway?" he groused. "A convention?"

Young Salveter walked down the stairs and approached us with a startled, questioning air. He gave Scarlett a curt, cold nod; then he caught sight of Vance.

"How do you do?" he said, obviously surprised at Vance's presence. "It's been a long time since I saw you...in Egypt... What's all the excitement about? Have we been invested by the military?" His pleasantry did not ring true.

Salveter was an earnest, aggressive-looking man of about thirty, with sandy hair, wide-set gray eyes, a small nose, and a thin, tight mouth. He was of medium height, stockily built, and might have been an athlete in his college days. He was dressed simply in a tweed suit that did not fit him, and the polka-dot tie in his soft-shirt collar was askew. I doubt if his cordovan blucher oxfords had ever been polished. My first instinct was to like him. The impression he gave was that of boyish frankness; but there was a quality in his make-up,—I could not analyze it at the time,—that signalled to one to be wary and not attempt to force an issue against his stubbornness.

As he spoke to Vance his eyes shifted with intense curiosity about the room, as if he were looking for something amiss.

Vance, who had been watching him appraisingly, answered after a slight pause in a tone that struck me as unnecessarily devoid of sympathy.

"No, it's not the milit'ry, Mr. Salveter. It's the police. The fact is, your uncle is dead—he has been murdered."

"Uncle Ben!" Salveter appeared stunned by the news; but presently an angry scowl settled on his forehead. "So—that's it!" He drew in his head and squinted pugnaciously at Doctor Bliss. "He had an appointment with you this morning, sir... When—and how—did it happen?"

It was Vance, however, who made reply.

"Your uncle, Mr. Salveter, was struck over the head with that statue of Sakhmet, about ten o'clock. Mr. Scarlett found the body here at the foot of Anûbis, and notified me. I, in turn, notified the District Attorney... This, by the by, is Mr. Markham—and this is Sergeant Heath of the Homicide Bureau."

Salveter scarcely glanced in their direction.

"A damned outrage!" he muttered, setting his square, heavy jaw.

"An outrage—yes!" Bliss lifted his head, and his eyes, pitifully discouraged, met Salveter's. "It means the end of all our excavations, my boy—"

"Excavations!" Salveter continued to study the older man. "What do they matter? I want to lay my hands on the dog who did this thing." He swung about aggressively and faced Markham. "What can I do, sir, to help you?" His eyes were mere slits—he was like a dangerous wild beast waiting to pounce.

"Too much energy, Mr. Salveter," Vance drawled, sitting down indolently. "Far too much energy. I can apprehend exactly how you feel, don't y'know. But aggressiveness, while bein' a virtue in some circumstances, is really quite futile in the present situation... I say; why not walk round the block vigorously a couple of times, and then return to us? We crave a bit of polite intercourse with you, but calmness and self-control are most necess'ry."

Salveter glared ferociously at Vance, who met his gaze with languid coldness; and for fully thirty seconds there was an unflinching ocular clash between them. But I have seen other men attempt to stare Vance out of countenance—without the least success. His quiet power and strength of character were colossal, and I would wish no one the task of outgazing him.

Finally Salveter shrugged his broad shoulders. A slight, compromising grin flickered along his set mouth.

"I'll pass up the promenade," he said, with admiring sheepishness. "Fire away."

Vance took a deep inhalation on his cigarette, and let his eyes wander lazily along the great frieze of Pen-ta-Weret's Rhapsody.

"What time did you leave the house this morning, Mr. Salveter?"

"About half past nine." Salveter was now standing relaxed, his hands in his coat pockets. All of his aggressiveness was gone, and, though he watched Vance closely, there was neither animosity nor tenseness in his manner.

"And you did not, by any chance, leave the front door unlatched—or open?"

"No!... Why should I?"

"Really, y'know, I couldn't say." Vance conferred on him a disarming smile. "A more or less vital question, however. Mr. Scarlett, d'ye see, found the door open when he arrived between ten and ten-thirty."

"Well, *I* didn't leave it that way... What next?"

"You went to the Metropolitan Museum of Art, I understand."

"Yes. I went to inquire about some reproductions of the tomb furniture of Hotpeheres."

"And you got the information?"

"I did."

Vance looked at his watch.

"Twenty-five after one," he read. "That means you have been absent about four hours. Did you, by any hap, walk to Eighty-second Street and back?"

Salveter clamped his teeth tight for a moment, and stared antagonistically at Vance's nonchalant figure.

"I didn't walk either way, thank you." (I could not determine whether he was merely exerting great self-control or whether he was actually frightened.) "I took a 'bus up the Avenue, and came back in a taxi."

"Let us say one hour coming and going, then. That allowed you three hours to obtain your information, eh, what?"

"Mathematically correct." Again Salveter grinned savagely. "But it happened I dropped into the rooms on the right of the entrance to take a look at Per-nêb's Tomb. I'd heard recently that they'd added some objects to their collection of the contents of the burial-chamber... Per-nêb, you see, was Fifth Dynasty—"

"Yes, yes... And as Khufu, Hetep-hir-es' offspring, belonged to the preceding dynasty, you were æsthetically interested in the burial-chamber contents. Quite natural... And how long did you prowl and commune among the Per-nêb fragments?"

"See here, Mr. Vance"—Salveter was growing apprehensive—"I don't know what you're trying to get at; but if it's going to help you in your investigation of Uncle Ben's death, I'll take your gaff... I hung around the cabinets in the Egyptian rooms for nearly an hour. Got interested and didn't hurry—I knew Uncle Ben had an appointment with Doctor Bliss this morning, and I figured that if I got back at lunch time it would be all right."

"But you didn't get back at lunch time," Vance remarked.

"What if I didn't? I had to cool my feet for nearly an hour in the Curator's outer office after I went up-stairs—Mr. Lythgoe was talking with Lindsley Hall about some drawings. And then I had to hang around another half hour or so while he was phoning to Doctor Reisner at the Boston Museum of Fine Arts. I'm lucky to be back now."

"Quite... I know how those things are. Very tryin'."

Vance apparently accepted his story without question. He rose lazily and drew a small note-book from his pocket, at the same time feeling in his waistcoat as if for something with which to write.

"Sorry and all that, Mr. Salveter; but could you lend me a pencil? Mine seems to have disappeared."

(I immediately became interested, for I knew Vance never carried a pencil but invariably used a small gold fountain-pen which he always wore on his watch-chain.)

"Delighted." Salveter reached in his pocket and held out a long hexagonal yellow pencil.

Vance took it and made several notations in his book. Then, as he was about to return the pencil, he paused and looked at the name printed on it.

"Ah, a Mongol No. 1, what?" he said. "Popular pencils, these Fabers-482... Do you always use them?"

"Never anything else…"

"Thanks awfully." Vance returned the pencil, and dropped the note-book into his pocket. "And now, Mr. Salveter, I'd appreciate it if you'd go to the drawing-room and wait for us. We'll want to question you again… Mrs. Bliss, by the by, is there," he added casually.

Salveter's eyelids dropped perceptibly, and he gave Vance a swift sidelong glance.

"Oh, is she? Thanks… I'll wait for you in the drawing-room." He went up to Bliss. "I'm frightfully sorry, sir," he said. "I know what this means to you…" He was going to add something but halted himself. Then he walked doggedly toward the front door.

He was half-way up the stairs when Vance, who now stood regarding the statue of Sakhmet meditatively, suddenly turned and called to him.

"Oh, I say, Mr. Salveter. Tell Hani we'd like to see him here—there's a good fellow."

Salveter made a gesture of assent, and passed through the great steel door without looking back.

CHAPTER SEVEN

The Finger-Prints
(Friday, July 13; 1.30 p.m.)

Hani JOINED US a few moments later.

"I am at your service, gentlemen," he announced, looking from one to the other of us superciliously.

Vance had already drawn up a second chair beside the one on which he had stood during his inspection of the top of the cabinet; and he now made a beckoning gesture to the Egyptian.

"We appreciate your passionate spirit of co-operation, Hani," he replied lightly. "Would you be so amiable as to stand on this chair and point out to me exactly where you set the statue of Sakhmet yesterday?"

I was watching Hani closely, and I could have sworn that his eyebrows contracted slightly. But there was almost no hesitation in his compliance with Vance's request. Making a slow, deep bow, he approached the cabinet.

"Don't put your hands on the woodwork," Vance admonished. "And don't touch the curtain."

Awkwardly, because of his long flowing kaftan, Hani mounted one of the chairs; and Vance stepped upon the seat of the other.

The Egyptian squinted for a moment at the top of the cabinet, and then pointed a bony finger to a spot near the edge, exactly half-way across the two-and-a-half-foot opening.

"Just here, *effendi*," he said. "If you look closely you can see where the base of Sakhmet disturbed the dust..."

"Oh, quite." Vance, though in an attitude of concentration, was nevertheless studying Hani's face. "But if one looks even more closely one can see other disturbances in the dust."

"The wind, perhaps, from yonder window..."

Vance chuckled.

"*Blasen ist nicht flöten, ihr müsst die Finger bewegen*—to quote Goethe figuratively... Your explanation, Hani, is a bit too poetic." He indicated a point near the moulding at the edge of the cabinet. "I doubt if even your simoon—or, as you may prefer to call it, samûm*—could have made that scratch at the edge of the statue's base, what?... Or, it may be, you set down the statue with undue violence."

"It is possible, of course—though not likely."

"No, not likely—considerin' your superstitious reverence for the leonine lady." Vance descended from his perch. "However, Sakhmet seems to have been standing on the very edge of the cabinet, directly in the centre, when Mr. Kyle arrived this morning to inspect the new treasures."

We had all been watching him with curiosity. Heath and Markham were especially interested, and Scarlett—frowning and immobile—had not taken his eyes from Vance. Even Bliss, who had seemed utterly broken by the tragedy and in a state of

---

* *I am not quite sure why Vance added this parenthetical phrase, unless it was because the word* simoon *comes from the Arabic* samma *(meaning to be poisoned), and he thought that Hani would better recognize the word in its correct etymological form.*

complete hopelessness, had followed the episode with intentness. That Vance had discovered something of importance was evident. I knew him too well to underestimate his persistence, and I waited, with a sense of inner excitement, for the time when he would share his new knowledge with us.

Markham, however, voiced his impatience.

"What have you in mind, Vance?" he asked irritably. "This is hardly the time to be secretive and dramatic."

"I'm merely delving into the subtler possibilities of this inveiglin' case," he replied, in an offhand manner. "I'm a complex soul, Markham old dear. I don't, alas! possess a simple, forthright nature. I'm a sworn enemy of the obvious and the trite... You remember what the heart of the young man said to the Psalmist?—'Things are not what they seem.'"

Markham had long since come to understand this kind of evasive garrulousness on Vance's part, and no further question was asked. Moreover, there was an interruption at this moment, which was to place an even more complicated and more sinister aspect on the entire case.

The front door was opened by Hennessey, and Captain Dubois and Detective Bellamy, the finger-print experts, clattered down the stairs.

"Sorry to keep you waiting, Sergeant," Dubois said, shaking hands with Heath; "but I was tied up with a safe-breaking job on Fulton Street." He looked about him. "How d'ye do, Mr. Markham?" He extended his hand to the District Attorney... "And Mr. Vance, is it?" Dubois spoke civilly but without enthusiasm: I believe his tiff with Vance during the "Canary" murder case still rankled in him.

"There ain't much of a job for you here, Captain," Heath interrupted impatiently. "The only thing I want you to check up on is that black statue laying there."

Dubois at once became seriously professional.

"That won't take long," he muttered, bending over the diorite figure of Sakhmet. "What might it be, Sergeant?—one of those Futuristic works of art that don't mean anything?"

"It don't mean anything to me," the Sergeant growled, "unless you can find some nice identifiable prints on it."

Dubois grunted and snapped his fingers toward his assistant. Bellamy, who had stood imperturbably in the background during the exchange of greetings, came ponderously forward and opened a black hand-bag which he had brought with him. Dubois, using a large handkerchief and the palms of his hands, carefully lifted the statue and placed it upright on the seat of a chair. Then he reached in the hand-bag and took out an insufflator, or tiny hand-bellows, and puffed a fine pale-saffron powder over the entire figure. Following this operation, he gently blew away all the surplus powder, and fixing a jeweller's-glass in his eye, knelt down and made a close inspection of every part of the statue.

Hani had watched the performance with the keenest interest. He had slowly moved toward the finger-print men until now he stood within a few feet of them. His eyes were concentrated on their labors, and his hands, which hung at his sides, were tightly flexed.

"You'll find no finger-prints of mine on Sakhmet, gentlemen," he proclaimed in a low, tense voice. "I polished them off... Nor will there be any finger-prints to guide you. The Goddess of Vengeance strikes of her own volition and power, and no human hands are needed to assist her in her acts of justice."

Heath threw the Egyptian a glance of scathing contempt; but Vance turned in his direction with a considerable show of interest.

"How do you know, Hani," he asked, "that your sign-manuals will not appear on the statue? It was you who placed it upon the cabinet yesterday."

"Yes, *effendi*," the man answered, without taking his eyes from Dubois. "I placed it there—but with reverence. I rubbed and polished it from top to bottom when it was unpacked. And then I took it in my hands and stood it on the top of the cabinet, as Bliss *effendi* had directed. But when it was in place I could see where my hands had made marks upon its polished surface; and again I rubbed it with a chamois cloth so that it would be pure and untouched while the spirit of Sakhmet looked down sorrowfully over the stolen treasures of this room... There was no mark or print on it when I left it."

"Well, my friend, there's finger-prints on it now," declared Dubois unemotionally. He had taken out a powerful magnifying glass and was centring his gaze on the thick ankles of the statue. "And they're damn clear prints, too... Looks to me like they'd been made by some guy who'd lifted up this statue... Both hands show around the ankles... Pass me the camera, Bellamy."

Bliss had paid scant heed to the entrance of the finger-print men, but when Hani had begun to speak, he had roused himself from his despondent lethargy and concentrated his attention on the Egyptian. Then, when Dubois had announced the presence of finger-prints, he had stared, with terrible intentness, at the statue. A startling change had come over him. He was like a man in the grip of some consuming fear; and before Dubois had finished speaking he leapt to his feet and stood in a frozen attitude of stark horror.

"*God help me!*" he cried; and the sound of his voice sent a chill over me. "Those are *my* finger-prints on that statue!"

The effect of this admission was dumbfounding. Even Vance seemed momentarily shaken out of his habitual calm, and going to a small standard ash-tray he abstractedly crushed out his cigarette, though he had smoked less than half of it.

Heath was the first to break the electric silence that followed Bliss's cry of anguish. He took his dead cigar from his lips, and thrust out his chin.

"Sure, they're your finger-prints!" he snapped unpleasantly. "Who else's would they be?"

"Just a moment, Sergeant!" Vance had wholly recovered himself, and his voice was casual. "Finger-prints can be very misleadin', don't y'know. And a few digital signatures on a lethal weapon don't mean that their author is necessarily a murderer. It's most important, d'ye see, to ascertain when and under what circumstances the signatures were made."

He approached Bliss, who had remained staring at the statue of Sakhmet like a stricken man.

"I say, doctor;"—he had assumed an easy, off-hand manner—"how do you know those finger-prints are yours?"

"How do I know?" Bliss repeated the question in a resigned, colorless tone. He appeared to have aged before our very eyes; and his white, sunken cheeks made him resemble a death's-head. "Because—oh, my God!—because I made them!... I made them last night—or, rather, early this morning, before I turned in. I took hold of the statue—around the ankles—exactly where that gentleman says there are the marks of two hands."

"And how did you happen to do that, doctor?" Vance asked quietly.

"I did it without thought—I'd even forgotten doing it till the finger-prints were mentioned." Bliss spoke with feverish earnestness: he seemed to feel that his very life depended on his being believed. "When I had finished arranging all the figures of the report early this morning, at about three o'clock, I came down here to the museum. I'd told Kyle about the new shipment, and I wanted to make sure that everything was in order for his inspection... You see, Mr. Vance, a great deal depended on the impression the new treasures made on him... I looked over the items in that end cabinet, and then re-drew the curtain. Just as I was about to depart I noticed that the statue of Sakhmet had not been placed evenly on the top of the cabinet—it was not in the exact centre, and was slightly sidewise. So I reached up and straightened it—taking hold of it by the ankles..."

"Pardon me for intruding, Vance,"—Scarlett, a troubled look on his face, had stepped forward—"but I can assure you that such an act was quite natural with Doctor Bliss. He's a stickler for orderliness—it's a good-natured joke among the rest of us. We never dare leave anything out of place: he's constantly criticising us and rearranging things after us."

Vance nodded.

"Then, as I understand you, Scarlett, if a statue was left a bit askew, it would be practically inevitable that Doctor Bliss, on seeing it, would set it right."

"Yes—I think that's a reasonable conclusion."

"Many thanks." Vance turned again to Bliss. "Your explanation is that you adjusted the statue of Sakhmet, by taking hold of its ankles, and forthwith went to bed?"

"That's the truth—so help me God!" The man searched Vance's eyes eagerly. "I turned out the lights and went up-stairs. And I've not set foot in the museum till you knocked on my study door."

Heath was obviously not satisfied with this story. It was plain that he had no intention of relinquishing his belief in Bliss's guilt.

"The trouble with that alibi," he retorted doggedly, "is that you haven't got any witnesses. And it's the sort of alibi any one would pull when they'd got caught with the goods."

Markham diplomatically intervened. He himself was patently not convinced one way or the other.

"I think, Sergeant," he said, "that it might be advisable to have Captain Dubois verify the identity of those finger-prints. We'll at least know definitely then if the prints are the ones Doctor Bliss made... Can you do that now, Captain?"

"Sure thing."

Dubois reached in the hand-bag and drew forth a tiny inked roller, a narrow glass slab, and a small paper pad.

"I guess the thumbs'll be enough," he said. "There's only one set of hands showing on the statue."

He ran the inked roller over the glass slab, and going to Bliss, asked him to hold out his hands.

"Press your thumbs on the ink and then put 'em down on this paper," he ordered.

Bliss complied without a word; and when the impressions had been made Dubois again placed the jeweller's-glass in his eye and inspected the marks.

"Looks like 'em," he commented. "Ulnar loops—same like those on the statue... Anyhow, I'll check 'em."

He knelt down beside the statue and held the pad close to its ankles. For a minute or so he studied the two sets of finger-prints.

"They match," he announced at length. "No doubt about it... And there ain't another visible mark on the statue. This gentleman"—he gestured contemptuously toward Bliss—"is the only person who's laid hands on the statue, so far as I can see."

"That's bully with me," grinned Heath. "Let me have the enlargements as soon as you can—I got a feeling I'm going to need 'em." He took out a fresh cigar and bit the end off with gloating satisfaction. "I guess that'll be all, Captain. Many thanks... Now you can go and victual up."

"And let me tell you I need it." Dubois passed his camera and paraphernalia to Bellamy, who packed them with stodgy precision; and the two of them walked noisily out of the museum.

Heath finally got his cigar going, and for several moments stood puffing on it voluptuously, one eye cocked at Vance.

"That sorta sews things up—don't it, sir?" he asked. "Or maybe you've swallowed the doctor's alibi." He addressed himself to Markham. "I put it up to you, sir. There's only one set of finger-prints on that statue; and if those prints were made last night, I'd like to have somebody drive up in a hearse and tell me what became of the finger-prints of the bird who cracked Kyle over the head. Kyle was hit with the top of the statue, and whoever did it musta had hold of it by the legs... Now, Mr. Markham, I ask you: is any one going to rub off his own finger-prints and leave those of the doctor? He couldn't have done it if he'd wanted to."

Before Markham could reply, Vance spoke. "How do you know, Sergeant, that the person who killed Mr. Kyle actually wielded the statue?"

Heath gave Vance a look of amazement.

"Say! You don't seriously think, do you, that this lion-headed dame did the job by herself—like this Yogi says?" He jerked his thumb at Hani without turning his eyes.

"No, Sergeant." Vance shook his head. "I haven't yet gone in for the supernatural. And I don't think the murderer erased his finger-prints and left those of Doctor Bliss. But I do think, d'ye see, that there's some explanation which will account for all the contradict'ry phases of this astonishin' case."

"Maybe there is." Heath felt that he could be tolerant and magnanimous. "But I'm pinning my opinion on finger-prints and tangible evidence."

"A very dangerous procedure, Sergeant," Vance told him, with unwonted seriousness. "I doubt if you could ever get a conviction against Doctor Bliss on the evidence you possess. It's far too obvious—too imbecile. You're bogged with an *embarras de richesse*—meanin' that no sane man would commit a crime and leave so many silly bits of damnin' evidence around... And I believe Mr. Markham will agree with me."

"I'm not so sure," said Markham dubiously. "There's something in what you say, Vance; but on the other hand—"

"Excuse *me*, gentlemen!" Heath had suddenly become animated. "I gotta see Hennessey—I'll be back in a minute." And he stalked with vigorous determination to the front door and disappeared.

Bliss, to all appearances, had taken no interest in this discussion of his possible guilt. He had sunk back in his chair, where he sat staring resignedly at the floor—a tragic, broken figure. When the Sergeant had left us he moved his head slowly toward Vance.

"Your detective is fully justified in his opinion," he said. "I can see his point of view. Everything is against me—everything!" His tone, though flat and colorless, was bitter. "If only I hadn't fallen asleep this morning, I'd know the meaning of all this... My scarab-pin, that financial report, those finger-prints..." He shook his head like a man in a daze. "It's damnable—damnable!" His trembling hands went to his face, and he placed his elbows on his knees, bending forward in an attitude of utter despair.

"It's too damnable, doctor," Vance replied soothingly. "Therein lies our hope of a solution."

Again he walked to the cabinet and remained for some time in *distrait* contemplation. Hani had returned to his ascetic adoration of Teti-shiret; and Scarlett, frowning and unhappy, was pacing nervously up and down between the delicate state chair and the shelves holding the *shawabtis*. Markham stood in a brown study, his hands clasped behind him, gazing at the shaft of sunshine which had fallen diagonally through the high rear windows.

I noted that Hennessey had silently entered the main door and taken his post on the stair landing, one hand resting ominously in his right coat pocket.

Then the little metal door at the head of the iron spiral stairs swung open, and Heath appeared at the entrance to Doctor Bliss's study. One hand was behind him, out of sight, as he descended to the floor of the museum. He walked directly to Bliss and stood for a moment glowering grimly at the man whose guilt he believed in. Suddenly his hand shot forward—it was holding a white canvas tennis shoe.

"That yours, doctor?" he barked.

Bliss gazed at the shoe with perplexed astonishment.

"Why...yes. Certainly it's mine..."

"You bet your sweet life it's yours!" The Sergeant strode to Markham and held up the sole of the shoe for inspection. I was standing at the District Attorney's side, and I saw that the rubber sole was criss-crossed with ridges and that there was a pattern of small hollow circles on the heel. But that which sent an icy breath of horror through me was the fact that the entire sole was red with dried blood.

"I found that shoe in the study, Mr. Markham," Heath was saying. "It was wrapped in a newspaper at the bottom of the waste-basket, covered up with all kinds of trash... hidden!"

It was several moments before Markham spoke. His eyes moved from the shoe to Bliss and back again; finally they rested on Vance.

"I think that clinches it." His voice was resolute. "I have no alternative in the matter now—"

Bliss sprang to his feet and hurried toward the Sergeant, his hypnotized gaze fastened on the shoe.

"What is it?" he cried. "What has that shoe to do with Kyle's death…?" He caught sight of the blood. "Oh, God in Heaven!" he moaned.

Vance placed his hand on the man's shoulder.

"Sergeant Heath found foot-prints here, doctor. They were made by one of your canvas shoes…"

"How can that be?" Bliss's fascinated eyes were riveted on the bloody sole. "I left those shoes up-stairs in my bedroom last night, and I came down this morning in my slippers… *There's something diabolical going on in this house.*"

"Something diabolical, yes!—something unspeakably devilish… And rest assured, Doctor Bliss, I am going to find out what it is…"

"I'm sorry, Vance," Markham's stern voice rang forth ominously. "I know you don't believe Doctor Bliss is guilty. But I have a duty to perform. I'd be betraying the people who elected me if, in view of the evidence, I didn't take action.— And, after all, you may be wrong." (He said this with the kindliness of an old friend.) "In any event, my duty is clear."

He nodded to Heath.

"Sergeant, place Doctor Bliss under arrest, and charge him with the murder of Benjamin H. Kyle."

CHAPTER EIGHT

In the Study
(Friday, July 18; 2 p.m.)

I HAD OFTEN SEEN Vance in crucial moments of violent disagreement with Markham's judgment, but, whatever his feelings had been, he had always assumed a cynical and nonchalant attitude. Now, however, no lightness or playfulness marked his manner. He was grim and serious: a deep frown had settled on his forehead, and a look of baffled exasperation had come into his cold gray eyes. He compressed his lips tightly and crammed his hands deep into his coat pockets. I expected him to protest vigorously against Markham's action, but he remained silent, and I realized that he was confronted by one of the most difficult and unusual problems in his career.

His eyes drifted from Bliss to the immobile back of Hani and rested there. But they were unseeing eyes—eyes that were turned inward as if seeking for some means of counteracting the drastic step about to be taken against the great Egyptologist.

Heath, on the contrary, was elated. A grin of satisfaction had overspread his dour face at Markham's order, and without moving from in front of Bliss, he called stridently to the ominous figure of the detective on the stair landing.

"Hey, Hennessey! Tell Snitkin to phone Precinct Station 8 for a wagon... Then go out back and get Emery, and bring him in here."

Hennessey disappeared, and Heath stood watching Bliss like a cat, as though he expected the doctor to make a dash for liberty. Had the situation not been so tragic the Sergeant's attitude would have appeared humorous.

"You needn't book and finger-print the doctor at the local station," Markham told him. "Send him direct to Headquarters. I'll assume all responsibility."

"That's fine with me, sir." The Sergeant seemed greatly pleased. "I'll want to talk confidentially with this baby myself later on."

Bliss, once the blow had fallen, had drawn himself together. He sat upright, his head thrown slightly back, his eyes gazing defiantly out of the rear windows. There was no cowering, no longer any fear, in his manner. Faced with the inevitable, he had apparently decided to accept it with stoical intrepidity. I could not help admiring the man's fortitude in extremity.

Scarlett stood like a man paralyzed, his mouth hanging partly open, his eyes fixed on his employer with a kind of unbelieving horror. Hani, of all the persons in the room, was the least perturbed: he had not even turned round from his rapt contemplation of Teti-shiret.

Vance, after several moments, dropped his chin on his chest, and his perplexed frown deepened. Then, as if on sudden impulse, he swung about and walked to the end cabinet. He stood absorbed, leaning against the statue of Anûbis; but soon his head moved slowly up and down and from side to side as he inspected various parts of the cabinet and its partly-drawn curtain.

Presently he came back to Heath.

"Sergeant, let me have another look at that tennis slipper." His voice was low and strained.

Heath, without relaxing his vigilance, reached in his pocket and held out the shoe. Vance took it and, again adjusting his monocle, scrutinized the sole. Then he returned the shoe to the Sergeant.

"By the by," he said; "the doctor has more than one foot... What about the other slipper?"

"I didn't look for it," snapped Heath. "This one was enough for me. It's the right shoe—the one that made the foot-prints."

"So it is." Vance's drawl informed me that his mind was more at ease. "Still, I could bear to know where the other shoe is."

"I'll find it—don't worry, sir." Heath spoke with contemptuous cocksureness. "I've got a little investigating to do as soon as I get the doctor safely booked at Headquarters."

"Typical police procedure," murmured Vance. "Book your man and then investigate. A sweet practice."

Markham was ruffled by this comment.

"It seems to me, Vance," he remarked with angry dignity, "that the investigation has already led to something fairly definite. Whatever else we find will be in the nature of supplementary evidence."

"Oh, will it, now? Fancy that!" Vance smiled tauntingly. "I observe you've gone in for fortune-telling. Do you crystal-gaze in your moments of leisure, by any chance?... I myself am not what you'd call clairvoyant, but, Markham old dear, I can read the future better than you. And I assure you that when this investigation is continued there will be no supplement'ry evidence against Doctor Bliss. Indeed, you'll be amazed at what will turn up."

He came nearer to the District Attorney and dropped his scoffing tone.

"Can't you see, Markham, that you're playing into the murderer's hands? The person who killed Kyle planned the affair so you'd do exactly what you are doing... And, as I've already told you, you'll never get a conviction with the preposterous evidence you have."

"I'll come mighty close to it," Markham retorted. "In any event, my duty is plain. I'll have to take a chance on the conviction... But for once, Vance, I think you've permitted your theories to override a simple, obvious fact."

Before Vance could reply Hennessey and Emery came into the museum.

"Here, boys," the Sergeant ordered, "take this bird up-stairs and get some clothes on him, and bring him back here. Make it snappy."

Bliss went out between the two detectives.

Markham turned to Scarlett.

"You'd better wait in the drawing-room. I'll want to question every one, and I think you can give us some of the information we want... And take Hani with you."

"I'll be glad to do what I can." Scarlett spoke in an awed voice. "But you're making a terrible mistake—"

"I'll settle that point for myself," Markham interrupted coldly. "Be good enough to wait in the drawing-room."

Scarlett and Hani walked slowly up the museum and passed out through the great steel door.

Vance had gone to the front of the spiral stairs and was pacing up and down with suppressed anxiety. A tense atmosphere had settled over the room. No one spoke. Heath was inspecting the small statue of Sakhmet with forced curiosity; and Markham had lapsed into a state of solemn abstraction.

A few minutes later Hennessey and Emery returned with Doctor Bliss in street clothes. They had hardly reached the rear of the museum when Snitkin put his head in the front door and called:

"The wagon's here, Sergeant."

Bliss turned immediately, and the two detectives swung about alertly. The three men had taken only a few steps when Vance's voice cracked out like a whip.

"Stop!" He looked squarely at Markham. "You can't do this! The thing is a farce. You're making an unutterable ass of yourself."

I had never seen Vance so fiery—he was quite unlike his usual frigid self—and Markham was noticeably taken aback.

"Give me ten minutes," Vance hurried on. "There's something I want to find out—there's an experiment I want to make. Then, if you're not satisfied, you can go ahead with this imbecile arrest."

Heath's face grew red with anger.

"Look here, Mr. Markham," he protested; "we've got the goods—"

"Just a minute, Sergeant." Markham held up his hand: he had obviously been impressed by Vance's unusual earnestness. "Ten minutes is not going to make any material difference. And if Mr. Vance has any evidence we don't know of, we might as well learn it now." He turned brusquely to Vance. "What's on your mind? I'm willing to give you ten minutes... Has your request anything to do with what you found on top of the cabinet and put in your pocket?"

"Oh, a great deal." Vance had again assumed his habitual easy-going manner. "And many thanks for the respite... I'd suggest, however, that these two myrmidons take the doctor into the front hall and hold him there for further instructions."

Markham, after a brief hesitation, nodded to Heath, who gave Hennessey and Emery the necessary order.

When we were alone Vance turned toward the spiral stairs.

"*Imprimis,*" he said almost gaily, "I passionately desire to make a curs'ry inspection of the doctor's study. I've a premonition that we will find something there of the most entrancin' interest."

He was now half-way up the stairs, with Markham, Heath and me following.

The study was a spacious room, about twenty feet square. It had two large windows at the rear and a smaller window on the east side giving on a narrow court. There were several massive embayed bookcases about the walls; and stacked in the corners were piles of paper pamphlets and cardboard folders. Along the wall which contained the door leading into the hall, stretched a long divan. Between the two rear windows stood a large flat-topped mahogany desk, before which was a cushioned swivel chair. Several other chairs were drawn up about the desk—evidences of the conference that had been held the previous night.

It was an orderly room, and there was a striking neatness about all of its appointments. Even the papers and books on the desk were carefully arranged, attesting to Bliss's meticulous nature. The only untidiness in the study was where Heath had upset the wicker waste-basket in his search for the tennis shoe. The curtains of the rear windows were up, and the afternoon sunlight flooded in.

Vance stood for a while just inside the door glancing slowly about him. His eyes tarried for a moment on the disposition of the chairs, but more especially, I thought, on the doctor's swivel seat, which stood several feet away from the desk. He looked at the heavily padded hall door, and let his gaze rest on the drawn curtain of the side window. After a pause he went to the window and raised the shade,—the window was shut.

"Rather strange," he commented. "A torrid day like this— and the window closed. Bear that in mind, Markham... You observe, of course, that there's a window opposite, in the next house."

"What possible significance could that have?" asked Markham irritably.

"I haven't the foggiest notion, don't y'know... Unless," Vance added whimsically, "something went on in here that the occupant—or occupants—of the room didn't wish the neighbors to know about. The trees in the yard completely preclude any spying through the rear windows."

"Huh! That looks like a point in our favor," Heath rejoined. "The doc shuts the side window and pulls the shade down so's nobody'll hear him going in and out of the museum, or'll see him hiding the shoe."

Vance nodded.

"Your reasoning, Sergeant, is good as far as it goes. But you might carry the equation to one more decimal point. Why, for instance, didn't your guilty doctor open the window and throw up the shade after the dire deed was done? Why should he leave another obvious clew indicating his guilt?"

"Guys who commit murder, Mr. Vance," argued the Sergeant pugnaciously, "don't think of everything."

"The trouble with this crime," Vance returned quietly, "is that the murderer thought of too many things. He erred on the side of prodigality, so to speak."

He stepped to the desk. On one end lay a low starched turn-over collar with a dark-blue four-in-hand pulled through it.

"Behold," he said, "the doctor's collar and cravat which he removed last night during the conference. The scarab pin was in the cravat. Any one might have taken it—eh, what?"

"So you remarked before." Markham's tone held a note of bored sarcasm. "Did you bring us here to show us the necktie? Scarlett told us it was here. Forgive me, Vance, if I confess that I am not stunned by your discovery."

"No, I didn't lead you here to exhibit the doctor's neck-wear." Vance spoke with calm assurance. "I merely mentioned the four-in-hand *en passant*."

He brushed the spilled papers of the waste-basket back and forth with his foot.

"I am rather anxious to know where the doctor's other tennis shoe is. I have a feelin' its whereabouts might tell us something."

"Well, it ain't in the basket," declared Heath. "If it had been I'd have found it."

"Ah! But, Sergeant, why wasn't it in the basket? That's a point worth considerin', don't y'know."

"Maybe it didn't have any blood on it. And that being the case, there wasn't any use in hiding it."

"But, my word! It strikes me that the blameless left shoe is hidden even better than was the incriminatin' right shoe." (During the discussion Vance had made a fairly thorough search of the study for the missing tennis shoe.) "It's certainly not round here."

Markham, for the first time since we quitted the museum, showed signs of interest.

"I see your point, Vance," he conceded reluctantly. "The telltale shoe was hidden here in the study, and the other one has disappeared... I admit that's rather odd. What's your explanation?"

"Oh, I say! Let's locate the shoe before we indulge in speculation..." Vance then addressed himself to Heath. "Sergeant, if you should get Brush to conduct you to Doctor Bliss's bedchamber, I'm rather inclined to think you'll find the missing shoe there. You remember the doctor said he wore his tennis shoes up-stairs last night and came down this morning in his house slippers."

"Huh!" Heath scouted the suggestion. Then he gave Vance a sharp, calculating look. After a moment he changed his mind. Shrugging his shoulders in capitulation, he went swiftly out into the hall, and we could hear him calling down the rear stairs for the butler.

"If the Sergeant finds the shoe up-stairs," Vance observed to Markham, "it will be fairly conclusive evidence that the doctor didn't wear his tennis shoes this morning; for we know that he did not return to his bedroom after descending to his study before breakfast."

Markham looked perplexed.

"Then who brought the other shoe from his room this morning? And how did it get in the waste-basket? And how did it become blood-stained?... Surely the murderer wore the shoe that Heath found here..."

"Oh, yes—there can be no doubt of that." Vance nodded gravely. "And my theory is that the murderer wore only the one tennis shoe and left the other up-stairs."

Markham clicked his tongue with annoyance.

"Such a theory doesn't make sense."

"Forgive me, Markham, for disagreeing with you," Vance returned dulcetly. "But I think it makes more sense than the clews on which you're so trustfully counting to convict the doctor."

Heath burst into the room at this moment, holding the left tennis shoe in his hand. His expression was sheepish, but his eyes blinked with excitement.

"It was there, all right," he announced, "—at the foot of the bed... Now, how did it get there?"

"Perhaps," softly suggested Vance, "the doctor wore it up-stairs last night, as he said."

"Then how the hell did the other shoe get down here?" The Sergeant was now holding the two shoes, one in each hand, staring at them in wrathful bewilderment.

"If you knew who brought that other shoe down-stairs this morning," returned Vance, "you'd know who killed Kyle." Then he added: "Not that it would do us any particular good at the present moment."

Markham had been standing scowling at the floor and smoking furiously. The shoe episode had disconcerted him. But now he looked up and made an impatient gesture.

"You're making a mountain out of this affair, Vance," he asserted aggressively. "A number of simple explanations suggest themselves. The most plausible one seems to be that Doctor Bliss, when he came down-stairs this morning, picked up his tennis shoes to have them handy in his study, and in his nervousness—or merely accidentally—dropped one, or even failed to pick both of them up, and did not discover the fact until he was here—"

"And then," continued Vance, with a japish grin, "he took off one slipper and put on the tennis shoe, murdered Kyle, re-exchanged it for his temporarily discarded slipper, and tucked the tennis shoe in the waste-basket."

"It's possible."

Vance sighed audibly.

"Possible—yes. I suppose that almost anything is possible in this illogical world. But really, Markham, I can't subscribe enthusiastically to your touchin' theory of the doctor's having picked up one shoe instead of two and not having known the difference. He's much too orderly and methodical—too conscious of details."

"Let us assume then," Markham persisted, "that the doctor actually wore one tennis shoe and one bedroom slipper when he came to the study this morning. Scarlett told us his feet troubled him a great deal."

"If that hypothesis is correct," countered Vance, "how did the other bedroom slipper get down-stairs? He would hardly have put it in his pocket and carried it along."

"Brush perhaps…"

Heath had been following the discussion closely, and now he went into action.

"We can check that point *pronto*, Mr. Vance," he said; and going briskly to the hall door, he called down the stairs to the butler.

But no help came from Brush. He declared that neither he nor any member of the household had been near the study after Bliss had gone there at eight o'clock, with the one exception of the time when he carried the doctor's breakfast to him. When asked what shoes the doctor was wearing, Brush answered that he had taken no notice.

When the butler had gone Vance shrugged his shoulders.

"Let's not fume and whirret ourselves over the mysteriously separated pair of tennis shoes. My prim'ry reason for luring you to the study was to inspect the remains of the doctor's breakfast."

Markham gave a perceptible start, and his eyes narrowed.

"Good Heavens! You don't believe…? I'll confess I thought of it, too. But then came all that other evidence…"

"Thought of what, sir?" Heath was frankly exasperated, and his tone was irritable.

"Both Mr. Markham and I," explained Vance soothingly, "noted the dazed condition of Doctor Bliss when he appeared this morning in answer to my continued pounding on the door."

"He'd been asleep. Didn't he tell us so?"

"Quite. And that's why I'm so dashed interested in his matutinal coffee."

Vance walked to the end of the desk upon which rested a small silver tray containing a rack of toast and a cup and saucer. The toast had not been touched, but the cup was practically empty. Only the congealed brown dregs of what had evidently been coffee remained in the bottom. Vance leant over and looked into the cup. Then he lifted it to his nose.

"There's a slightly acrid odor here," he remarked. He touched the tip of his finger to the inside of the cup and placed it on his tongue.

"Yes!... Just what I thought," he nodded, setting the cup down. "Opium. And it's powdered opium—the kind commonly used in Egypt. The other forms and derivatives of opium—such as laudanum, morphine, heroin, thebain, and codein—are not easily obtainable there."

Heath had come forward and stood peering belligerently into the cup.

"Well, suppose there was opium in the coffee," he rumbled. "What does that mean?"

"Ah, who knows?" Vance was lighting a cigarette, his eyes in space. "It might, of course, account for the doctor's long siesta this morning and for his confused condition when he answered my knock. Also, it might indicate that some one narcotized his coffee for a purpose. The fact is, Serge-ant, the opium in the doctor's coffee might mean various things. At the present moment I'm expressing no opinion. I'm merely calling Mr. Markham's attention to the drug... I'll say this, however: as soon as I saw the doctor this morning and observed the way he acted, I guessed that there would be evidences of an opiate in the study. And, being fairly familiar with conditions in Egypt, I surmised that the opiate would prove to be powdered opium—*opii pulvis*. Opium makes one very thirsty: that is why I wasn't in the least astonished when the doctor asked for a drink of water." He looked at Markham. "Does this discovery of the opium affect the doctor's legal status?"

"It's certainly a strong point in his favor," Markham returned after several moments.

That he was deeply perplexed was only too apparent. But he was loath to forgo his belief in Bliss's guilt; and when he spoke again it was obvious that he was arguing desperately against Vance's new discovery.

"I realize that the presence of the opium will have to be explained away before a conviction can be assured. But, on the other hand, we don't know how much opium he took. Nor do we know when he took it. He may have drunk the coffee *after* the murder—we have only his word that he drank it at nine o'clock... No, it certainly doesn't affect the fundamental issue—though it does raise a very grave question. But the evidence against him is too strong to be counterbalanced by this one point in his favor. Surely, you must see, Vance, that the mere presence of opium in that cup is not conclusive evidence that Bliss was asleep from nine o'clock until you knocked on the study door."

"The perfect Public Prosecutor," sighed Vance. "But a shrewd defense lawyer could sow many fecund seeds of doubt in the jurors' so-called minds—eh, what?"

"True." The admission came after a moment's thought. "But we can't overlook the fact that Bliss was practically the only person who had the opportunity to kill Kyle. Every one else was out of the house, with the exception of Hani; and Hani impresses me as a harmless fanatic who believes in the supernatural power of his Egyptian deities. So far as we know, Bliss was the only person who was actually on hand when Kyle was murdered."

Vance studied Markham for several seconds. Then he said: "Suppose it had not been necess'ry for the murderer to have been anywhere near the museum when Kyle was killed with the statue of Sakhmet."

Markham took his cigar slowly from his mouth.

"What do you mean? How could that statue have been wielded by an absent person? It strikes me you're talking nonsense."

"Perhaps I am." Vance was troubled and serious. "And yet, Markham, I found something on top of that end cabinet which makes me think that maybe the murder was planned with diabolical cleverness... As I told you, I want to make an experiment. Then, when I have made it, your course of action must rest entirely on your own convictions... There's something both terrible and subtle about this crime. All its outward appearances are misleading—deliberately so."

"How long will this experiment take?" Markham was patently impressed by Vance's tone.

"Only a few minutes..."

Heath had taken a sheet of newspaper from the basket and was carefully wrapping up the cup.

"This goes to our chemist," he explained sullenly. "I'm not doubting you, Mr. Vance, but I want an expert analysis."

"You're quite right, Sergeant."

Vance's eye at that moment caught sight of a small bronze tray on the desk, containing several yellow pencils and a fountain pen. Leaning over casually, he picked up the pencils, glanced at them, and put them back on the tray. Markham noted the action, as did I, but he refrained from asking any question.

"The experiment will have to be made in the museum," Vance said; "and I'll need a couple of sofa pillows for it."

He walked to the divan and tucked two large pillows under his arm. Then he went to the steel door and held it open.

Markham and Heath and I passed down the spiral stairs; and Vance followed us.

CHAPTER NINE

Vance Makes an Experiment
(Friday, July 13; 2.15 p.m.)

VANCE WENT DIRECT to the end cabinet before which Kyle's body had been found, and dropped the two sofa pillows on the floor. Then he looked again speculatively at the upper edge of the cabinet.

"I wonder...," he murmured. "Dash it all! I'm almost afraid to carry on. If I should be wrong, this entire case would come topplin' about my head..."

"Come, come!" Markham was growing impatient. "Soliloquies have gone out of date, Vance. If you have anything to show me, let's get it over with."

"Right you are."

Vance stepped to the ash-tray and resolutely crushed out his cigarette. Returning to the cabinet he beckoned to Markham and Heath.

"By way of *præludium*," he began, "I want to call your attention to this curtain. You will observe that the brass ring at the end has been slipped off of the rod and is now hanging down."

For the first time I noticed that the small ring on the corner of the curtain was not strung on the rod, and that the left edge of the curtain sagged correspondingly.

"You will also observe," Vance continued, "that the curtain of this cabinet is only half drawn. It's as if some one had started to draw the curtain and, for some reason, had stopped. When I saw the partly-drawn curtain this morning it struck me as a bit peculiar, for obviously the curtain should have been entirely closed or else entirely open. We may assume that the curtain was closed when Kyle arrived here—we have Hani's word for it that he had pulled shut the curtain of this particular cabinet because of the disorder of its contents; and Doctor Bliss mentioned to Kyle on the telephone that the new treasures were in the end cabinet—*the cabinet with the drawn curtain*... Now, in order to open the curtain, one has only to make a single motion of the arm—that is to say, one has only to take hold of the left-hand edge of it and pull it to the right: the brass rings would slide easily over the metal pole... But what do we find? We find the curtain only half drawn! Kyle unquestionably would not have opened the curtain half-way to inspect the contents of the cabinet. Therefore, I concluded that something must have halted the curtain at the half-way point, and that Kyle died before he could draw the curtain entirely open... I say, Markham; are you with me?"

"Go on." Markham had become interested. Heath, too, was watching Vance with close attention.

"Perpend, then. Kyle was found dead directly in front of this end cabinet; and he had died as the result of having been struck over the head by the heavy diorite statue of Sakhmet. This statue, as we know, had been placed by Hani on the top of the cabinet. When I observed that the curtain of the cabinet had been only partly opened and then discovered that the first brass ring of the curtain—the ring on the extreme left end—was not on the rod, I began to speculate—especially as I was familiar with Doctor Bliss's orderly habits. Had that ring been off of the rod last night when Doctor Bliss came into the museum, you may rest assured he would have seen it..."

"Are you suggesting, Vance," asked Markham, "that the ring was deliberately taken off of the rod some time this morning—and for a purpose?"

"Yes! At some time between Doctor Bliss's phone call to Kyle last night and Kyle's arrival this morning, I believe that some one removed that ring from the rod—and, as you say, for a purpose!"

"What purpose?" Heath put the question. His voice was aggressive and antagonistic.

"That remains to be seen, Sergeant." Vance spoke with scarcely any modulation of tone. "I'll admit I have a rather definite theory about it. In fact, I had a theory about it the moment I saw the position in which Kyle's body lay and learned that Hani had placed the statue atop the end cabinet. The partly drawn curtain and the unstrung brass ring substantiated that theory."

"I think I understand what's in your mind, Vance." Markham nodded slowly. "Was that why you inspected the top of the cabinet and got Hani to show you exactly where he had placed the statue?"

"Precisely. And not only did I find what I was looking for, but Hani confirmed my suspicions when he pointed to the spot where he had set the statue. That spot was several inches back from the edge of the cabinet; but there was also a deep scratch at the very edge and a second outline of the statue's base in the dust, showing that the statue had been moved forward after Hani had put it in place."

"But Doctor Bliss admitted he moved it last night before retiring," suggested Markham.

"He said only that he had straightened the statue," Vance answered. "And the two impressions made in the dust by the front of the statue's base are exactly parallel, so that the adjustment to which Doctor Bliss referred could not have been the moving of the statue six inches forward."

"I see what you mean... Your theory is that some one moved the statue to the very edge of the cabinet after Doctor Bliss had straightened it. And it's not an unreasonable assumption."

Heath, who had been listening sullenly with half-shut eyes, suddenly mounted one of the chairs in front of the cabinet and peered over the moulding.

"I want to see this," he mumbled. Presently he descended and wagged his head heavily at Markham. "It's like Mr. Vance says, all right... But what's all this hocus-pocus got to do with the case?"

"That's what I'm endeavorin' to ascertain, Sergeant," smiled Vance. "It may have nothing to do with it. On the other hand..."

He leaned over and, with considerable effort, lifted the statue of Sakhmet. (As I have said, the statue was about two feet high. It was solidly sculptured and had a heavy thick base. I later lifted the statue to test it, and I should say it weighed at least thirty pounds.) Vance, stepping on a chair, placed the statue, with great precision, on top of the cabinet at the very edge of the moulding. Having carefully superimposed its base over the outlines in the dust, he drew the curtain shut. Then he took the free brass ring in his left hand, turned the corner of the curtain back until the ring reached the left-hand edge of the statue, tipped the statue to the right, and placed the ring just under the forward edge of the statue's base.

Having done this, he reached into his coat pocket and drew forth the object he had found on the top of the cabinet. He held it up to us.

"What I discovered, Markham," he explained, "was a three-inch section of a pencil, carefully cut and trimmed. I assumed that it was a home-made 'upright' such as is used in figure-4 traps... Let us see if it works."

He tipped the statue forward and propped the piece of pencil under the rear edge of the statue's base. He took his hands away, and the statue stood leaning toward us, perilously balanced. For a moment it seemed as if it might topple over of its own accord, but the prepared pencil was apparently the exact length necessary to tilt the statue forward without quite upsetting its equilibrium.

"So far my theory checks." Vance stepped down from the chair. "Now, we will proceed with the experiment."

He moved the chair to one side, and arranged the two sofa pillows over the spot where Kyle's head had lain at the foot of Anûbis. Then he straightened up, and faced the District Attorney.

"Markham," he said sombrely, "I present you with a possibility. Regard the position of that curtain; consider the position of the loose brass ring—under the edge of the statue; observe the tilting attitude of Our Lady of Vengeance; and then picture the arrival of Kyle this morning. He had been informed that the new treasures were in the end cabinet, with the curtain drawn. He told Brush not to disturb Doctor Bliss because he was going into the museum to inspect the contents of the recent shipment."

He paused and deliberately lighted a cigarette. By his slow, lazy movements I knew that his nerves were tense.

"I am not suggesting," he continued, "that Kyle met his end as the result of a death trap. In fact, I do not even know if my reconstructed trap will work. But I am advancing the theory as a possibility; for if the defense attorneys can show that Kyle could have been murdered by some one other than Doctor Bliss—that is, *by an absent person*—then your case against him would receive a decided setback..."

He stepped over to the statue of Anûbis. Lifting up the lower left-hand corner of the curtain, he stood close against the west wall of the museum.

"Let us say that Kyle, after taking his position before this end cabinet, reached out and drew the curtain aside. Now, what would have happened—provided the death trap had actually been set?..."

He gave the curtain a sharp jerk to the right. It moved over the rod until it was caught and held half-way across by the brass ring that had been inserted beneath Sakhmet's base. The jar dislodged the statue from its perilously balanced position. It toppled forward and fell with a terrific thud upon the sofa pillows, in the exact spot where Kyle's head had lain.

There were several moments of silence. Markham continued to smoke, his eyes focussed on the fallen statue. He was frowning and thoughtful. Heath, however, was frankly astounded. Apparently he had not considered the possibility of a death trap, and Vance's demonstration had everted, to a great extent, all his set theories. He glared at the statue of Sakhmet with perplexed amazement, his cigar held tightly between his teeth.

Vance was the first to speak.

"The experiment seems to have worked, don't y'know. Really, I think I've demonstrated the possibility of Kyle's having been killed while alone in the museum... Kyle was rather short in stature, and there was sufficient distance between the top of the cabinet and Kyle's head for the statue to have gained a deadly momentum. The width of the cabinet is only a little over two feet, so that it would have been inevitable that the statue would hit him on the head, provided he had been standing in front of it. And he obviously would have stood directly in front of it when he pulled the curtain. The weight of the statue is sufficient to have caused the terrific fracture of his skull; and the position of the statue across the back of his head is wholly consistent with his having been killed by a carefully planned trap."

Vance made a slight gesture of emphasis.

"You must admit, Markham, that the demonstration I've just given you makes plausible the guilt of any absent person, and consequently removes one of your strongest counts against Doctor Bliss—namely, proximity and opportunity... And this fact, taken in connection with the opium found in the coffee, gives him a convincing, though not an absolute, alibi."

"Yes..." Markham spoke with deliberate and pensive slowness. "The negative clews you have found tend to counteract the direct clews of the scarab and the financial report and the bloody foot-prints. There's no doubt about it: the doctor could present a strong defense..."

"A reasonable doubt, as it were—eh, what?" Vance grinned. "A beautiful phrase—meaningless, of course, but typically legal. As if the mind of man were ever capable of being reasonable!... And don't overlook the fact, Markham, that, if the doctor had merely intended to brain Kyle with the statue of Sakhmet, the evidences of the death trap would not have been present. If his object was only to kill Kyle, why should the whittled pencil—in the shape of an 'upright'—have been on top of the cabinet?"

"You're perfectly right," Markham admitted. "A shrewd defense attorney could make a shambles of the case I have against the doctor."

"And consider your direct evidence for a moment." Vance seated himself and crossed his legs. "The scarab pin, which was found beside the body, could have been palmed by any one at the conference last night, and deliberately placed beside the murdered body. Or, if the doctor had been put to sleep by the opium in his coffee, it would have been an easy matter for the murderer to have taken the pin from the desk this morning— the door into the study, y'know, was never locked. And what would have been simpler than to have taken the financial report at the same time, and slipped it into Kyle's dead hand?... As for the bloody foot-prints: any member of the household could have taken the tennis shoe from Doctor Bliss's bedroom and made the prints in the blood and then chucked the shoe in the waste-basket while the doctor slept under the influence of the opiate... And that closed east window on the court: doesn't that closed window, with its drawn shade, indicate that some one in the study didn't want the neighbors next door to see what was going on?"

Vance took a slow draw on his cigarette and blew out a long spiral of smoke.

"I'm no Demosthenes, Markham, but I'd take Doctor Bliss's case in any court, and guarantee him an acquittal."

Markham had begun walking up and down, his hands behind his back.

"The presence of this death trap and of the opium in the coffee cup," he conceded at length, "casts an entirely new light on the case. It throws the affair wide open and makes possible and even plausible some one else's guilt." He stopped suddenly and looked sharply at Heath. "What's your opinion, Sergeant?"

Heath was obviously in a quandary.

"I'm going cuckoo," he confessed, after a pause. "I thought we had the damn affair sewed up in an air-tight bag, and now Mr. Vance pulls a lot of his subtle stuff and hands the doc a loophole." He gave Vance a belligerent glare. "Honest to Gawd, Mr. Vance, you shoulda been a lawyer." His contempt was devastating.

Markham could not help smiling, but Vance shook his head sadly and looked at the Sergeant with an exaggeratedly injured air.

"Oh, I say, Sergeant; must you be insultin'?" he protested whimsically. "I'm only tryin' to save you and Mr. Markham from making a silly blunder. And what thanks do I get? I'm told I should have been a lawyer! Alack and welladay!"

"Let's forgo the cynicism." Markham was too upset to fall in with Vance's frivolous attitude. "You've made your point. And, in doing so, you've saddled me with a serious and weighty problem."

"Still and all," pursued Heath, "there's plenty of evidence against Bliss."

"Quite true, Sergeant." Vance had again become thoughtful. "But I'm afraid that evidence will not bear the closest scrutiny."

"You think, I take it," said Markham, "that the evidence was deliberately planted—that the actual murderer maliciously placed these clews so that they would point to Doctor Bliss."

"Is such a technic so unusual?" asked Vance. "Hasn't many a murderer sought to throw suspicion on some one else? Isn't criminal history filled with cases of innocent men being convicted on convincing circumstantial evidence? And is it not entirely possible that the misleading evidence in such cases was deliberately planted by the real culprits?"

"Still," Markham returned, "I can't afford, at this stage of the game, to ignore entirely the indicatory evidence pointing to Doctor Bliss. I must be able to prove a plot against him before I can completely exonerate him."

"And the arrest?"

Markham hesitated. He realized, I think, the hopelessness of his case now that Vance had unearthed so many contradictory bits of evidence.

"It's impossible, of course," he concluded, "to order the doctor's arrest at present, in view of the extenuating factors you've brought to light… But," he added grimly, "I'm certainly not going to ignore altogether the evidence against him."

"And just what does one do in such legalistically complicated circumstances?"

Markham smoked for a while in troubled silence.

"I'm going to keep Bliss under close surveillance," he pronounced finally. Then he turned to Heath. "Sergeant, you may order your men to release the doctor. But make arrangements to have him followed day and night."

"That suits me, sir." Heath started toward the front stairs.

"And Sergeant," Markham called; "tell Doctor Bliss he is not to leave the house until I have seen him."

Heath disappeared on his errand.

CHAPTER TEN

The Yellow Pencil
(Friday, July 13; 2.30 p.m.)

Markham SLOWLY LIGHTED a fresh cigar and sat down heavily on one of the folding chairs near the inlaid coffer, facing Vance.

"The situation is beginning to look serious—and complex," he said, with a weary sigh.

"More serious than you think," Vance returned. "And far more complex... I assure you, Markham, that this murder is one of the most astounding and subtle criminal plots you have ever been faced with. Superficially it appears simple and direct—it was intended to appear that way, d'ye see—and your first reading of the clews was exactly what the murderer counted on."

Markham regarded Vance shrewdly.

"You have an idea of what that plot is?" His words were more a statement than a question.

"Yes...oh, yes." Vance at once became aloof. "An idea?...
Quite. But not what you'd term a blindin' illumination. I immediately suspected a plot; and all the subsequent findings verified
my theory. But I've only a nebulous idea regardin' it. And the
precise object of the plot is totally obfuscated. However, since
I know that the surface indications are deliberately misleading,
there's a chance of getting at the truth."

Markham sat up aggressively.

"What's in your mind?"

"Oh, my dear chap! You flatter me abominably." Vance
smiled blandly. "My mind is beclouded and adumbrated. It is
shot with mist and mizzle, with vapor and haze and steam; it is
cirrous and nubiferous, cumulous and vaporous; it is filled with
wool-packs, mare's-tails, colt's-tails, cat's-tails, frost smoke, and
spindrift. 'The lowring element scowls o'er the darkened land-
scip.'... My mind, in fact, is nephological—"

"Spare me your meteorological vocabulary. Remember,
I'm only an ignorant District Attorney." Markham's sarcasm
was measured by his exasperation. "Perhaps, however, you can
suggest our next step. I frankly admit that, aside from cross-
examining the members of the Bliss household, I can't see any
means of approach to this problem; for, if Bliss isn't guilty, the
crime was obviously committed by some one who was not only
intimate with the domestic situation here but who had access
to the house."

"I think, don't y'know," suggested Vance, "that we should
first acquaint ourselves with the conditions and relationships
existing in the ménage. It would give us a certain equipment,
what? And it might indicate some fertile line of inquiry." He
bent forward in his chair. "Markham, the solution of this
problem depends almost entirely on our finding the motive.
And there are sinister ramifications to that motive. Kyle's
murder was no ordin'ry crime. It was planned with a finesse
and a cunning amounting to genius. Only a tremendous
incentive could have produced it. There's fanaticism behind
this crime—a powerful, devastating *idée fixe* that is cruel

and unspeakably ruthless. The actual murder was merely a prelimin'ry to something far more devilish—it was the means to an end. And that ultimate object was infinitely more terrible and despicable than Kyle's precipitous demise... A nice, clean, swift murder can sometimes be justified, or at least extenuated. But the criminal in this instance did not stop with murder: he used it as a weapon to crush and ruin an innocent person..."

"Granted what you say is true,"—Markham rose uneasily and leaned against the shelves containing the *shawabtis*—"how can we discover the interrelationships of this household without interviewing its members?"

"By questioning the one man who stands apart from the actual inmates."

"Scarlett?"

Vance nodded.

"He undoubtedly knows more than he has told us. He has been with the Bliss expedition for two years. He has lived in Egypt, and is acquainted with the family history... Why not have him in here for a brief *causerie* before tackling the members of the establishment? There are several points I could endure to know ere the investigation proceeds."

Markham was watching Vance closely. Presently he moved his head up and down slowly.

"You've something in mind, Vance, and it's neither nimbus, cumulus, stratus, nor cirrus... Very well. I'll get Scarlett here and let you question him."

Heath returned to the museum at this moment.

"Doc Bliss has gone to his bedroom, with orders to stay there," he reported. "The rest of 'em are in the drawing-room, and Hennessey and Emery are keeping their eye on things. Also, I sent the wagon away—and Snitkin's watching the front door." I had rarely seen Heath in so discouraged a mood.

"How did Doctor Bliss act when you ordered his release?" Vance asked.

"Didn't seem to care one way or another," the Sergeant told him, with an intonation of disgust. "Didn't even say anything. Just went up-stairs with his head down, stunned-like... Queer bird, if you ask me."

"Most Egyptologists are queer birds, Sergeant," Vance remarked consolingly.

Markham was again growing impatient. He addressed himself curtly to Heath.

"Mr. Vance and I have decided to find out what Mr. Scarlett can tell us before going on with the investigation. Will you ask him to step here?"

The Sergeant extended his arms and let them fall in a broad gesture of resignation. Then he went from the museum. In a few moments he returned with Scarlett in tow.

Vance drew up several chairs. By his serious, deliberate manner I realized that he regarded the conference with Scarlett as highly important. At the time I was not aware of what was in his mind; nor did I understand why he had chosen Scarlett as his chief source of information. But before the day was over it was only too clear to me. With subtle accuracy and precision he had chosen the one man who could supply the data that were needed to solve the murder of Kyle. And the things Vance learned from Scarlett that afternoon proved to be the determining factors in his solution of the case.

Without preliminaries Vance informed Scarlett of the altered status of Doctor Bliss.

"Mr. Markham has decided to postpone the doctor's arrest. The evidence at present is most conflicting. We've discovered several things, which, from the legal point of view, throw serious doubt on his guilt. The fact is, Scarlett, we've come to the conclusion that further investigation is necess'ry before we can make any definite move."

Scarlett appeared greatly relieved.

"By Jove, Vance, I'm frightfully glad of that!" he exclaimed with complete conviction. "Doctor Bliss's guilt is unthinkable. What could possibly have been the man's motive? Kyle was his benefactor—"

"Have you any ideas on the subject?" Vance interrupted.

Scarlett shook his head emphatically.

"Not the ghost of an idea. The thing has stunned me. I can't imagine how it could have happened."

"Yes...most mysterious," Vance murmured. "We'll have to get at the matter by tryin' to discover the motive... That's why we're appealin' to you. We want to know just what the inner workings are in the Bliss ménage. You, bein' more or less of an outsider, can possibly lead us to the truth... For instance, you mentioned an intimate relationship between Kyle and Mrs. Bliss's father. Let us have the whole story."

"It's a bit romantic, but quite simple." Scarlett paused and took out his briar pipe. When he had got it going he continued: "You know the story of old Abercrombie, Meryt's father. He went to Egypt in 1885, and became Grébaut's assistant the following year when Sir Gaston Maspero returned to France to resume his chair at the Collège de France. Maspero returned to Egypt in 1899 and retained his position as head of the Egyptian *Service des Antiquités* at Cairo until his resignation in 1914, at which time he was elected permanent Secretary of the Académie des Inscriptions et Belles-Lettres in Paris. Abercrombie then succeeded Maspero as Director of Antiquities at the Cairo Museum. In 1898, however, Abercrombie had fallen in love with a Copt lady, and had married her. Meryt was born two years later—in 1900."

Scarlett seemed to be having difficulty with his pipe, and used two matches to relight it.

"Kyle entered the picture four years before Meryt's birth," he went on. "He came to Egypt in 1896 as a representative of a group of New York bankers who had become financially interested in the proposed Nile irrigation system.* He met Abercrombie—then Grébaut's assistant—and their acquaintance developed into a close friendship. Kyle returned to Egypt nearly every year during the process of the dam's

---

* *The irrigation to which Scarlett referred was the system that resulted in the Aswan Dam, the Asyût Weir, and the Esneh Barrage.*

construction—that is, until 1902. He naturally met the Coptic lady whom Abercrombie subsequently married, and, I have every reason to believe, was much smitten with her. But being Abercrombie's friend and a gentleman, he refrained from any trespassing. However, when the lady died, at Meryt's birth, he quite openly transferred his affections from the mother to the daughter. He became Meryt's godfather and, in a big-hearted way, looked out for her as though she had been his own child... Kyle wasn't a bad scout."

"And Bliss?"

"Bliss first went to Egypt in the winter of 1913. He met Abercrombie at that time, and they became friendly. He also met Meryt, who was then only thirteen years old. Seven years later—in 1920—young Salveter introduced Bliss to Kyle; and the first expedition to Egypt was made in the winter of 1921–22. Abercrombie died in Egypt in the summer of 1922, and Meryt was fathered, after a fashion, by Hani, who had been an old family retainer. The second Bliss expedition was in 1922–23; and Bliss again met Meryt. She was now twenty-three; and the following spring Bliss married her... You met Meryt, Vance, on the third Bliss expedition in 1924... Bliss brought Meryt back to America with him after the second expedition; and last year he added Hani to his personal staff. Hani had then been made an under inspector by the Egyptian Government... That sums up the relationship between Bliss and Kyle and Abercrombie and Meryt. Is it what you wanted?"

"Exactly." Vance looked at the tip of his cigarette thoughtfully. "Briefly, then, Kyle was interested in Mrs. Bliss because of his love for her mother and his friendship for her father; and no doubt he had an added interest in financing Bliss's later expeditions because of the fact that Bliss married the daughter of his lost love."

"Yes, the assumption is perfectly reasonable."

"That bein' the case, Kyle probably has not forgotten Mrs. Bliss in his will. Do you happen to know, Scarlett, if he made any provision for her?"

"As I understand it," Scarlett explained, "he left a very considerable fortune to Meryt. I have only Hani's word for it; but he once mentioned to me that Kyle had willed her a large amount. Hani was elated over the fact, for there's no doubt he has a very deep, dog-like affection for her."

"And what of Salveter?"

"I presume that Kyle has taken care of him generously. Kyle was not married—whether his loyalty to Meryt's mother was responsible for his bachelorhood, I can't say—and Salveter was his only nephew. Moreover, he liked Salveter immensely. I'm inclined to think that, when the will is read, it'll be found he left Meryt and Salveter equal amounts."

Vance turned to Markham.

"Could you have one of your various diplomatic coadjutors find out confidentially about Kyle's will? I've a notion the data would help us materially."

"It might be done," Markham returned. "The moment this thing breaks in the papers Kyle's attorneys will come forward. I'll use a little pressure."

Vance again addressed Scarlett.

"I believe you told me that Kyle had recently begun to balk at the expenses of the Bliss expeditions.—Can you suggest any reason for his deflection other than lack of immediate results?"

"No—o." Scarlett pondered a moment. "You know, expeditions such as Doctor Bliss had planned are deucedly expensive luxuries, and the results, of course, are highly problematic. Furthermore, however successful they are, it takes a long time to produce any tangible evidence of their value. Kyle was getting impatient; he was not an Egyptologist and knew little of such matters; and he may have thought that Doctor Bliss was on an extravagant wild-goose chase at his expense. Fact is, he intimated last year that unless some definite results were obtained during the new excavations he'd not go on doling out money. That was why the doctor was so anxious last night to present a financial report and to have Kyle see the new treasures that arrived yesterday."

"There was nothing personal in Kyle's attitude?"

"To the contrary. All the relationships were very friendly. Kyle liked Bliss personally and respected him immensely. And Bliss had only praise and gratitude for Kyle... No, Vance, you'll find nothing by going at it from that angle."

"How did the doctor feel last night about the possible outcome of his interview with Kyle?—Was he worried or sanguine?"

Scarlett knit his brows and puffed at his pipe.

"Neither, I should say," he answered at length. "His state of mind was what might be described as philosophic. He's inclined to be easy-going—takes things as they come—and he has a rare amount of self-control. The serious scholar at all times—if you comprehend me."

"Quite..." Vance put out his cigarette and folded his hands behind his head. "But what do you think would have been the effect on Doctor Bliss if Kyle had refused to finance the expedition further?"

"That's hard to say... He'd probably have looked for capital elsewhere—remember, he had made great strides in his work despite the fact that he had not actually entered Intef's tomb."

"And what was young Salveter's attitude in the face of a possible cessation of the excavations?"

"He was more upset about it than the doctor. Salveter has unbounded enthusiasm, and he made several pleas to his uncle to continue financing the work. If Kyle had refused to go on, it would have come pretty near breaking the lad's heart. I understand he even offered to forgo his inheritance if Kyle would see the expedition through."

"There's no mistakin' Salveter's earnestness," Vance acceded. Then he was silent for a considerable time. Finally he reached for his cigarette-case; but he did not open it, and sat tapping it with his fingers. "There's another point I want to ask you about, Scarlett," he said presently. "How does Mrs. Bliss regard her husband's work?"

The question was vague—purposely so, I imagine; and Scarlett was a little puzzled. But after a moment he replied:

"Oh, Meryt is quite the loyal wife. During the first year or so of her marriage she was most interested in all the doctor did—in fact, she accompanied him, as you know, on his 1924 expedition. Lived in a tent and all that sort of thing, and seemed perfectly happy. But—to tell you the truth, Vance—her interest has been waning of late. A racial reaction, I take it. The Egyptian blood in her is a powerful influence. Her mother was almost fanatical on the subject of Egyptian sanctity, and very proud; resented the so-called desecration of the tombs of her ancestors by western barbarians—as she designated all Occidental scientists. But Meryt has never voiced her own opinion,—I'm merely assuming that some of her mother's antagonism has recently cropped out in her. Nothing serious though, please understand. Meryt has been absolutely loyal to Bliss and his chosen work."

"Hani may have had something to do with her state of mind," commented Vance.

Scarlett shot him a questioning look.

"It's barely possible," he admitted reluctantly, and lapsed into silence.

Vance tenaciously pursued the subject.

"Most probable, I'd say. And I'd go even further. I've a suspicion that Doctor Bliss himself recognized Hani's influence on his wife, and became bitterly resentful. You recall the tirade he launched against Hani when he came into the museum this morning. He openly accused Hani of poisoning Mrs. Bliss's mind."

Scarlett moved uneasily in his chair and chewed the stem of his pipe.

"There's never been any love between the doctor and Hani," he remarked evasively. "Bliss brought him to America solely because Meryt insisted on it. I think he believes Hani is spying on him for the Egyptian Government."

"Is it entirely unlikely?" Vance put the question offhandedly.

"Really, Vance, I can't answer that." Scarlett suddenly leaned forward, and his features became tense. "But I'll tell you this: Meryt is incapable of any fundamental disloyalty to her husband. Even though she may think she made a mistake in marrying Doctor Bliss—who's much older than she is and completely absorbed in his work—she'd stand by her bargain... like a thoroughbred."

"Ah...just so." Vance nodded slightly and selected a *Régie* from his case. "And that brings me to a most delicate question... Do you think that Mrs. Bliss has any—what shall I say?—interests outside of her husband? That is, aside from Doctor Bliss's life work, is it possible that her more intimate emotions are involved elsewhere?"

Scarlett got to his feet and began spluttering.

"Oh, really, Vance... Dash it all!... You've no right to ask me such a question... I'm no quidnunc... One doesn't talk about such things; it's not done—really it isn't, old man... You put me in a most embarrassing position..." (Scarlett's predicament roused my sympathy.)

"Neither is murder done in the best circles," returned Vance equably. "We're dealin' with a most unusual situation. And somebody translated Kyle from this world into the hereafter in a very distressin' fashion... But since your sensitivities are so deuced lacerated I'll withdraw the question." He smiled disarmingly. "You're not entirely impervious to the lady's charms yourself—eh, what, Scarlett?"

The man whirled about and glared at Vance ferociously. Before he could answer, Vance stood up and looked him steadily in the eyes.

"A man has been murdered," he said quietly; "and a devilish plot has been introduced into that murder. Another human life is at stake. And I'm here to find out who concocted this hideous scheme and to save an innocent person from the electric chair. Therefore I'm not going to let any squeamish conventional taboos stand in my way." His voice softened somewhat. "I appreciate your reticence. Under ordin'ry circumstances it would be most admirable. But just now it's rather silly."

Scarlett met Vance's gaze squarely, and after a few seconds he sat down again.

"You're quite right, old man," he acquiesced, in a low voice. "I'll tell you anything you want to know."

Vance nodded indifferently and smoked for a while.

"I think you've told me everything," he said finally. "But we may call on you later… It's far past lunch time. Suppose you toddle along home."

Scarlett drew a deep sigh of relief and got to his feet.

"Thanks awfully." And without another word he went out.

Heath followed him, and we could hear him giving instructions to Snitkin to let Scarlett leave the house.

"Well," said Markham to Vance, when the Sergeant had returned; "how has Scarlett's information helped you? I can't see that it has thrown any very dazzling light on our problem."

"My word!" Vance shook his head with commiserating incredulity. "Scarlett has put us infinitely forrader. He was most revealin'. We now have a definite foundation on which to stand when we chivy the members of the household."

"I'm glad you feel so confident." Markham rose and regarded Vance sternly. "You can't really believe—?" He broke off, as if he did not quite dare to articulate his thought.

"Yes, I believe this crime was merely a means to an end," Vance returned. "Its real object, I'm convinced, was to involve an innocent person and thus wash the slate clean of several annoyin' elements."

Markham stood stock-still for several seconds.

"I think I see what you mean," he nodded. "It's possible of course."

He walked up the museum and back again, his head clouded in cigar smoke.

"See here;"—he stood looking grimly down at Vance—"I want to ask you a question. I recall your asking Salveter for a pencil... What make of pencil was used for that 'upright' which you found on top of the end cabinet?—Was it a Mongol No. 1?"

Vance shook his head.

"No. It was not a Mongol. It was a Koh-i-noor—an HB, a much harder lead than the No. 1 Mongol, which is very soft... Y'know, Mongols and Koh-i-noors look exactly alike: they're both hexagonal and yellow. The Koh-i-noor is made by Hardtmuth in Czecho-Slovakia—one of the oldest firms in Europe. Originally the Koh-i-noors were Austrian pencils, but after the World War the old Austrian empire was divided—"

"Never mind the kindergarten lesson in history." Markham's face became suddenly overcast. "So it wasn't a Mongol that was used in the death trap..." He came closer to Vance. "Another question—and all your garrulousness about the Austrian Successor States can't divert me: What make of pencil were those you looked at on Doctor Bliss's desk in the study?"

Vance sighed.

"I feared you'd ask that question. And, y'know, I'm almost afraid to tell you—you're so impulsive..."

Markham glowered with exasperation and started toward Bliss's study.

"Oh, it won't be necess'ry for you to trudge up the spiral stairs," Vance called after him. "I'll tell you... They were Koh-i-noors."

"Ah!"

"But I say; are you goin' to let that fact influence you?"

There was a slight pause before Markham answered.

"No... After all, the pencil is not a particularly convincing piece of evidence, especially as every one had access to the study."

Vance grinned and looked puckish.

"Such broadmindedness in a district attorney is positively amazin'," he said.

CHAPTER ELEVEN

The Coffee Percolator
(Friday, July 13; 2.45 p.m.)

M ARKHAM RESUMED HIS seat. He was far too dismayed to resent Vance's good-natured irony. The murder of Kyle, which at first had appeared so straightforward and simple, was becoming more and more involved. Subtle and terrible undercurrents were beginning to make themselves felt; and it was now clear to every one, I think, that the crime, instead of being a mere brutal braining, was a sinister factor in a deep, ramified plot. Even Heath had at last begun to sense the hidden significations of the obvious clews to which he had at first pinned his hope for a speedy solution.

"Yes," he admitted, his cigar bobbing up and down between his thin lips; "that pencil don't mean anything in particular... This case—as you'd say, Mr. Vance—is getting a bit thick. Nobody with a brain is going to smear the whole works with clews pointing to himself, if he's guilty." He frowned at Markham. "What about that opium in the coffee, Chief?"

Markham pursed his lips.

"I was just thinking about that. And it might be advisable to try to find out at once who could have drugged Bliss... What's your opinion, Vance?"

"A coruscatin' idea." Vance was smoking thoughtfully. "It's most essential to know who could have put the sleepin' powder in the doctor's coffee, for there's no doubt that the person who did it is the one who sent Kyle on his long pilgrimage. In fact, the key to the whole plot lies in the question of who had the opportunity to meddle with that cup of coffee."

Markham sat up decisively.

"Sergeant, get the butler. Bring him through the study so that the people in the drawing-room won't see him come in."

Heath rose with alacrity and swung up the spiral stairs three steps at a time. A minute or two later he reappeared at the study door, unceremoniously urging Brush before him.

The man was palpably in a state of fright; his face was very pale and he held his hands tightly clinched. He approached us unsteadily, but bowed with instinctive correctness and stood quite erect, like a well-trained servant waiting for orders.

"Sit down and relax, Brush." Vance busied himself with lighting a fresh cigarette. "I can't blame you for being wrought up, don't y'know. A most tryin' situation. If you'll try to be calm you can help us... I say, stop fidgetin'!..."

"Yes, sir." The man sat down on the edge of a chair, and gripped his knees tensely with his hands. "Very good, sir. But I'm very much upset. I've been in the employ of gentlemen for fifteen years, and never before—"

"Oh, quite. I fully sympathize with your predicament." Vance smiled pleasantly. "Emergencies do arise, though. And this may be your great opportunity to enlarge your field of activities. The fact is, Brush, you may be able to lead us to the truth concerning this unfortunate affair."

"I hope so, sir." The butler had perceptibly calmed down under Vance's casual attitude.

"Tell us, then, about the breakfast arrangements in the house." Vance, with Markham's tacit consent, assumed the role of interrogator. "Where does the family indulge in its morning coffee?"

"In the breakfast-room down-stairs." Brush was now controlling himself admirably. "There's a small room at the front of the house in the basement, which Mrs. Bliss had decorated in Egyptian style. Only luncheon and dinner are served in the main dining-room up-stairs."

"Ah! And does the family break its fast together?"

"Generally, sir. I call every one at eight; and at eight-thirty breakfast is served."

"And just who appears at this unearthly hour?"

"Doctor and Mrs. Bliss, and Mr. Salveter—and Mr. Hani."

Vance's eyebrows went up slightly.

"Does Hani eat with the family?"

"Oh, no, sir." Brush seemed perplexed. "I don't exactly understand Mr. Hani's status—if you know what I mean, sir. He is treated by Doctor Bliss as a servant, and yet he calls the mistress by her first name... He has his meals in an alcove off the kitchen—he will not eat with me and Dingle." There was a certain resentment in his tone.

Vance sought to console him.

"Hani, you must realize, is a very old retainer of Mrs. Bliss's family—and he is also an official of the Egyptian Government..."

"Oh, the arrangement suits Dingle and me perfectly, sir," was the evasive answer.

Vance did not pursue the subject, but asked:

"Does Mr. Scarlett ever breakfast with the Blisses?"

"Quite often, sir—especially when there's work to be done in the museum."

"Did he come this morning?"

"No, sir."

"Then, if Hani was in his room all the morning and Doctor Bliss was in his study, Mrs. Bliss and Mr. Salveter must have breakfasted alone together, what?"

"That's correct, sir. Mrs. Bliss came down-stairs a little before half past eight and Mr. Salveter a few minutes later. The doctor had told me at eight o'clock on his way to the study that he had work to do and the others should not wait for him."

"And who informed you of Hani's indisposition?"

"Mr. Salveter, sir. He told me that Mr. Hani had asked him to tell me he wouldn't be down for breakfast... Their rooms, you see, face each other on the third floor, and I have noticed that Mr. Hani always leaves his door open at night."

Vance nodded approvingly.

"You're most limpid, Brush... Therefore, as I understand it, at half past eight this morning the disposition of the members of the house was as follows:—Mrs. Bliss and Mr. Salveter were in the breakfast-room down-stairs; Hani was in his bedroom on the third floor; and Doctor Bliss was in his study. Mr. Scarlett was presumably at home... And where were you and Dingle?"

"Dingle was in the kitchen, and I was between the kitchen and the breakfast-room, serving."

"And to your knowledge there was no one else in the house?"

The butler appeared mildly surprised.

"Oh, no, sir. There could not have been any one else in the house."

"But if you were down-stairs," Vance persisted, "how do you know no one came in the front door?"

"It was locked."

"You are quite sure?"

"Positive, sir. One of my duties is to see that the latch is thrown the last thing before retiring each night; and no one rang the bell or used the door this morning before nine o'clock."

"Very good." Vance smoked meditatively for several moments. Then he lay back lazily in his chair and closed his eyes. "By the by, Brush, how and where is the morning coffee prepared?"

"The coffee?" The man gave a start of astonishment, but quickly recovered himself. "The coffee is a fad of the doctor's— if you understand me, sir. He orders it from some Egyptian firm on Ninth Avenue. It's very black and damp, and somewhat burnt in the roasting. It tastes like French coffee—if you know how French coffee tastes."

"Unfortunately I do." Vance sighed and made a wry face. "An excruciatin' beverage. No wonder the French fill it full of hot milk... And do you yourself drink this coffee, Brush?"

The butler looked a trifle disconcerted.

"No, sir. I can't say that I care for the taste of it. Mrs. Bliss has kindly given me and Dingle permission to make our own coffee in the old-fashioned way."

"Oh!" Vance half-closed his eyes. "So Doctor Bliss's coffee is not made in the old-fashioned way."

"Well, sir, I may have used the wrong word, but it's certainly not made in the customary way."

"Tell us about it." Vance again relaxed. "There's so much pother in this world about the correct way to make coffee. People get positively fanatical on the subject. I shouldn't be surprised if one day we had a civil war between the boilers and the non-boilers, or perhaps the drippers and the percolaters. Silly notion...as if coffee were of any importance. Now, tea, on the other hand... But go ahead and unfold the doctor's ideas on the subject."

Markham had begun beating an irritable tattoo with his foot, and Heath was wagging his head with elaborate impatience. But Vance, by his irrelevant loquacity, had produced exactly the effect he desired. He had succeeded in allaying Brush's nervousness and diverting his mind from the direct object of the interrogation.

"Well, sir," the man explained, "the coffee is made in a kind of percolator like a large samovar—"

"And where is this outlandish machine situated?"

"It always stands on the end of the breakfast-table... It has a spirit lamp under it to keep the coffee hot after it has—has—"

"'Trickled' is probably the word."

"Trickled, sir. The percolator is in two sections—one fits into the other like a French coffee pot. You first lay a piece of filter paper over the holes and then put in the pulverized coffee—which Dingle grinds fresh every morning. Then there's a small plate which you set over the coffee—Doctor Bliss calls it the water-distributor. When that's in place you pour boiling water into the top of the samovar, and the coffee drips into the bottom. It is drawn off by a little spigot."

'Very interestin'.... And if one lifts off the top section of this apparatus one would have direct access to the liquid itself, what?"

Brush was frankly puzzled by this question. "Yes, sir—but that isn't necessary because the spigot—"

"I can visualize the process perfectly, Brush. I was just wonderin' how one might go about doctorin' the coffee before it was drawn off."

"Doctoring the coffee?" The man appeared genuinely amazed.

"Just a passin' fancy." Vance spoke with utter negligence. "And now, Brush, to return to this morning's breakfast.—You say that Mrs. Bliss and Mr. Salveter were the only persons present. How much of the time were you actually in the breakfast-room during the repast?"

"Very little, sir. I merely brought in the breakfast and retired at once to the kitchen. Mrs. Bliss always serves the coffee herself."

"Did Hani go breakfastless this morning?"

"Not exactly, sir. Mrs. Bliss asked me to take him a cup of coffee."

"At what time was this?"

Brush thought a moment.

"At about quarter of nine, I should say, sir."

"And you of course took it to him."

"Certainly, sir. Mrs. Bliss had already prepared it when she called me."

"And what about the doctor's breakfast?"

"Mrs. Bliss suggested that I take his coffee and toast to the study. I would not have disturbed him myself unless he rang for me."

"And when was this suggestion made by Mrs. Bliss?"

"Just before she and Mr. Salveter left the breakfast-room."

"At about nine, I think you said."

"Yes, sir—perhaps a few minutes before."

"Did Mrs. Bliss and Mr. Salveter leave the breakfast-room together?"

"I couldn't say, sir. The fact is, Mrs. Bliss called me in just as she had finished breakfast, and told me to take some coffee and toast to the doctor. When I returned to the breakfast-room to get the coffee, she and Mr. Salveter had gone."

"And had Mrs. Bliss prepared the coffee for the doctor?"

"No, sir. I drew it myself."

"When?"

"The toast was not quite ready, sir; but I drew the coffee within five minutes after Mrs. Bliss and Mr. Salveter had gone up-stairs."

"And during those five minutes you were, I presume, in the kitchen?"

"Yes, sir. That is to say, except when I was in the rear hall telephoning—the usual daily orders to the tradespeople."

Vance roused himself from his apparent lethargy and crushed out his cigarette.

"The breakfast-room, then, was empty for about five minutes between the time when Mrs. Bliss and Mr. Salveter went up-stairs and the time when you went in to draw Doctor Bliss's coffee?"

"Just about five minutes, sir."

"Now, focus your brain on those five minutes, Brush.—Did you hear any sound in the breakfast-room during that time?"

The butler looked critically at Vance, and made an attempt at concentration.

"I wasn't paying much attention, sir," he replied at length. "And I was telephoning most of the time. But I can't recall hearing any sound. As a matter of fact, no one could have been in the breakfast-room during those five minutes."

"Mrs. Bliss or Mr. Salveter might have returned for some reason," Vance suggested.

"It's possible, sir," Brush admitted dubiously.

"Moreover, could not Hani have come down-stairs in the interim?"

"But he was not well, sir. I took him his coffee—"

"So you told us... I say, Brush, was Hani in bed when you presented him with this abominable coffee?

"He was lying down—on the sofa."

"Dressed?"

"He had on that striped robe he usually wears round the house."

Vance was silent for several moments. Presently he turned to Markham.

"It's not what one would call a crystalline situation," he commented. "The samovar containing the coffee seems to have been in an almost indecent state of exposure this morning. Observe that Mrs. Bliss and Salveter were alone with it during breakfast, and that either one of 'em might have lingered behind for a few moments at the conclusion of the meal, or perhaps returned. Also, Hani could have descended to the breakfast-room as soon as Mrs. Bliss and Salveter came up-stairs. In fact, every one in the house had an opportunity to meddle with the coffee before Brush took the doctor's breakfast to him."

"It looks that way." Markham considered the matter morosely for a while. Then he addressed himself to the butler. "Did you notice anything unusual about the coffee you drew for Doctor Bliss?"

"Why no, sir." Brush sought unsuccessfully to hide his astonishment at the question. "It seemed perfectly all right, sir."

"The usual color and consistency?"

"I didn't see anything wrong with it, sir." The man's apprehension was growing, and again an unhealthy pallor overspread his sallow features. "It might have been a little strong," he added nervously. "But Doctor Bliss prefers his coffee very strong."

Vance got to his feet and yawned.

"I could bear to have a peep at this breakfast-room and its weird percolator. A bit of observation might help us, don't y'know."

Markham readily acceded.

"We'd better go through the doctor's study," said Vance, "so as not to rouse the curiosity of the occupants of the drawing-room…"

Brush led the way silently. He looked ghastly, and as he ascended the spiral stairs ahead of us I noticed that he held tightly to the iron railing. I could not figure him out. At times he appeared to be entirely dissociated from the tragic events of the forenoon; but at other times I got the distinct impression that some racking secret or suspicion was undermining his poise.

The breakfast-room extended, except for a small hallway, across the entire front of the house; but it was no more than eight feet deep. The front windows, which gave on the areaway of the street, were paned with opaque glass and heavily curtained. The room was fitted in exotic fashion and decorated with Egyptian designs. The breakfast-table was at least twelve feet long and very narrow, inlaid and painted in the decadent, rococo-esque style of the New Empire—not unlike the baroque furniture found in the tomb of Tut-ankh-Amûn.

On the end of the table stood the coffee samovar. It was of polished copper and about two feet high, elevated on three sprawling legs. Beneath it was an alcohol lamp.

Vance, after one glance, paid scant attention to it, much to my perplexity. He seemed far more interested in the arrangement of the lower rooms. He put his head in the butler's pantry between the breakfast-room and the kitchen, and stood for several moments in the main doorway looking up and down the narrow hallway which led from the rear stairs to the front of the house.

"A simple matter for any one to come to the breakfast-room without being seen," he observed. "I note that the kitchen door is behind the staircase."

"Yes, sir—quite so, sir." Brush's agreement was almost eager.

Vance appeared not to notice his manner.

"And you say you took the doctor's coffee to him about five minutes after Mrs. Bliss and Mr. Salveter had gone up-stairs... What did you do after that, Brush?"

"I went in to tidy up the drawing-room, sir."

"Ah, yes—so you told us." Vance was running his finger over the inlaid work of one of the chairs. "And I believe you said Mrs. Bliss left the house shortly after nine. Did you see her go?"

"Oh, yes, sir. She stopped at the drawing-room door on her way out and said she was going shopping, and that I should so inform Doctor Bliss in case he asked for her."

"You're sure she went out?"

Brush's eyes opened wide: the question seemed to startle him.

"Quite sure, sir," he replied with much emphasis. "I opened the front door for her... She walked toward Fourth Avenue."

"And Mr. Salveter?"

"He came down-stairs fifteen or twenty minutes later, and went out."

"Did he say anything to you?"

"Only, 'I'll be back for lunch.'"

Vance sighed deeply and looked at his watch.

"Lunch!... My word! I'm positively famished." He gave Markham a doleful look. "It's nearly three o'clock...and I've had nothing today but tea and muffins at ten... I say; must one starve to death simply because a silly crime has been committed?"

"I can serve you gentlemen—" Brush began, but Vance cut him short.

"An excellent idea. Tea and toast would sustain us. But let us speak to Dingle first."

Brush bowed and went to the kitchen. A few moments later he reappeared with a corpulent, placid woman of about fifty.

"This is Dingle, sir," he said. "I took the liberty of informing her of Mr. Kyle's death."

Dingle regarded us stolidly and waited, unperturbed, her hands on her generous hips.

"Good-afternoon, Dingle." Vance sat on the edge of the table. "As Brush has told you, a serious accident has happened in this house…"

"An accident, is it?" The woman nodded her head sagely. "Maybe. Anyhow, you couldn't knock me over with a feather. What surprises me is that something didn't happen long ago—what with young Mr. Salveter living in the house, and Mr. Scarlett hanging around, and the doctor fussing with his mummies day and night. But I certainly didn't expect anything to happen to Mr. Kyle,—he was a very nice and liberal gentleman."

"To whom did you expect something to happen, Dingle?"

The woman set her face determinedly.

"I'm not saying—it's none of my business. But things here ain't according to nature…" Again she wagged her head shrewdly. "Now, I've got a young good-looking niece who wants to marry a man of fifty, and I says to her—"

"I'm sure you gave her excellent advice, Dingle," Vance interrupted; "but we'd much prefer to hear your views on the Bliss family."

"You've heard 'em." The woman's jaws went together with a click, and it was obvious that neither threats nor wheedling could get any more out of her on the subject.

"Oh, that's quite all right." Vance treated her refusal as of no importance. "But there's one other matter we'd like to know about. It won't compromise you in the slightest to tell us.—Did you hear any one in this room after Mrs. Bliss and Mr. Salveter had gone up-stairs this morning—that is, during the time you were making the toast for the doctor's breakfast?"

"So that's it, is it?" Dingle squinted and remained silent for several moments. "Maybe I did and maybe I didn't," she said at length. "I wasn't paying any particular attention... Who could've been in here?"

"I haven't the faintest notion." Vance smiled engagingly. "That's what we're tryin' to find out."

"Is it, now?" The woman's eyes drifted to the percolator. "Since you ask me," she returned, with a malevolence I could not understand at the time, "I'll tell you that I thought I heard some one drawing a cup of coffee."

"Who did you think it was?"

"I thought it was Brush. But at that moment he came out of the rear hall and asked me how the toast was getting along. So I knew it wasn't him."

"And what did you think then?"

"I didn't do any thinking."

Vance nodded abruptly and turned to Brush.

"Maybe we could have that toast and tea now."

"Certainly, sir." He started toward the kitchen, waving Dingle before him; but Markham halted them.

"Bring me a small container of some kind, Brush," he ordered. "I want to take away the rest of the coffee in this percolator."

"There ain't no coffee in it," Dingle informed him aggressively. "I cleaned that pesky contraption out and polished it at ten o'clock this morning."

"Thank Heaven for that," sighed Vance. "Y'know, Markham, if you had any of that coffee to analyze, you'd be farther away from the truth than ever."

With this cryptic remark he slowly lighted a cigarette and began inspecting one of the stencilled figures on the wall.

CHAPTER TWELVE

The Tin of Opium
(Friday, July 13; 3.15 p.m.)

A FEW MINUTES LATER Brush served us tea and toast.

"It is oolong tea, sir—Taiwan," he explained proudly to Vance. "And I did not butter the toast."

"You have rare intuition, Brush." Vance spoke appreciatively. "And what of Mrs. Bliss and Mr. Salveter? They have had no lunch."

"I took tea to them a little while ago. They did not wish anything else."

"And Doctor Bliss?"

"He has not rung for me, sir. But then, he often goes without lunch."

Ten minutes later Vance called Brush in from the kitchen.

"Suppose you fetch Hani."

The butler's eyelids fluttered.

"Yes, sir." He bowed stiffly and departed.

"There are one or two matters," Vance explained to Markham, "that we should clear up at once; and Hani may be able to enlighten us... The actual murder of Kyle is the least devilish thing about this plot. I'm countin' extravagantly on what we'll learn from Salveter and Mrs. Bliss—which is why, d'ye see, I want to accumulate beforehand as much ammunition as possible."

"Still and all," put in Heath, "a guy was bumped off, and if I could put my hands on the bird who did it I wouldn't lay awake nights worrying about plots."

"You're so dashed pristine, Sergeant." Vance sipped his tea dolefully. "Findin' the murderer is simple. But even if you had him gyved, it wouldn't do you a tittle of good. He'd have you apologizin' to him within forty-eight hours."

"The hell he would!" snapped Heath. "Slip me the baby that croaked Kyle, and I'll show you some inside stuff that don't get into the newspapers."

"If you were to arrest the murderer now," Vance returned mildly, "both of you would get into the newspapers—and the stories would all go against you. I'm savin' you from your own impetuosity."

Heath snorted, but Markham looked at Vance seriously.

"I'm beginning to fall in with your views," he said. "The elements in this case are damnably confused."

At this moment soft, measured footsteps sounded in the hall, and Hani appeared at the door. He was calm and aloof as usual, and his immobile face registered not the least surprise at our being in possession of the breakfast-room.

"Come in and sit down, Hani." Vance's invitation was almost too pleasant.

The Egyptian moved slowly toward us, but he did not take a seat.

"I prefer to stand, *effendi*."

"It's of course more comfortin' to stand in moments of stress," Vance commented.

Hani inclined his head slightly, but made no answer. His poise, typically Oriental, was colossal.

"Mr. Scarlett tells us," Vance began, without looking up, "that Mrs. Bliss has been well provided for in Mr. Kyle's will. This information, Mr. Scarlett said, came from you."

"Is it not natural," asked Hani, in a quiet voice, "that Mr. Kyle should have provided for his god-child?"

"He told you he had done so?"

"Yes. He always confided in me, for he knew I loved Meryt-Amen like a father."

"When did he give you his confidence?"

"Years ago—in Egypt."

"Who else, Hani, knew of this bequest?"

"I think every one knew of it. He told me in the presence of Doctor Bliss. And naturally I told Meryt-Amen."

"Did Mr. Salveter know about it?"

"I told him myself." There was a curious note in Hani's voice, which I could not understand at the time.

"And you also told Mr. Scarlett." Vance raised his eyes and studied the Egyptian impersonally. "You're not what I'd call the ideal reposit'ry for a secret."

"I did not consider the matter a secret," Hani returned.

"Obviously not." Vance rose and walked languidly to the samovar.

"Do you happen to know if Mr. Salveter was also to be an object of Mr. Kyle's benefactions?"

"I could not say with assurance." Hani's eyes rested dreamily on the opposite wall. "But from certain remarks dropped by Mr. Kyle, I gathered that Mr. Salveter was also well provided for in the will."

"You like Mr. Salveter—eh, what, Hani?" Vance lifted the top of the samovar and peered into its interior.

"He is, I have reason to think, an admirable young man."

"Oh, quite." Vance smiled faintly, and replaced the samovar's lid. "And he is much nearer Mrs. Bliss's age than Doctor Bliss."

Hani's eyes flickered, and it seemed to me that he gave a slight start. It was a momentary reaction, however. Slowly he folded his arms, and stood like a sphinx, silent and detached.

"Mrs. Bliss and Mr. Salveter will both be rich, now that Mr. Kyle is dead." Vance spoke casually without glancing toward the Egyptian. After a pause he asked: "But what of Doctor Bliss's excavations?"

"They are probably at an end, *effendi*." Despite Hani's monotonous tone there was a discernible note of triumphal satisfaction in his words. "Why should the sacred resting-places of our noble Pharaohs be ravaged?"

"I'm sure I don't know," Vance said blandly. "The art unearthed is scarcely worth considerin'. The only true art of antiquity is Chinese; and all modern æsthetic beauty stems from the Greeks... But this isn't an appropriate time to discuss the creative instinct... Speakin' of the doctor's researches, isn't it possible that Mrs. Bliss will continue to finance her husband's work?"

A black cloud fell across Hani's face.

"It's possible. Meryt-Amen is a loyal wife... And no one can tell what a woman will do."

"So I've been told—by those unversed in feminine psychology." Vance's manner was light and almost flippant. "Still, even should Mrs. Bliss decline to assist in the continuance of the work, Mr. Salveter—with his fanatical enthusiasm for Egyptology—might be persuaded to act as the doctor's financial angel."

"Not if it offended Meryt-Amen—" began Hani, and then stopped abruptly.

Vance appeared not to notice the sudden break in the other's response.

"You would, I suppose," he remarked, "attempt to influence Mrs. Bliss against helping her husband complete his excavations."

"Oh, no, *effendi*." Hani shook his head. "I would not presume to advise her. She knows her own mind—and her loyalty to Doctor Bliss would dictate her decision, whatever I might say."

"Ah!... Tell me, Hani, who do you consider was most benefited by the death of Mr. Kyle?"

"The *ka* of Intef."*

Vance raised his eyes and gave an exasperated smile.

"Ah, yes—of course... Most helpful," he murmured.

"For that reason," Hani continued, a visionary look on his face, "the spirit of Sakhmet returned to the museum this morning and struck down the desecrator—"

"And," interjected Vance, "put the financial report in the desecrator's hand, placed the doctor's scarab pin beside the body, and made bloody foot-prints leading to the study... Not very fair-minded, your lady of vengeance—in fact, a rather bad sport, don't y'know, tryin' to get some one else punished for her little flutter in crime." He studied the Egyptian closely through narrowed eyes; then he leaned forward over the end of the table. When he spoke again his voice was severe and resonant. "You're trying to shield some one, Hani!... Who is it?"

The other took a deep breath, and the pupils of his eyes dilated.

"I have told you all I know, *effendi*." His voice was scarcely audible. "I believe that Sakhmet—"

"Rubbish!" Vance cut him short. Then he shrugged his shoulders and grinned. "*Jawâb ul ahmaq sakût.*"†

---

*   Sir E.A. Wallis Budge defines ka (or, more correctly, ku) both as "the double of a man" and "a divine double." Breasted, explaining the ka, says it was the "vital force" which was supposed to animate the human body and also to accompany it into the next world. G. Elliot Smith calls the ka "one of the twin souls of the dead." (The other soul, ba, became deified in identification with Osiris.) Ka was the spirit of a mortal person, which remained in the tomb after death; and if the tomb were violated or destroyed, the ka had no resting-place. Our own word "soul" is not quite an accurate rendition of ka, but is perhaps as near as we can come to it in English. The German word Doppelgänger, however, is an almost exact translation.

†   An old Arabic proverb meaning: "The only answer to a fool is silence."

A shrewd gleam came into Hani's eyes, and I thought I detected a sneer on his mouth.

Vance was in no wise disconcerted, however. Somehow I felt that, despite the Egyptian's evasiveness, he had learned what he wanted. After a brief pause he tapped the samovar.

"Leaving mythology to one side," he said complaisantly, "I understand that Mrs. Bliss sent Brush to you this morning with a cup of coffee."

Hani merely nodded.

"What, by the by, was the nature of your illness?" Vance asked.

"Since coming to this country," the man returned, "I have suffered from indigestion. When I awoke this morning—"

"Most unfortunate," Vance murmured sympathetically. "And did you find that the one cup of coffee was sufficient for your needs?"

Hani obviously resented the question, but there was no indication of his feeling in his answer.

"Yes, *effendi*. I was not hungry…"

Vance looked mildly surprised.

"Indeed! I was rather under the impression you came downstairs and drew yourself a second cup from this percolator."

Once more a cautious expression came over Hani's face, and he hesitated perceptibly before answering.

"A second cup?" he repeated. "Here in the breakfast-room?… I was not aware of the fact."

"It doesn't matter in the least," Vance returned. "Some one was alone with the percolator this morning. And whoever it was—that is to say, whoever might have been alone with it—was involved in the plot of Mr. Kyle's death."

"How could that be, *effendi*?" Hani, for the first time, appeared vitally worried.

Vance did not answer his query. He was leaning over the table, looking critically at the inlay.

"Dingle said she thought she heard some one in here after Mrs. Bliss and Mr. Salveter had gone up-stairs after breakfast, and it occurred to me it might have been you…" He glanced up sharply. "It's possible, of course, that Mrs. Bliss returned for another cup of coffee…or even Mr. Salveter…"

"It was I who was here!" Hani spoke with slow and impressive emphasis. "I came down-stairs almost immediately after Meryt-Amen had returned to her room. I drew myself another cup of coffee, and at once went back up-stairs. It was I whom Dingle heard… I lied to you a moment ago because I had already told you, in the museum, that I had remained in my room all the morning—my trip to the breakfast-room had slipped my mind. I did not regard the matter as of any importance."

"Well, well! That explains everything." Vance smiled musingly. "And now that you have recalled your little pilgrimage for coffee, will you tell us who in the house possesses powdered opium?"

I was watching Hani, and I expected to see him show some sign of fear at Vance's question. But only an expression of profound puzzlement came over his stolid features. A full half minute passed before he spoke.

"At last I comprehend why you have questioned me concerning the coffee," he said. "But you are being cleverly deceived."

"Fancy that!" Vance stifled a yawn.

"Bliss *effendi* was not put to sleep this morning," the Egyptian continued; and, despite the oracular monotone of his voice, there was an undercurrent of hatred beneath his words.

"Really, now!… And who said he had been put to sleep, Hani?"

"Your interest in the coffee…your question regarding the opium…" His voice trailed off.

"Well?"

"I have no more to say."

"Opium," Vance informed him, "was found in the bottom of the doctor's coffee cup."

Hani appeared genuinely startled by this news.

"You are sure, *effendi*?… I cannot understand."

"Why should you understand?" Vance stepped forward and stood before the man, searching him with a fixed look. "How much do you know about this crime, Hani?"

The veil of detachment again fell over the Egyptian.

"I know nothing," he returned sullenly.

Vance made a gesture of impatient resignation.

"You at least know who owned powdered opium hereabouts."

"Yes, I know that. Powdered opium was part of the medical equipment on our tours of exploration in Egypt. Bliss *effendi* had charge of it."

Vance waited.

"There is a large cabinet in the hall up-stairs," Hani continued. "All the medical supplies are kept there."

"Is the door kept locked?"

"No, I do not believe so."

"Would you be so good as to toddle up-stairs and see if the opium is still there?"

Hani bowed and departed without a word.

"Look here, Vance";—Markham had risen and was pacing up and down—"what earthly good can it do us to know whether the rest of the opium is in the cabinet?... Moreover, I don't trust Hani."

"Hani has been most revealin'," Vance replied. "Let me dally with him in my own way for a time,—he has ideas, and they're most interestin'... As for the opium, I have a distinct feelin' that the tin of brown powder in the medicine chest will have disappeared—"

"But why," interrupted Markham, "should the person who extracted some of the opium remove it all from the cabinet? He wouldn't leave the container on his dressing-table for the purpose of leading us directly to him."

"Not exactly." Vance's tone was grave. "But he may have sought to throw suspicion on some one else... That's mere theory, however. Anyway, I'll be frightfully disappointed if Hani finds the tin in the cabinet."

Heath was glowering.

"It looks to me, sir," he complained, "that one of *us* oughta looked for that opium. You can't trust anything that Swami says."

"Ah, but you can trust his reactions, Sergeant," Vance answered. "Furthermore, I had a definite object in sending Hani up-stairs alone."

Again came the sound of Hani's footsteps in the hall outside. Vance walked to the window. Under his drooping lids he was watching the door eagerly.

The Egyptian entered the room with a resigned, martyr-like air. In one hand he held a small circular tin container bearing a white-paper label. He placed it solemnly on the table and lifted heavy eyes to Vance.

"I found the opium, *effendi*."

"Where?" The word was spoken softly.

Hani hesitated and dropped his gaze.

"It was not in the cabinet," he said. "The place on the shelf where it was generally kept, was empty... And then I remembered—"

"Most convenient!" There was a sneer in Vance's tone. "You remembered that you yourself had taken the opium some time ago—eh, what?... Couldn't sleep—or something of the kind."

"The *effendi* understands many things." Hani's voice was flat and expressionless. "Several weeks ago I was lying awake—I had not slept well for nights—and I went to the cabinet and took the opium to my room. I placed the container in the drawer of my own cabinet—"

"And forgot to return it," Vance concluded. "I do hope it cured your insomnia." He smiled ironically. "You are an outrageous liar, Hani. But I do not blame you altogether—"

"I have told you the truth."

"*Se non è vero, è molto ben trovato.*" Vance sat down, frowning.

"I do not speak Italian..."

"A quotation from Bruno." He inspected the Egyptian speculatively. "Clawed into the vulgate, it means that, although you have not spoken the truth, you have invented your lie very well."

"Thank you, *effendi*."

Vance sighed and shook his head with simulated weariness. Then he said:

"You were not gone long enough to have made any extensive search for the opium. You probably found it in the first place you looked—you had a fairly definite idea where you'd find it..."

"As I told you—"

"Dash it all! Don't be so persistent. You're becoming very borin'..." Menacingly Vance rose and stepped toward the Egyptian. His eyes were cold and his body was tense. "Where did you find that tin of opium?"

Hani shrank away and his arms fell to his sides.

"Where did you find the opium?" Vance repeated the question.

"I have explained, *effendi*." Despite the doggedness of Hani's manner, his tone was not convincing.

"Yes! You've explained—but you haven't told the truth. The opium was not in your room—although you have a reason for wanting us to think so... A reason! What is it?... Perhaps I can guess that reason. You lied to me because you found the opium—"

"*Effendi*!... Don't continue. You are being deceived..."

"I am not being deceived by you, Hani." (I had rarely seen Vance so earnest.) "You unutterable ass! Don't you understand that I knew where you'd find the opium? Do you think I'd have sent you to look for it if I hadn't been pretty certain where it was? And you've told me—in your circuitous Egyptian way you've informed me most lucidly." Vance relaxed and smiled. "But my real reason for sending you to search for the sleeping-powder was to ascertain to what extent you were involved in the plot."

"And you found out, *effendi*?" There were both awe and resignation in the Egyptian's question.

"Yes...oh, yes." Vance casually regarded the other. "You're not at all subtle, Hani. You're only involved—you have characteristics in common with the ostrich, which is erroneously said to bury its head in the sand when in danger. You have merely buried your head in a tin of opium."

"Vance *effendi* is too erudite for my inferior comprehension..."

"You're extr'ordin'rily tiresome, Hani." Vance turned his back and walked to the other end of the room. "Go away, please—go quite away."

At this moment there was a disturbance in the hall outside. We could hear angry voices at the end of the corridor. They became louder, and presently Snitkin appeared at the door of the breakfast-room holding Doctor Bliss firmly by the arm. The doctor, fully clothed and with his hat on, was protesting volubly. His face was pale, and his eyes had a hunted, frightened look.

"What's the meaning of this?" He addressed no one in particular. "I wanted to go out to get a bit of fresh air, and this bully dragged me down-stairs—"

Snitkin looked toward Markham.

"I was told by Sergeant Heath not to let any one leave the house, and this guy tries to make a getaway. Full of hauchoor, too... Whaddya want done with him?"

"I see no reason why the doctor shouldn't take an airin', don't y'know." Vance spoke to Markham. "We sha'n't want to confer with him till later."

"It's bully with me," Heath agreed. "There's too many people in this house anyway."

Markham nodded to Snitkin.

"You may let the doctor go for a walk, officer." He shifted his gaze to Bliss. "Please be back, sir, in half an hour or so. We'll want to question you."

"I'll be back before that,—I only want to go over in the park for a while." Bliss seemed nervous and distraught.

"I feel unusually heavy and suffocated. My ears are ringing frightfully."

"And, I take it," put in Vance, "you've been inordinately thirsty."

The doctor regarded him with mild surprise.

"I've consumed at least a gallon of water since going to my room. I hope I'm not in for an attack of malaria..."

"I hope not, sir. I believe you'll feel perfectly normal later on."

Bliss hesitated on the door-sill.

"Anything new?" he asked.

"Oh, much." Vance spoke without enthusiasm. "But we'll talk of that later."

Bliss frowned and was about to ask another question; but he changed his mind, and bowing, went away, Snitkin trailing after him sourly.

CHAPTER THIRTEEN

An Attempted Escape
(Friday, July 13; 3.45 p.m.)

IT WAS HANI who broke the silence after Bliss's departure.

"You wish me to go away, *effendi*?" he asked Vance, with a respect that struck me as overdone.

"Yes, yes." Vance had become *distrait* and introspective. I knew something was preying on his mind. He stood near the table, his hands in his pockets, regarding the samovar intently. "Go up-stairs, Hani. Take some sodium bicarbonate—and meditate. Divinely bend yourself, so to speak; indulge in a bit of 'holy exercise,' as Shakespeare calls it in—is it *Richard III*?"

"Yes, *effendi*—in Act III. Catesby uses the phrase to the Duke of Buckingham."

"Astonishin'!" Vance studied the Egyptian critically. "I had no idea the fellahîn were so well versed in the classics."

"For hours at a time I read to Meryt-Amen when she was young—"

"Ah, yes." Vance dropped the matter. "We'll send for you when we need you. In the meantime wait in your room."

Hani bowed and moved toward the hall.

"Do not be deceived by appearances, *effendi*," he said solemnly, turning at the door. "I do not fully understand the things that have happened in this house to-day; but do not forget—"

"Thanks awfully." Vance waved his hand in dismissal. "I at least shall not forget that your name is Anûpu."

With a black look the man went out.

Markham was growing more and more impatient.

"Everything in this case seems to peter out," he complained. "Any one in the household could have put the opium in the coffee—which leaves us just where we were before we came here to the breakfast-room... By the way, where do you think Hani found the can of opium?"

"Oh, that? Why, in Salveter's room, of course... Rather obvious, don't y'know."

"I'm damned if I see anything obvious about it. Why should Salveter have left it there?"

"But he didn't leave it there, old dear... My word! Don't you see that some one in the house had ideas? There's a *deus ex machina* in our midst, and he's troublin' himself horribly about the situation. The plot has been far too clever; and there's a tutelary genius who's attempting to simplify matters for us."

Heath made a throaty noise of violent disgust.

"Well, I'm here to tell you he's making a hell of a job of it."

Vance smiled sympathetically.

"A hellish job, let us say, Sergeant."

Markham regarded him with a quizzical frown.

"Do you believe, Vance, that Hani was in this room after Mrs. Bliss and Salveter had gone up-stairs?"

"It's possible. In fact, it seems more likely that it was Hani than either Mrs. Bliss or Salveter."

"If the front door had been unlatched," Markham offered, "it might conceivably have been some one from the outside."

"Your hypothetical thug?" asked Vance dryly. "Dropped in here, perhaps, for a bit of caffein stimulant before tackling his victim in the museum." He did not give Markham time to reply, but went to the door. "Come. Let's chivy the occupants of the drawing-room. We need more data—oh, many more data."

He led the way up-stairs. As we walked along the heavily carpeted upper hall toward the drawing-room door, the sound of an angry high-pitched voice came to us. Mrs. Bliss was speaking; and I caught the final words of a sentence.

"...should have waited."

Then Salveter answered in a hoarse, tense tone: "Meryt! You're insane..."

Vance cleared his throat, and there was silence.

Before we entered the room, however, Hennessey beckoned mysteriously to Heath from the front of the hall. The Sergeant stepped forward past the drawing-room door, and the rest of us, sensing some revelation, followed him.

"You know that bird Scarlett who you told me to let go," Hennessey reported in a stage whisper; "well, just as he was going out he turned suddenly and ran up-stairs. I was going to chase him, but since you O.K.'d him, I thought it was all right. A coupla minutes later he came down and went away without a word. Then I got to thinking that maybe I shoulda followed him up-stairs..."

"You acted correctly, Hennessey." Vance spoke before the Sergeant could reply. "No reason why he shouldn't have gone up-stairs—probably went there to speak to Doctor Bliss."

Hennessey appeared relieved and looked hopefully toward Heath, who merely grunted disdainfully.

"And, by the by, Hennessey," Vance continued; "when the Egyptian came up-stairs the first time, did he go directly to the floor above, or did he tarry in the drawing-room *en route*?"

"He went in and spoke to the missus..."

"Did you hear anything he said?"

"Naw. It sounded to me like they was parleying in one of those foreign languages."

Vance turned to Markham and said in a low voice: "That's why I sent Hani up-stairs alone. I had an idea he'd grasp the opportunity to commune with Mrs. Bliss." He again spoke to Hennessey. "How long was Hani in the drawing-room?"

"A minute or two maybe—not long." The detective was growing apprehensive. "Shouldn't I have let him go in?"

"Oh, certainly... And then what happened?"

"The guy comes outa the room, looking worried, and goes up-stairs. Pretty soon he comes down again carrying a tin can in his hand. 'What you got there, Abdullah?' I asks. 'Something Mr. Vance sent me to get. Any objection?' he says. 'Not if you're on the level; but I don't like your looks,' I answers. And then he gives me the high hat and goes down-stairs."

"Perfect, Hennessey." Vance nodded encouragingly and, taking Markham by the arm, walked back toward the drawing-room. "I think we'd better question Mrs. Bliss."

As we entered the woman rose to greet us. She had been sitting by the front window, and Salveter was leaning against the folding doors leading to the dining-room. They had obviously taken these positions when they heard us in the hall, for as we came up-stairs they had been speaking at very close quarters.

"We are sorry to have to annoy you, Mrs. Bliss," Vance began, courteously. "But it's necess'ry that we question you at this time."

She waited without the slightest movement or change of expression, and I distinctly received the impression that she was resentful of our intrusion.

"And you, Mr. Salveter," Vance went on, shifting his gaze to the man, "will please go to your room. We'll confer with you later."

Salveter seemed disconcerted and worried.

"May I not be present—?" he began.

"You may not," Vance cut in with unwonted severity; and I noticed that even Markham was somewhat surprised at his manner. "Hennessey!" Vance called toward the door, and the detective appeared almost simultaneously. "Escort this gentleman to his room, and see that he communicates with no one until we send for him."

Salveter, with an appealing look toward Mrs. Bliss, walked out of the room, the detective at his side.

"Pray be seated, madam." Vance approached the woman and, after she had sat down, took a chair facing her. "We are going to ask you several intimate questions, and if you really want the murderer of Mr. Kyle brought to justice you will not resent those questions but will answer them frankly."

"The murderer of Mr. Kyle is a despicable and unworthy creature," she answered in a hard, strained voice; "and I will gladly do anything I can to help you." She did not look at Vance, but concentrated her gaze on an enormous honey-colored carnelian ring of intaglio design which she wore on the fore-finger of her right hand.

Vance's eyebrows went up slightly.

"You think, then, we did right in releasing your husband?"

I could not understand the purport of Vance's question; and the woman's answer confused me still further. She raised her head slowly and regarded each one of us in turn. Finally she said:

"Doctor Bliss is a very patient man. Many people have wronged him. I am not even sure that Hani is altogether loyal to him. But my husband is not a fool—he is even too clever at times. I do not put murder beyond him—or beyond any one, for that matter. Murder may sometimes be the highest form of courage. However, if my husband had killed Mr. Kyle he would not have been stupid about it—certainly he would not have left evidence pointing to himself..." She glanced again at her folded hands. "But if he had been contemplating murder, Mr. Kyle would not have been the object of his crime. There are others whom he had more reason for wanting out of the way."

"Hani, for instance?"

"Perhaps."

"Or Mr. Salveter?"

"Almost any one but Mr. Kyle," the woman answered, without a perceptible modulation of voice.

"Anger could have dictated the murder." Vance spoke like a man discussing a purely academic topic. "If Mr. Kyle had refused to continue financing the excavations—"

"You do not know my husband. He has the most equable temper I have ever seen. Passion is alien to his nature. He makes no move without long deliberation."

"The scholar's mind," Vance murmured. "Yes, I have always had that impression of him." He took out his cigarette-case. "Do you mind if I smoke?"

"Do you mind if *I* do?"

Vance leapt to his feet and extended his case.

"Ah—*Régies!*" She selected a cigarette. "You are very fortunate, Mr. Vance. There were none left in Turkey when I applied for a shipment."

"I am doubly fortunate that I am able to offer you one." Vance lighted her cigarette and resumed his seat. "Who, do you think, Mrs. Bliss, was most benefited by Mr. Kyle's death?" He put the question carelessly, but I could see he was watching her closely.

"I couldn't say." The woman was clearly on her guard.

"But surely," pursued Vance, "some one benefited by his death. Otherwise he would not have been murdered."

"That point is one the police should ascertain. I can give you no assistance along that line."

"It may be that the police have satisfied themselves, and that I merely asked you for corroboration." Vance, while courteous, spoke with somewhat pointed significance. "Lookin' at the matter coldly, the police might argue that the sudden demise of Mr. Kyle would remove a thorn from Hani's side and end the so-called desecration of his ancestors' tombs. Then again, the police might hold that Mr. Kyle's death would enrich both you and Mr. Salveter."

I expected the woman to resent this remark of Vance's, but she only glanced up with a frigid smile and said in a dispassionate tone:

"Yes, I do believe there was a will naming Mr. Salveter and myself as the principal beneficiaries."

"Mr. Scarlett informed us to that effect," Vance returned. "Quite understandable, don't y'know... And by the by, would you be willing to use your inheritance to perpetuate Doctor Bliss's work in Egypt?"

"Certainly," she replied with unmistakable emphasis. "If he asked me to help him, the money would be his to do with as he desired... Especially now," she added.

Vance's face had grown cold and stern, and after a quick upward glance he dropped his eyes and contemplated his cigarette.

Markham rose at this moment.

"Who, Mrs. Bliss," he asked, with what I regarded as unnecessary aggression, "would have had an object in attempting to saddle your husband with this crime?"

The woman's gaze faltered, but only momentarily.

"I'm sure I don't know," she returned. "Did some one really try to do that?"

"You suggested as much yourself, madam, when the scarab pin was called to your attention. You said quite positively that some one had placed it beside Mr. Kyle's body."

"What if I did?" She became suddenly defiant. "My initial instinct was naturally to defend my husband."

"Against whom?"

"Against you and the police."

"Do you regret that 'initial instinct'?" Markham put the question brusquely.

"Certainly not!" The woman stiffened in her chair and glanced surreptitiously toward the door. Vance noted her action and drawled:

"It is only one of the detectives in the hall. Mr. Salveter is sojourning in his boudoir—quite out of hearing."

Quickly she covered her face with her hands, and a shudder ran over her body.

"You are torturing me," she moaned.

"And you are watching me through your fingers," said Vance with a mild grin.

She rose swiftly and glared ferociously at him.

"Please don't say 'How dare you?'" Vance spoke banteringly. "The phrase is so trite. And do sit down again... Hani informed you, I believe—in your native language—that Doctor Bliss was supposed to have been given opium in his coffee this morning. What else did he tell you?"

"That was all he said." The woman resumed her seat: she appeared exhausted.

"Did you know that opium was kept in the cabinet up-stairs?"

"I wasn't aware of it," she replied listlessly; "though I'm not surprised."

"Did Mr. Salveter know of it?"

"Oh, undoubtedly—if it was actually there. He and Mr. Scarlett had charge of the medical supplies."

Vance shot her a quick look.

"Although Hani would not admit it," he said, "I am pretty sure that the tin of opium was found in Mr. Salveter's room."

"Yes?" (I could not help feeling that she rather expected this news. Certainly, it was no surprise to her.)

"On the other hand," pursued Vance, "it might have been found by Hani in *your* room."

"Impossible! It couldn't have been in my room!" She flared up, but on meeting Vance's steady gaze, subsided. "That is, I don't see how it could be possible," she ended weakly.

"I'm probably wrong," Vance murmured. "But tell me, Mrs. Bliss: did you return to the breakfast-room this morning for another cup of coffee, after you and Mr. Salveter had gone up-stairs?"

"I—I..." She took a deep breath. "Yes!... Was there any crime in that?"

"Did you meet Hani there?"

After a brief hesitation she answered:

"No. He was in his room—ill... I sent him his coffee."

Heath grunted disgustedly.

"A lot we're finding out," he growled.

"Quite right, Sergeant," Vance agreed pleasantly. "An amazin' amount. Mrs. Bliss is helpin' us no end." He turned to the woman again. "You know, of course, who killed Mr. Kyle?" he asked blandly.

"Yes… I know!" The words were spoken with impulsive venom.

"And you also know why he was killed?"

"I know that, too." A sudden change had come over her. A strange combination of fear and animus possessed her; and the tragic bitterness of her attitude stunned me.

Heath let forth a queer, inarticulate ejaculation.

"You tell us who it was," he blurted vindictively, shaking his cigar in her face, "or I'll arrest you as an accessory, or as a material witness…"

"Tut, tut, Sergeant!" Vance rose and placed his hand pacifyingly on the other's shoulder. "Why be so precipitate? It wouldn't do you the slightest good to incarcerate Mrs. Bliss at this time… And, d'ye see, she may be wholly wrong in her diagnosis of the case."

Markham projected himself into the scene.

"Have you any definite reasons for your opinion, Mrs. Bliss?" he asked. "Have you any specific evidence against the murderer?"

"Not legal evidence," she answered quietly. "But—but…" Her voice faltered, and her head fell forward.

"You left the house about nine o'clock this morning, I believe." Vance's calm voice seemed to steady her.

"Yes—shortly after breakfast."

"Shopping?"

"I took a taxi at Fourth Avenue to Altman's. I didn't see what I wanted there, and walked to the subway. I went to Wanamaker's, and later returned to Lord and Taylor's. Then I went to Saks's, and finally dropped in at a little shop on Madison Avenue…"

"The usual routine," sighed Vance. "You of course bought nothing?"

"I ordered a hat on Madison Avenue..."

"Remarkable!" Vance caught Markham's eye and nodded significantly. "I think that will be all for the present, Mrs. Bliss," he said. "You will kindly go to your room and wait there."

The woman pressed a small handkerchief to her eyes, and left us without a word.

Vance walked to the window and gazed out into the street. He was, I could see, deeply troubled as a result of the interview. He opened the window, and the droning summer noises of the street drifted in to us. He stood for several minutes in silence, and neither Markham nor Heath interrupted his meditations. At length he turned and, without looking at us, said in a quiet, introspective tone:

"There are too many cross-currents in this house—too many motives, too many objects to be gained, too many emotional complications. A plausible case could be made out against almost any one..."

"But who could have benefited by Bliss's entanglement in the crime?" Markham asked.

"Oh, my word!" Vance leaned against the centre-table and gazed at a large oil portrait of the doctor which hung on the east wall. "Every one apparently. Hani doesn't like his employer and writhes in psychic agony at each basketful of sand that is excavated from Intef's tomb. Salveter is infatuated with Mrs. Bliss, and naturally her husband is an obstacle to his suit. As for the lady herself: I do not wish to wrong her, but I'm inclined to believe she returns the young gentleman's affection. If so, the elimination of Bliss would not drive her to suicidal grief."

Markham's face clouded.

"I got the impression, too, that Scarlett was not entirely impervious to her charms and that there was a chilliness between him and Salveter."

"Quite. *Ça crève les yeux.*" Vance nodded abstractedly. "Mrs. Bliss is undeniably fascinatin'.... I say; if only I could find the clew I'm looking for! Y'know, Markham, I've an idea that something new is going to happen anon. The plot thus far has gone awry. We've been led into a Moorish maze by the murderer, but the key hasn't yet been placed in our hands. When it is, I'll know which door it'll unlock—and it won't be the door the murderer intends us to use it on. Our difficulty now is that we have too many clews; and not one of 'em is the real clew. That's why we can't make an arrest. We must wait for the plot to unfold."

"It's unfolding, as you call it, too swift for me," Heath retorted impatiently. "And I don't mind admitting that I think we're getting sidetracked. After all's said and done, weren't Bliss's finger-prints found on the statue, and no one else's? Wasn't his stick-pin found beside the body? And didn't he have every opportunity to bump Kyle off?..."

"Sergeant,"—Vance spoke patiently—"would a man of intelligence and profound scientific training commit a murder and not only overlook his finger-prints on the weapon, but also be so careless as to drop his scarf-pin at the scene of the murder, and then calmly wait in the next room for the police to arrest him, after having made bloody foot-prints to guide them?"

"And there's the opium, too, Sergeant," added Markham. "It seems pretty clear to me that the doctor was drugged."

"Have it your own way, sir." Heath's tone bordered on impoliteness. "But I don't see that we're getting anywheres."

As he spoke Emery came to the door.

"Telephone call for you, Sergeant," he announced. "Down-stairs."

Heath hurried eagerly from the room and disappeared down the hall. Three or four minutes later he returned. His face was wreathed in smiles, and he swaggered as he walked toward Vance.

"Huh!" He inserted his thumbs in the armholes of his waistcoat. "Your good friend Bliss has just tried to make a getaway. My man, Guilfoyle,* who I'd phoned to tail the doctor, picked him up as he came out of this house for his walk in the park. But he didn't go to the park, Mr. Vance. He beat it over to Fourth Avenue and went to the Corn Exchange Bank at Twenty-ninth Street. It was after hours, but he knew the manager and didn't have no trouble getting his money…"

"Money?"

"Sure! He drew out everything he had in the bank—got it in twenties, fifties and hundreds—and then took a taxi. Guilfoyle hopped another taxi and followed him up-town. He got off at Grand Central Station and hurried to the ticket office. 'When's the next train for Montreal?' he asked. 'Four forty-five,' the guy told him. 'Gimme a through ticket,' he said… It was then four o'clock; and the doc walked to the gate and stood there, waiting. Guilfoyle came up to him and said: 'Going for a jaunt to Canada?' The doc got haughty and refused to answer. 'Anyway,' said Guilfoyle, 'I don't think you'll leave the country to-day.' And taking the doc by the arm, he led him to a tele-phone booth… Guilfoyle's on his way here with your innocent friend." The Sergeant rocked back and forth on his feet. "What do you think of that, sir?"

Vance regarded him lugubriously.

"And that is taken as another sign of the doctor's guilt?" He shook his head hopelessly. "Is it possible that you regard such a childish attempt of escape as incriminating?… I say, Sergeant; mightn't that come under the head of panic on the part of an impractical scientist?"

"Sure it might." Heath laughed unpleasantly. "All crooks and killers get scared and try to make a getaway. But it don't prove their lily-white innocence."

"Still, Sergeant,"—Vance's voice was discouraged—"a murderer who accidentally left clews on every hand pointing

---

*   *Guilfoyle, I recalled, was the detective of the Homicide Bureau who was set to watch Tony Skeel in the "Canary" murder case, and who reported on the all-night light at the Drukker house in the Bishop murder case.*

directly to himself and then indulged in this final stupid folly of trying to escape would not be exactly bright. And, I assure you, Doctor Bliss is neither an imbecile nor a lunatic."

"Them's mere words, Mr. Vance," declared the Sergeant doggedly. "This bird made a coupla mistakes and, seeing he was caught, tried to get outa the country. And, I'm here to tell you, that's running true to form."

"Oh, my aunt—my precious, dodderin' aunt!" Vance sank into a large chair and let his head fall back wearily against the lace antimacassar.

CHAPTER FOURTEEN

A Hieroglyphic Letter
(Friday, July 13; 4.15 p.m.)

MARKHAM GOT UP irritably and walked the length of the room and back. As always in moments of perplexity his hands were clasped behind him, and his head was projected forward.

"Damn your various aunts!" he growled, as he came abreast of Vance. "You're always calling on an aunt. Haven't you any uncles?"

Vance opened his eyes and smiled blandly.

"I know how you feel." Despite the lightness of his tone there was unmistakable sympathy in his words. "No one is acting as he should in this case. It's as if every one were in a conspiracy to confuse and complicate matters for us."

"That's just it!" Markham fumed. "On the other hand, there's something in what the Sergeant says. Why should Bliss—?"

"Too much theory, Markham old dear," Vance interrupted. "Oh, much too much theory…too much speculation…too many futile questions. There's a key coming, and it'll explain everything. Our immediate task, it seems to me, is to find that key."

"Sure!" Heath spoke with heavy sarcasm. "Suppose I begin punching the furniture with hat-pins and ripping up the carpets…"

Markham snapped his fingers impatiently, and Heath subsided.

"Let's get down to earth." He regarded Vance with vindictive shrewdness. "You've got some pretty definite idea; and all your maunderings couldn't convince me to the contrary.— What do you suggest we do next?—interview Salveter?"

"Precisely." Vance nodded with unwonted seriousness. "That bigoted lad fits conspicuously into the picture; and his presence on the tapis now is, as the medicos say, indicated."

Markham made a sign to Heath, who immediately rose and went to the drawing-room door and bellowed up the staircase.

"Hennessey!… Bring that guy down here. We got business with him."

A few moments later Salveter was piloted into the room. His eyes were flashing, and he planted himself aggressively before Vance, cramming his hands violently into his trousers' pockets.

"Well, here I am," he announced with belligerence. "Got the handcuffs ready?"

Vance yawned elaborately and inspected the newcomer with a bored expression.

"Don't be so virile, Mr. Salveter," he drawled. "We're all worn out with this depressin' case, and simply can't endure any more vim and vigor. Sit down and let the joints go free… As for the manacles, Sergeant Heath has 'em beautifully polished. Would you like to try 'em on?"

"Maybe," Salveter returned, watching Vance calculatingly. "What did you say to Meryt—to Mrs. Bliss?"

"I gave her one of my *Régies*," Vance told him carelessly. "Most appreciative young woman… Would you care for one yourself? I've two left."

"Thanks—I smoke Deities."

"Ever dip 'em in opium?" Vance asked dulcetly.

"Opium?"

"The concrete juice of the poppy, so to speak—obtained from slits in the cortex of the capsule of *Papaver somniferum*. Greek word: *opion*—to wit: omicron, pi, iota, omicron, nu."

"No!" Salveter sat down suddenly and shifted his gaze. "What's the idea?"

"There seems to be an abundance of opium in the house, don't y'know."

"Oh, is there?" The man looked up warily.

"Didn't you know?" Vance selected one of his two remaining cigarettes. "We thought you and Mr. Scarlett had charge of the medical supplies."

Salveter started and remained silent for several moments.

"Did Meryt-Amen tell you that?" he asked finally.

"Is it true?" There was a new note in Vance's voice.

"In a way," the other admitted. "Doctor Bliss—"

"What about the opium?" Vance leaned forward.

"Oh, there has always been opium in the cabinet up-stairs—nearly a canful."

"Have you had it in your room lately?"

"No…yes… I—"

"Thanks awfully. We take our choice of answers, what?"

"Who said there was opium in my room?" Salveter squared his shoulders.

Vance leaned back in his chair.

"It really doesn't matter. Anyway, there's no opium there now… I say, Mr. Salveter; did you return to the break-fast-room this morning after you and Mrs. Bliss had gone up-stairs?"

"I did not!… That is," he amended, "I don't remember…"

Vance rose abruptly and stood menacingly before him.

"Don't try to guess what Mrs. Bliss told us. If you don't care to answer my questions, I'll turn you over to the Homicide Bureau—and God help you!... We're here to learn the truth, and we want straight answers.—Did you return to the breakfast-room?"

"No—I did not."

"That's much better—oh, much!" Vance sighed and resumed his seat. "And now, Mr. Salveter, we must ask you a very intimate question.—Are you in love with Mrs. Bliss?"

"I refuse to answer!"

"Good! But you would not be entirely broken-hearted if Doctor Bliss should be gathered to his fathers?"

Salveter clamped his jaws and said nothing.

Vance contemplated him ruminatingly.

"I understand," he said amicably, "that Mr. Kyle has left you a considerable fortune in his will... If Doctor Bliss should ask you to finance the continuation of his excavations in Egypt, would you do it?"

"I'd insist upon it, even if he did not ask me." A fanatical light shone in Salveter's eyes. "That is," he added, as a reasoned afterthought, "if Meryt-Amen approved. I would not care to go against her wishes."

"Ah!" Vance had lit his cigarette and was smoking dreamily. "And do you think she would disapprove?"

Salveter shook his head.

"No, I think she would do whatever the doctor wanted."

"A dutiful wife—quoi?"

Salveter bristled and sat up.

"She's the straightest, most loyal—"

"Yes, yes." Vance exhaled a spiral of cigarette smoke. "Spare me your adjectives... I take it, however, she's not entirely ecstatic with her choice of a life mate."

"If she wasn't," Salveter returned angrily, "she wouldn't show it."

Vance nodded uninterestedly.

"What do you think of Hani?" he asked.

"He's a dumb beast—a good soul, though. Adores Mrs. Bliss..." Salveter stiffened and his eyes opened wide. "Good God, Mr. Vance! You don't think—" He broke off in horror; then he shook himself. "I see what you're getting at. But... but... Those degenerate modern Egyptians! They're all alike— Oriental dogs, every one of 'em. No sense of right and wrong—superstitious devils—but loyal as they make 'em. I wonder..."

"Quite. We're all wonderin'." Vance was apparently unimpressed by Salveter's outbreak. "But, as you say, he's pretty close to Mrs. Bliss. He'd do a great deal for her—eh, what? Might even risk his neck, don't y'know, if he thought her happiness was at stake. Of course, he might need a bit of coaching..."

A hard light shone in Salveter's eyes.

"You're on the wrong tack. Nobody coached Hani. He's capable of acting for himself..."

"And throwing the suspicion on some one else?" Vance looked at the other. "I'd say the planting of that scarab pin was a bit too subtle for a mere fellah."

"You think so?" Salveter was almost contemptuous. "You don't know those people the way I do. The Egyptians were working out intricate plots when the Nordic race were arboreans."

"Bad anthropology," murmured Vance. "And you're doubt-less thinkin' of Herodotus's silly story of the treasure house of King Rhampsinitus. Personally, I think the priests were spoofing the papa of history... By the by, Mr. Salveter; do you know any one round here, besides Doctor Bliss, who uses Koh-i-noor pencils?"

"Didn't even know the doctor used 'em." The man flicked his cigarette ashes on the carpet and brushed his foot over them.

"You didn't by any chance see Doctor Bliss this morning?"

"No. When I came down to breakfast Brush told me he was working in the study."

"Did you go into the museum this morning before you went on your errand to the Metropolitan?"

Salveter's eyes blinked rapidly.

"Yes!" he blurted finally. "I generally go into the museum every morning after breakfast—a kind of habit. I like to see that everything is all right—that nothing has happened during the night. I'm the assistant curator; and, aside from my responsibility, I'm tremendously interested in the place. It's my duty to keep an eye on things."

Vance nodded understandingly.

"What time did you enter the museum this morning?"

Salveter hesitated. Then throwing his head back he looked challengingly at Vance.

"I left the house a little after nine. When I got to Fifth Avenue it suddenly occurred to me I hadn't made an inspection of the museum; and for some reason I was worried. I couldn't tell you why I felt that way—but I did. Maybe because of the new shipment that arrived yesterday. Anyway, I turned back, let myself in with my key, and went into the museum—"

"About half past nine?"

"That would be about right."

"And no one saw you re-enter the house?"

"I hardly think so. In any event, I didn't see any one."

Vance gazed at him languidly.

"Suppose you finish the recital... If you don't care to, I'll finish it for you."

"You won't have to." Salveter tossed his cigarette into a cloisonné dish on the table and drew himself resolutely to the edge of his chair. "I'll tell you all there is to tell. Then if you're not satisfied, you can order my arrest—and the hell with you!"

Vance sighed and let his head fall back.

"Such energy!" he breathed. "But why be vulgar?... I take it you saw your uncle before you finally quitted the museum for the Great American Mausoleum on the Avenue."

"Yes—I saw him!" Salveter's eyes flashed and his chin shot forward. "Now, make something out of that."

"Really, I can't be bothered. Much too fatiguin'." Vance did not even look at the man: his eyes, half closed, were resting on an old-fashioned crystal chandelier which hung low over the centre-table. "Since you saw your uncle," he said, "you must have remained in the museum for at least half an hour."

"Just about." Salveter obviously could not understand Vance's indifferent attitude. "The fact is I got interested in a papyrus we picked up last winter, and tried to work out a few of the words that stumped me. There were the words *ankhet*, *wash*, and *tema* that I couldn't translate."

Vance frowned slightly; then his eyebrows lifted.

"*Ankhet...wash...tema...*" He iterated the words slowly. "Was the *ankhet* written with or without a determinative?"

Salveter did not answer at once.

"With the animal-skin determinative," he said presently.

"And was the next word really *wash* and not *was*?"

Again he hesitated, and looked uneasily at Vance.

"It was *wash*, I think... And *tema* was written with a double flail."

"Not the sledge ideogram, eh?... Now, that's most interestin'.—And during your linguistic throes your uncle walked in."

"Yes. I was sitting at the little desk-table by the obelisk when Uncle Ben opened the door. I heard him say something to Brush, and I got up to greet him. It was rather dark, and he didn't see me till he'd reached the floor of the museum."

"And then?"

"I knew he wanted to inspect the new treasures; so I ran along. Went to the Metropolitan—"

"Your uncle seemed in normal good spirits when he came into the museum?"

"About as usual—a bit grouchy perhaps. He was never over-pleasant in the forenoons. But that didn't mean anything."

"You left the museum immediately after greeting him?"

"At once. I hadn't realized I'd been so long fussing over the papyrus; and I hurried away. Another thing, I knew he'd come to see Doctor Bliss on a pretty important matter, and I didn't want to be in the way."

Vance nodded but gave no indication whether or not he unreservedly accepted the other's statements. He sat smoking lazily, his eyes impassive and mild.

"And during the next twenty minutes," he mused, "—that is between ten o'clock and ten-twenty, at which time Mr. Scarlett entered the museum—your uncle was killed."

Salveter winced.

"So it seems," he mumbled. "But"—he shot his jaw out—"I didn't have anything to do with it! That's straight,—take it or leave it."

"There, now; don't be indelicate," Vance admonished him quietly. "I don't have to take it and I don't have to leave it, d'ye see? I may choose merely to dally with it."

"Dally and be damned!"

Vance got to his feet leisurely, and there was a chilly smile on his face—a smile more deadly than any contortion of anger could have been.

"I don't like your language, Mr. Salveter," he said slowly.

"Oh, don't you!" The man sprang up, his fists clenched, and swung viciously. Vance, however, stepped back with the quickness of a cat, and caught the other by the wrist. Then he made a swift, pivotal movement to the right, and Salveter's pinioned arm was twisted upward behind his shoulder-blades. With an involuntary cry of pain, the man fell to his knees. (I recalled the way in which Vance had saved Markham from an attack in the District Attorney's office at the close of the Benson murder case.) Heath and Hennessey stepped forward, but Vance motioned them away with his free hand.

"I can manage this impetuous gentleman," he said. Then he lifted Salveter to his feet and shoved him back into his chair. "A little lesson in manners," he remarked pleasantly. "And now you will please be civil and answer my questions, or I'll be compelled to have you—*and Mrs. Bliss*—arrested for conspiring to murder Mr. Kyle."

Salveter was completely subdued. He looked at his antagonist in ludicrous amazement. Then suddenly Vance's words seemed to seep into his astonished brain.

"*Mrs. Bliss?...* She had nothing to do with it, I tell you!" His tone, though highly animated, was respectful. "If it'll save her from any suspicion, I'll confess to the crime..."

"No need for any such heroism." Vance had resumed his seat and was again smoking calmly. "But you might tell us why, when you came into the museum this afternoon and learned of your uncle's death, you didn't mention the fact that you'd seen him at ten o'clock."

"I—I was too upset—too shocked," the man stammered. "And I was afraid. Self-protective instinct, maybe. I can't explain—really I can't. I should have told you, I suppose... but—but—"

Vance helped him out.

"But you didn't care to involve yourself in a crime of which you were innocent. Yes...yes. Quite natural. Thought you'd wait and find out if any one had seen you... I say, Mr. Salveter; don't you know that, if you had admitted being with your uncle at ten o'clock, it would have been a point in your favor?"

Salveter had become sullen, and before he could answer Vance went on.

"Leavin' these speculations to one side, could we prevail upon you to tell us exactly what you did in the museum between half past nine and ten o'clock?"

"I've already told you." Salveter was troubled and *distrait*. "I was comparing an Eighteenth-Dynasty papyrus recently found by Doctor Bliss at Thebes with Luckenbill's translation of the hexagonal prism of the Annals of Sennacherib* in order to determine certain values for—"

---

*   *The prism referred to by Salveter was the terra-cotta one acquired by the Oriental Institute of the University of Chicago during its reconnoitering expedition of 1919–20. The document was a variant duplicate of the Taylor prism in the British Museum, written about two years earlier under another eponym.*

"You're romancing frightfully, Mr. Salveter," Vance broke in quietly. "And you're indulgin' in an anachronism. The Sennacherib prism is in Babylonian cuneiform, and dates almost a thousand years later." He lifted his eyes sternly. "What were you doing in the museum this morning?"

Salveter started forward in his chair, but at once sank back.

"I was writing a letter," he answered weakly.

"To whom?"

"I'd rather not say."

"Naturally." Vance smiled faintly. "In what language?"

An immediate change came over the man. His face went pale, and his hands, which were lying along his knees, convulsed.

"What language?" he repeated huskily. "Why do you ask that?... What language would I be likely to write a letter in— Bantu, Sanskrit, Walloon, Ido...?"

"No—o." Vance's gaze came slowly to rest on Salveter. "Nor did I have in mind Aramaic, or Agao, or Swahili, or Sumerian... The fact is, it smote my brain a moment ago that you were composin' an epistle in Egyptian hieroglyphics."

The man's eyes dilated.

"Why, in Heaven's name," he asked lamely, "should I do a thing like that?"

"Why? Ah, yes—why, indeed?" Vance sighed deeply. "But, really, y'know, you were composin' in Egyptian—weren't you?"

"Was I? What makes you think so?"

"Must I explain?... It's so deuced simple." Vance put out his cigarette and made a slight deprecatory gesture. "I could even guess for whom the epistle was intended. Unless I'm hopelessly mistaken, Mrs. Bliss was to have been the recipient." Again Vance smiled musingly. "Y'see, you mentioned three words in the imagin'ry papyrus, which you have not yet satisfactorily translated—*ankhet*, *wash*, and *tema*. But since there are scores of Egyptian words that have thus far resisted accurate translation, I wondered why you should have mentioned these particular three. And I further wondered why you should have mentioned three words whose meaning you did not recall, which so closely approximate three very familiar words in Egyptian... And then I bethought me as to the meaning of these three familiar words. *Ankh*—without a determinative—can mean the 'living one.' *Was*—which is close to *wash*—means 'happiness' or 'good fortune'; though I realize there is some doubt about it,—Erman translates it, with a question-mark, as *Glück*. The *tema* you mentioned with a double flail is unknown to me. But I of course am familiar with *tem* spelt with a sledge ideograph. It means 'to be ended' or 'finished.'... Do you follow me?"

Salveter stared like a man hypnotized.

"Good God!" he muttered.

"And so," Vance continued, "I concluded that you had been dealin' in the well-known forms of these three words, and had mentioned them because, in their other approximate forms, their transliterative meanings are unknown... And the words fitted perfectly with the situation. Indeed, Mr. Salveter, it wouldn't take a great deal of imagination to re-construct your letter, being given the three verbal salients—to wit, *the living one, happiness* or *good fortune,* and *to be ended* or *finished.*"

Vance paused briefly, as if to arrange his words.

"You probably composed a communication in which you said that the 'living one' (*ankh*) was standing in the way of your 'happiness' or 'good fortune' (*was*), and expressed a desire for the situation 'to be ended' or 'finished' (*tem*)... I'm right, am I not?"

Salveter continued staring at Vance in a kind of admiring astonishment.

"I'm going to be truthful with you," he said at length. "That's exactly what I wrote. You see, Meryt-Amen, who knows the Middle Egyptian hieroglyphic language better than I'll ever know it, suggested long ago that I write to her at least once a week in the language of her ancestors, as a kind of exercise. I've been doing it for years; and she always corrects me and advises me—she's almost as well versed as any of the scribes who decorated the ancient tombs... This morning, when I returned to the museum, I realized that the Metropolitan did not open until ten o'clock, and on some sudden impulse I sat down and began working on this letter."

"Most unfortunate," Vance sighed; "for your phraseology in that letter made it appear that you were contemplating taking drastic measures."

"I know it!" Salveter caught his breath. "That's why I lied to you. But the fact is, Mr. Vance, the letter was innocent enough... I know it was foolish, but I didn't take it very seriously. Honest, sir, it was really a lesson in Egyptian composition—not an actual communication."

Vance nodded non-committally.

"And where is this letter now?" he asked.

"In the drawer of the table in the museum. I hadn't finished it when Uncle Ben came in; and I put it away."

"And you had already made use of the three words, *ankh* and *was* and *tem*?"

Salveter braced himself and took a deep breath.

"Yes! Those three familiar words were in it. And then, when you first asked me about what I'd been doing in the museum I made up the tale about the papyrus—"

"And mentioned three words which were suggested to you by the three words you had actually used—eh, what?"

"Yes, sir! That's the truth."

"We're most grateful for your sudden burst of honesty." Vance's tone was frigid. "Will you be so good as to bring me the uncompleted epistle? I'd dearly love to see it; and perhaps I can decipher it."

Salveter leapt to his feet and fairly ran out of the room. A few minutes later he returned, to all appearances dazed and crestfallen.

"It isn't there!" he announced. "It's gone!"

"Oh, is it, now?... Most unfortunate."

Vance lay back pensively for several moments. Then suddenly he sprang to his feet.

"It's not there!... It's gone!" he murmured. "I don't like this situation, Markham—I don't at all like it... Why should the letter have disappeared? Why...why?"

He swung about to Salveter.

"What kind of paper did you write that indiscreet letter on?" he asked, with suppressed excitement.

"On a yellow scratch-pad—the kind that's generally kept on the table..."

"And the ink—did you draw your characters with pen or pencil?"

"With a pen. Green ink. It's always in the museum..."

Vance raised his hand in an impatient gesture. "That's enough... Go up-stairs—go to your room...and stay there."

"But, Mr. Vance, I—I'm worried about that letter. Where do you think it is?"

"Why should I know where it is?—provided, of course, you ever wrote it. I'm no divining-rod." Vance was deeply troubled, though he sought to hide the fact. "Didn't you know better than to leave such a missive lying loosely about?"

"It never occurred to me—"

"Oh, didn't it?... I wonder." Vance looked at Salveter sharply. "This is no time to speculate... Please go to your room. I'll speak to you again... Don't ask any questions—do as I tell you!"

Salveter, without a word, turned and disappeared through the door. We could hear his heavy footsteps ascending the stairs.

CHAPTER FIFTEEN

Vance Makes a Discovery
(Friday, July 13; 4.45 p.m.)

VANCE STOOD FOR a long time in uneasy silence. At length he lifted his eyes to Hennessey.

"I wish you'd run up-stairs," he said, "and take a post where you can watch all the rooms. I don't want any communication between Mrs. Bliss and Salveter and Hani."

Hennessey glanced at Heath.

"Those are orders," the Sergeant informed him; and the detective went out with alacrity.

Vance turned to Markham.

"Maybe that priceless young ass actually wrote the silly letter," he commented; and a worried look came over his face. "I say; let's take a peep in the museum."

"See here, Vance,"—Markham rose—"why should the possibility of Salveter's having written a foolish letter upset you?"

"I don't know—I'm not sure." Vance went to the door; then pivoted suddenly. "But I'm afraid—I'm deuced afraid! Such a letter would give the murderer a loophole—that is, if what I think is true. If the letter was written, we've got to find it. If we don't find it, there are several plausible explanations for its disappearance—and one of 'em is fiendish... But come. We'll have to search the museum—on the chance that it was written, as Salveter says, and left in the table-drawer."

He went swiftly across the hall and threw open the great steel door.

"If Doctor Bliss and Guilfoyle return while we're in the museum," he said to Snitkin, who stood leaning against the front door, "take them in the drawing-room and keep them there."

We passed down the steps into the museum, and Vance went at once to the little desk-table beside the obelisk. He looked at the yellow pad and tested the color of the ink. Then he pulled open the drawer and turned out its contents. After a few minutes' inspection of the odds and ends, he restored the drawer to order and closed it. There was a small mahogany waste-basket beneath the table, and Vance emptied it on the floor. Going down on his knees he looked at each piece of crumpled paper. At length he rose and shook his head.

"I don't like this, Markham," he said. "I'd feel infinitely better if I could find that letter."

He strolled about the museum looking for places where a letter might have been thrown. But when he reached the iron spiral stairs at the rear he leaned his back against them and regarded Markham hopelessly.

"I'm becoming more and more frightened," he remarked in a low voice. "If this devilish plot should work!..." He turned suddenly and ran up the stairs, beckoning to us as he did so. "There's a chance—just a chance," he called over his shoulder. "I should have thought of it before."

We followed him uncomprehendingly into Doctor Bliss's study.

"The letter should be in the study," he said, striving to control his eagerness. "That would be logical...and this case is unbelievably logical, Markham—so logical, so mathematical, that we may eventually be able to read it aright. It's too logical, in fact—that's its weakness..."

He was already on all fours delving into the spilled contents of Doctor Bliss's waste-basket. After a moment's search he picked up two torn pieces of yellow paper. He glanced at them carefully, and we could see tiny markings on them in green ink. He placed them to one side, and continued his search. After several minutes he had amassed a small pile of yellow paper fragments.

"I think that's about all," he said, rising.

He sat down in the swivel chair and laid the torn bits of yellow paper on the blotter.

"This may take a little time, but since I know Egyptian hieroglyphs fairly well I ought to accomplish the task without too much difficulty, don't y'know."

He began arranging and fitting the scraps together, while Markham, Heath and I stood behind him looking on with fascination. At the end of ten minutes he had reassembled the letter. Then he took a large sheet of white paper from one of the drawers of the desk and covered it with mucilage. Carefully he transferred the reconstructed letter, piece by piece, to the gummed paper.

"There, Markham old dear," he sighed, "is the unfinished letter which Salveter told us he was working on this morning between nine-thirty and ten."

The document was unquestionably a sheet of the yellow scratch-pad we had seen in the museum; and on it were four lines of old Egyptian characters painstakingly limned in green ink.

Vance placed his finger on one of the groups of characters.

"That," he told us, "is the *ankh* hieroglyph." He shifted his finger. "And that is the *was* sign... And here, toward the end, is the *tem* sign."

"And then what?" Heath was frankly nonplussed, and his tone was far from civil. "We can't arrest a guy because he drew a lot of cock-eyed pictures on a piece of yellow paper."

"My word, Sergeant! Must you always be thinkin' of clappin' persons into oubliettes? I fear you haven't a humane nature. Very sad... Why not try to cerebrate occasionally?" He looked up and I was startled by his seriousness. "The young and impetuous Mr. Salveter confesses that he has foolishly penned a letter to his Dulcibella in the language of the Pharaohs. He tells us he has placed the unfinished *billet-doux* in the drawer of a table in the museum. We discover that it is not in the table-drawer, but has been ruthlessly dismembered and thrown into the waste-basket in Doctor Bliss's study... On what possible grounds could you regard the Paul of this epistle as a murderer?"

"I ain't regarding nobody as anything," retorted Heath violently. "But there's too much shenanigan going on around here to suit me. I want action."

Vance contemplated him gravely.

"For once I, too, want action, Sergeant. If we don't get some sort of action before long, we may expect something even worse than has already happened. But it must be intelligent action—not the action that the murderer wants us to take. We're caught in the meshes of a cunningly fabricated plot; and, unless we watch our step, the culprit will go free and we'll still be battling with the cobwebs."

Heath grunted and began poring over the reconstructed letter.

"That's a hell of a way for a guy to write to a dame," he commented, with surly disdain. "Give me a nice dirty shooting by a gangster. These flossy crimes make me sick."

Markham was scowling.

"See here, Vance," he said; "do you believe the murderer tore up that letter and threw it in Doctor Bliss's waste-basket?"

"Can there be any doubt of it?" Vance asked in return.

"But what, in Heaven's name, could have been his object?"

"I don't know—yet. That's why I'm frightened." Vance gazed out of the rear window. "But the destruction of that letter is part of the plot; and until we can get some definite and workable evidence, we're helpless."

"Still," persisted Markham, "if the letter was incriminating, it strikes me it would have been valuable to the murderer. Tearing it up doesn't help any one."

Heath looked first at Vance and then at Markham.

"Maybe," he offered, "Salveter tore it up himself."

"When?" Vance asked quietly.

"How do I know?" The Sergeant was nettled. "Maybe when he croaked the old man."

"If that were the case, he wouldn't have admitted having written it."

"Well," Heath persevered, "maybe he tore it up when you sent him to find it a few minutes ago."

"And then, after tearing it up, he came here and put it in the basket where it might be found... No, Sergeant. That's not entirely reasonable. If Salveter had been frightened and had decided to get rid of the letter, he'd have destroyed it completely—burned it, most likely, and left no traces of it about."

Markham, too, had become fascinated by the hieroglyphs Vance had pieced together. He stood regarding the conjoined bits of paper perplexedly.

"You think, then, we were intended to find it?" he asked.

"I don't know." Vance's far-away gaze did not shift. "It may be...and yet... No! There was only one chance in a thousand that we would come across it. The person who put it in the waste-basket here couldn't have known, or even guessed, that Salveter would tell us of having written it and left it lying about."

"On the other hand,"—Markham was loath to relinquish his train of thought—"the letter might have been put here in the hope of involving Bliss still further—that is, it might have been regarded by the murderer as another planted clew, along with the scarab pin, the financial report, and the foot-prints."

Vance shook his head.

"No. That couldn't be. Bliss, d'ye see, couldn't have written the letter,—it's too obviously a communication from Salveter to Mrs. Bliss."

Vance picked up the assembled letter and studied it for a time.

"It's not particularly difficult to read for any one who knows something of Egyptian. It says exactly what Salveter said it did." He tossed the paper back on the desk. "There's something unspeakably devilish behind this. And the more I think of it the more I'm convinced we were not intended to find the letter. My feeling is, it was carelessly thrown away by some one—*after it had served its purpose.*"

"But what possible purpose—?" Markham began.

"If we knew the purpose, Markham," said Vance with much gravity, "we might avert another tragedy."

Markham compressed his lips grimly. I knew what was going through his mind: he was thinking of Vance's terrifying predictions in the Greene and the Bishop cases—predictions which came true with all the horror of final and ineluctable catastrophe.

"You believe this affair isn't over yet?" he asked slowly.

"I know it isn't over. The plan isn't complete. We forestalled the murderer by releasing Doctor Bliss. And now he must carry on. We've seen only the dark preliminaries of his damnable scheme—and when the plot is finally revealed, it will be monstrous…"

Vance went quietly to the door leading into the hall and, opening it a few inches, looked out.

"And, Markham," he said, reclosing the door, "we must be careful—that's what I've been insisting on right along. We must not fall into any of the murderer's traps. The arrest of Doctor Bliss was one of those traps. A single false step on our part, and the plot will succeed."

He turned to Heath.

"Sergeant, will you be so good as to bring me the yellow pad and the pen and ink from the table in the museum?…

We, too, must cover up our tracks, for we are being stalked as closely as we are stalking the murderer."

Heath, without a word, went into the museum, and a few moments later returned with the requested articles. Vance took them and sat down at the doctor's desk. Then placing Salveter's letter before him he began copying roughly the phonograms and ideograms on a sheet of the yellow pad.

"It's best, I think," he explained as he worked, "that we hide the fact that we've found the letter. The person who tore it up and threw it in the basket may suspect that we've discovered it and look for the fragments. If they're not here, he will be on, his guard. It's merely a remote precaution, but we can't afford to make a slip. We're confronted by a mind of diabolical cleverness…"

When he had finished transcribing a dozen or so of the symbols, he tore the paper into pieces of the same size as those of the original letter, and mixed them with the contents of the waste-basket. Then he folded up Salveter's original letter and placed it in his pocket.

"Do you mind, Sergeant, returning the paper and ink to the museum?"

"You oughta been a crook, Mr. Vance," Heath remarked good-naturedly, picking up the pad and ink-stand and disappearing through the steel door.

"I don't see any light," Markham commented gloomily. "The farther we go, the more involved the case becomes."

Vance nodded sombrely.

"There's nothing we can do now but await developments. Thus far we've checked the murderer's king; but he still has several moves. It's like one of Alekhine's chess combinations— we can't tell just what was in his mind when he began the assault. And he may produce a combination that will clean the board and leave us defenseless…"

Heath reappeared at this moment, looking uneasy.

"I don't like that damn room," he grumbled. "Too many corpses. Why do these scientific bugs have to go digging up mummies and things? It's what you might call morbid."

"A perfect criticism of Egyptologists, Sergeant," Vance replied with a sympathetic grin. "Egyptology isn't an archæological science—it's a pathological condition, a cerebral visitation—*dementia scholastica*. Once the *spirillum terrigenum* enters your system, you're lost—cursed with an incurable disease. If you dig up corpses that are thousands of years old, you're an Egyptologist; if you dig up recent corpses you're a Burke or a Hare, and the law swoops down on you. It all comes under the head of body-snatching..."*

"Be that as it may,"—Heath was still troubled and was chewing his cigar viciously—"I don't like the things in that morgue. And I specially don't like that black coffin under the front windows. What's in it, Mr. Vance?"

"The granite sarcophagus? Really, I don't know, Sergeant. It's empty in all probability, unless Doctor Bliss uses it as a storage chest—which isn't likely, considerin' the weight of the lid."

There came a knock on the hall door, and Snitkin informed us that Guilfoyle had arrived with Doctor Bliss.

"There are one or two questions," Vance said, "that I want to ask him. Then, I think, Markham, we can toddle along: I'm fainting for muffins and marmalade..."

"Quit now?" demanded Heath in astonished disgust. "What's the idea? We've just begun this investigation!"

"We've done more than that," Vance told him softly. "We've avoided every snare laid for us by the murderer. We've upset all his calculations and forced him to reconstruct his trenches. As the case stands now, it's a stalemate. The board will have to be set up again—and, fortunately for us, the murderer gets the

---

*   *Vance was here indulging in hyperbole, and believed it no more than John Dennis believed that "a man who could make so vile a pun would not scruple to pick a pocket." Vance knew several Egyptologists and respected them highly. Among them were Doctor Ludlow Bull and Doctor Henry A. Carey of the Metropolitan Museum of Art, who had once generously assisted him in his work on the Menander fragments.*

white pieces. It's his first move. He simply has to win the game, d'ye see. We can afford to play for a draw."

"I'm beginning to understand what you mean, Vance." Markham nodded slowly. "We've refused to follow his false moves, and now he must rebait his trap."

"Spoken with a precision and clarity wholly unbecoming a lawyer," returned Vance, with a forced smile. Then he sobered again. "Yes, I think he will rebait the trap before he takes any final steps. And I'm hopin' that the new bait will give us a solution to the entire plot and permit the Sergeant to make his arrest."

"Well, all I've gotta say," Heath complained, "is that this is the queerest case I was ever mixed up in. We go and eat muffins, and wait for the guilty guy to spill the beans! If I was to outline that technic to O'Brien* he'd call an ambulance and send me to Bellevue."

"I'll see that you don't go to a psychopathic ward, Sergeant," Markham said irritably, walking toward the door.

---

*   Chief Inspector O'Brien was at that time in charge of the entire
    Police Department of the City of New York.

CHAPTER SIXTEEN

A Call After Midnight
(Friday, July 18; 5.15 p.m.)

WE FOUND DOCTOR Bliss in the drawing-room, slumped in a deep sprawling chair, his tweed hat pulled down over his eyes. Beside him stood Guilfoyle smirking triumphantly.

Vance was annoyed, and took no pains to hide the fact.

"Tell your efficient bloodhound to wait outside, will you, Sergeant?"

"O.K." Heath looked commiseratingly at Guilfoyle. "Out on the cement, Guil," he ordered. "And don't ask any questions. This ain't a murder case—it's a Hallowe'en party in a bug-house."

The detective grinned and left us.

Bliss lifted his eyes. He was a dejected-looking figure. His face was flushed, and apprehension and humiliation were written on his sunken features.

"Now, I suppose," he said in a quavering voice, "you'll arrest me for this heinous murder. But—oh, my God, gentlemen!—I assure you—"

Vance had stepped toward him.

"Just a moment, doctor," he broke in. "Don't upset yourself. We're not going to arrest you; but we would like an explanation of your amazin' action. Why should you, if you are innocent, attempt to leave the country?"

"Why...why?" The man was nervous and excited. "I was afraid—that's why. Everything is against me. All the evidence points toward me... There's some one here who hates me and wants me out of the way. It's only too obvious. The planting of my scarab pin beside poor Kyle's body, and that financial report found in the murdered man's hand, and those terrible foot-prints leading to my study—don't you think I know what it all means? It means that I must pay the price—I, *I*." He struck his chest weakly. "And other things will be found; the person who killed Kyle won't rest content until I'm behind the bars—or dead. I know it—I know it!... That's why I tried to get away. And now you've brought me back to a living death—to a fate more awful than the one that befell my old benefactor..."

His head dropped forward and a shudder ran through his body.

"Still, it was foolish to attempt to escape, doctor," Markham said gently. "You might have trusted us. I assure you no injustice will be done you. We have learned many things in the course of our investigation; and we have reason to believe that you were drugged with powdered opium during the period of the crime—"

"Powdered opium!" Bliss almost leapt out of his chair. "That's what I tasted! There was something the matter with the coffee this morning—it had a curious flavor. At first I thought Brush hadn't made it the way I'd instructed him. Then I got drowsy, and forgot all about it... Opium! I know the taste. I once had dysentery in Egypt, and took opium and capsicum—my Sun Cholera Mixture* had run out." His mouth sagged open, and he gave Markham a look of terrified appeal. "Poisoned in my own house!" Suddenly a grim vindictiveness shone in his eyes. "You're right, sir," he said, with metallic hardness. "I shouldn't have attempted to run away. My place is here, and my duty is to help you—"

"Yes, yes, doctor." Vance was palpably bored. "Regrets are very comfortin', but we're tryin' to deal with facts. And thus far you haven't been very helpful... I say, who had charge of the medical supplies?" He put the question abruptly.

"Why...why...let me see..." Bliss averted his eyes and began fidgeting with the crease in his trousers.

"We'll drop the matter." Vance made a resigned gesture. "Maybe you're willing to tell us how well Mrs. Bliss knows Egyptian hieroglyphs."

Bliss looked surprised, and it took him several moments to regain his equanimity.

"She knows them practically as well as I do," he answered at length. "Her father, Abercrombie, taught her the old Egyptian language when she was a child, and she has worked with me for years in the deciphering of inscriptions..."

"And Hani?"

"Oh, he has a smattering of hieroglyphic writing—nothing unusual. He lacks the trained mind—"

"And how well does Mr. Salveter know Egyptian?"

"Fairly well. He's weak on grammatical points, but his knowledge of the signs and the vocabulary is rather extensive. He has studied Greek and Arabic; and I believe he had a year or two of Assyrian. Coptic, too. The usual linguistic foundation for an archæologist—Scarlett, on the other hand, is something

---

*   *The Sun Cholera Mixture for dysentery (a recipe of Doctor G.W. Busteed) was so named because its formula had been published by the New York Sun during the cholera excitement in New York in June, 1849. It was admitted to the first edition of the National Formulary in 1883. Its constituents were tincture of capsicum, tincture of rhubarb, spirits of camphor, essence of peppermint, and opium.*

of a wizard, though he's a loyal adherent of Budge's system—
like many amateurs.* And Budge, of course, is antiquated.
Don't misunderstand me. Budge is a great man—his contribu-
tions to Egyptology are invaluable; and his publication of the
Book of the Dead—"

"I know." Vance nodded with impatience. "His Index
makes it possible to find almost any passage in the Papyrus of
Ani…"

"Just so." Bliss had begun to reveal a curious animation:
his scientific enthusiasm was manifesting itself. "But Alan
Gardiner is the true modern scholar. His 'Egyptian Grammar'
is a profound and accurate work. The most important *opus* on
Egyptology, however, is the Erman-Grapow 'Wörterbuch der
aegyptischen Sprache.'…"

Vance had become suddenly interested.

"Does Mr. Salveter use the Erman-Grapow 'Wörterbuch'?"
he asked.

"Certainly. I insisted upon it. I ordered three sets from
Leipzig—one for myself, and one each for Salveter and
Scarlett."

"The signs differ considerably, I believe, from the
Theinhardt type used by Budge."

"Oh, yes." Bliss removed his hat and threw it on the floor.
"The consonant transliterated *u* by Budge—the quail chick—
appears as *w* in the 'Wörterbuch' and every other modern
work. And, of course, there's the cursive spiral sign which is
also the hieroglyphic adaptation of the hieratic abbreviated
form of the quail…"

"Thank you, doctor." Vance took out his cigarette-case,
saw he had only one *Régie* left, and returned it to his pocket.
"I understand that Mr. Scarlett, before leaving the house this
afternoon, went up-stairs. I rather thought, don't y'know, that
he dropped in to see you."

---

*   Sir E.A. Wallis Budge was for many years Keeper of the Egyptian
     and Assyrian Antiquities in the British Museum.

"Yes." Bliss sank back in his chair. "A very sympathetic fellow, Scarlett."

"What did he say to you?"

"Nothing of any importance. He wished me good luck— said he'd stand by, in case I wanted him. That sort of thing."

"How long was he with you?"

"A minute or so. He went away immediately. Said he was going home."

"One more question, doctor," Vance said, after several moments' pause. "Who in this house would have any reason for wanting to saddle you with the crime of killing Mr. Kyle?"

A sudden change came over Bliss. His eyes glared straight ahead, and the lines of his face hardened into almost terrifying contours. He clutched the arms of his chair and drew in his feet. Both fear and hatred possessed him; he was like a man about to leap at a mortal enemy. Then he stood up, every muscle in his body tense.

"I can't answer that question; I refuse to answer it!... I don't know—I don't know! But there is some one—isn't there?" He reached out and grasped Vance's arm. "You should have let me escape." A wild look came into his eyes, and he glanced hurriedly toward the door as if he feared some imminent danger lurking in the hall. "Have me arrested, Mr. Vance! Do anything but ask me to stay here..." His voice had become pitifully appealing.

Vance drew away from him.

"Pull yourself together, doctor," he said in a matter-of-fact tone. "Nothing is going to happen to you... Go to your room and remain there till to-morrow. We'll take care of the criminal end of the case."

"But you have no idea who did this frightful thing," Bliss protested.

"Oh, but we have, don't y'know." Vance's calm assurance seemed to have a quieting effect on him. "It's only necess'ry for us to wait a bit. At present we haven't enough evidence to make an arrest. But since the murderer's main object has failed, it's almost inevitable that he will make another move. And when he does, we may get the necess'ry evidence against him."

"But suppose he takes direct action—against me?" Bliss remonstrated. "The fact that he has failed to involve me may drive him to more desperate measures."

"I hardly think so," returned Vance. "But if anything happens, you can reach me at this telephone number." He wrote his private number on a card and handed it to Bliss.

The doctor took the card eagerly, glanced at it, and slipped it into his pocket.

"I'm going up-stairs now," he said, and walked distractedly out of the room.

"Are you sure, Vance," Markham asked in a troubled voice, "that we're not subjecting Doctor Bliss to unnecessary risk?"

"Pretty sure." Vance had become thoughtful. "Anyway, it's a delicate game, and there's no other way to play it." He went to the window. "I don't know... ," he murmured. Then after several moments: "Sergeant, I'd like to speak to Salveter.— And there's no need for Hennessey to remain up-stairs. Let him go."

Heath, nonplussed and helpless, went into the hall and called to Hennessey.

When Salveter came into the drawing-room, Vance did not even glance in his direction.

"Mr. Salveter," he said, looking out at the dusty trees in Gramercy Park, "if I were you I'd lock my door to-night... And don't write any more letters," he added. "Also, keep out of the museum."

Salveter appeared frightened by these admonitions. He studied Vance's back for some time, and then set his jaw.

"If any one starts anything round here—" he began with an almost ferocious aggressiveness.

"Oh, quite." Vance sighed. "But don't project your personality so intensively. I'm fatigued."

Salveter, after a moment's hesitation, swung about and strode from the room.

Vance came to the centre-table and rested heavily against it.

"And now, a word with Hani, and we can depart."

Heath shrugged his shoulders resignedly, and went to the door.

"Hey, Snitkin, round up that Ali Baba in the kimono."

Snitkin leapt to the staircase, and a few minutes later the Egyptian stood before us, serene and detached.

"Hani," said Vance, with an impressiveness wholly uncharacteristic, "you will do well to watch over this household to-night."

"Yes, *effendi*. I comprehend perfectly. The spirit of Sakhmet may return and complete the task she has begun—"

"Exactly." Vance gave a tired smile. "Your feline lady foozled things this morning, and she'll probably be back to tie up a few loose ends... Watch for her—do you understand?"

Hani inclined his head.

"Yes, *effendi*. We understand each other."

"That's positively rippin'. And incidentally, Hani, what is the number of Mr. Scarlett's domicile in Irving Place?"

"Ninety-six." The Egyptian revealed considerable interest in Vance's question.

"That will be all... And give my regards to your lion-headed goddess."

"It may be Anûbis who will return, *effendi*," said Hani sepulchrally, as he left us.

Vance looked whimsically at Markham.

"The stage is set, and the curtain will go up anon... Let's move on. There's nothing more we can do here. And I'm totterin' with hunger."

As we passed out into Twentieth Street Vance led the way toward Irving Place.

"I rather think we owe it to Scarlett to let him know how things stand," he explained negligently. "He brought us the sad tidings and is probably all agog and aflutter. He lives just round the corner."

Markham glanced at Vance inquisitively, but made no comment. Heath, however, grunted impatiently.

"It looks to me like we're doing 'most everything but clean up this homicide," he groused.

"Scarlett's a shrewd lad; he may have conjured up an idea or two," Vance returned.

"I got ideas, too," the Sergeant declared maliciously. "But what good are they? If *I* was handling this case, I'd arrest the whole outfit, put 'em in separate cells, and let 'em sweat. By the time they got *habeas-corpus* proceedings started I'd know a damn sight more than I do now."

"I doubt it, Sergeant." Vance spoke mildly. "I think you'd know even less... Ah, here's number ninety-six."

He turned into the Colonial entrance of an old brick house a few doors from Twentieth Street, and rang the bell.

Scarlett's quarters—two small rooms with a wide, arched doorway between—were on the second floor at the front. They were furnished severely but comfortably in Jacobean style, and typified the serious-minded bachelor. Scarlett had opened the door at our knock and invited us in with the stiff cordiality of the English host. He seemed relieved to see us.

"I've been in a frightful stew for hours," he said. "Been trying to analyze this affair. I was on the point of running round to the museum and finding out what progress you gentlemen had made."

"We've made a bit of progress," Vance told him; "but it's not of a tangible nature. We've decided to let matters float for a while in the anticipation that the guilty person will proceed with his plot and thus supply us with definite evidence."

"Ah!" Scarlett took his pipe slowly from his mouth and looked sharply at Vance. "That remark makes me think that maybe you and I have reached the same conclusion. There was no earthly reason for Kyle's having been killed unless his demise was to lead to something else—"

"To what, for example?"

"By Jove, I wish I knew!" Scarlett packed his pipe with his finger and held a match to it. "There are several possible explanations."

"My word! Are there?... Several? Well, well! Could you bear to outline one of them? We're dashed interested, don't y'know."

"Oh, I say, Vance! Really, now, I'd hate like the Old Harry to wrong any one," Scarlett spluttered. "Hani, however, didn't care a great deal for Doctor Bliss—"

"Thanks awfully. Astonishin' as it may seem, I noted that fact myself this morning. Have you any other little beam of sunshine you'd care to launch in our direction?"

"I think Salveter is hopelessly smitten with Meryt-Amen."

"Fancy that!"

Vance took out his cigarette-case and tapped his one remaining *Régie* on the lid. Deliberately he lighted it and, after a deep inhalation, looked up seriously.

"Yes, Scarlett," he drawled, "it's quite possible that you and I have arrived at the same conclusion. But naturally we can't make a move until we have something definite with which to back up our hypotheses... By the by, Doctor Bliss attempted to leave the country this afternoon. If it hadn't been for one of Sergeant Heath's minions he presumably would be on his way to Montreal at this moment."

I expected to see Scarlett express astonishment at this news, but instead he merely nodded his head.

"I'm not surprised. He's certainly in a funk. Can't say that I blame him. Things appear rather black for him." Scarlett puffed on his pipe, and shot a surreptitious look at Vance. "The more I think about this affair, the more I'm impressed with the possibility that, after all—"

"Oh, quite." Vance cut him short. "But we're not pantin' for possibilities. What we crave is specific data."

"That's going to be difficult, I'm afraid." Scarlett grew thoughtful. "There's been too much cleverness—"

"Ah! That's the point—*too much cleverness*. Exactly! Therein lies the weakness of the crime. And I'm hopefully countin' on that *abundantia cautelœ*." Vance smiled. "Really, y'know, Scarlett, I'm not as dense as I've appeared thus far.

My object in stultifyin' my perceptions has been to wangle the murderer into new efforts. Sooner or later he'll overplay his hand."

Scarlett did not answer for some time. Finally he spoke.

"I appreciate your confidence, Vance. You're very sporting. But my opinion is, you'll never be able to convict the murderer."

"You may be right," Vance admitted. "Nevertheless, I'm appealing to you to keep an eye on the situation... But I warn you to be careful. The murderer of Kyle is a ruthless johnnie."

"You don't have to tell me that." Scarlett got up and, walking to the fireplace, leaned against the marble mantel. "I could tell you volumes about him."

"I'm sure you could." To my astonishment Vance accepted the other's startling statement without the slightest manifestation of surprise. "But there's no need to go into that now." He, too, rose, and going to the door gave a casual wave of farewell to Scarlett. "We're toddlin' along. Just thought we'd let you know how things stood and admonish you to be careful."

"Very kind of you, Vance. Fact is, I'm frightfully upset— nervous as a Persian kitten... Wish I could work; but all my materials are at the museum. I know I sha'n't sleep a wink to-night."

"Well, cheerio!" Vance turned the door-knob.

"I say, Vance!" Scarlett stepped forward urgently. "Are you, by any chance, going back to the Bliss house to-day?"

"No. We're through there for the time being." Vance's voice was quiet and droning, as with ennui. "Why do you ask?"

Scarlett fiddled at his pipe with a sort of sudden agitation.

"No reason." He looked at Vance with a constricted brow. "No reason at all. I'm anxious about the situation. There's no telling what may happen."

"Whatever happens, Scarlett," Vance said, with a certain abruptness, "Mrs. Bliss will be perfectly safe. I think we can trust Hani to see to that."

"Yes—of course," the man murmured. "Faithful dog, Hani... And who'd want to harm Meryt?"

"Who, indeed?" Vance was now standing in the hallway, holding the door open for Markham and Heath and me to pass through.

Scarlett, animated by some instinct of hospitality, came forward.

"Sorry you're going," he said perfunctorily. "If I can be of any help... So you've ended your investigation at the house?"

"For the moment, at least." Vance paused. The rest of us had passed him and were waiting at the head of the stairs. "We're not contemplatin' returning to the Bliss establishment until something new comes to light."

"Right-o." Scarlett nodded with a curious significance. "If I learn anything I'll telephone to you."

We went out into Irving Place, and Vance hailed a taxicab.

"Food—sustenance," he moaned. "Let us see... The Brevoort isn't far away..."

We had an elaborate tea at the old Brevoort on lower Fifth Avenue, and shortly afterward Heath departed for the Homicide Bureau to make out his report and to pacify the newspaper reporters who would be swarming in on him the moment the case went on record.

"You had better stand by," Vance suggested to the Sergeant, as he left us; "for I'm full of anticipations, and we couldn't push forward without you."

"I'll be at the office till ten to-night," Heath told him sulkily. "And after that Mr. Markham knows where to reach me at home. But, I'm here to tell you, I'm disgusted."

"So are we all," said Vance cheerfully.

Markham telephoned to Swacker* to close the office and go home. Then the three of us drove to Longue Vue for dinner. Vance refused to discuss the case and insisted upon

---

*   *Swacker, a bright, energetic youth, was Markham's secretary.*

talking about Arturo Toscanini, the new conductor of the Philharmonic-Symphony Orchestra.

"A vastly overrated *Kapellmeister*," he complained, as he tasted his *canard Molière*. "It strikes me he is temperamentally incapable of sensing the classic ideals in the great symphonic works of Brahms and Beethoven... I say, the tomato purée in this sauce is excellent, but the Madeira wine is too vineg'ry. Prohibition, Markham, worked devastatin' havoc on the food of this country: it practically eliminated gastronomic æsthetics... But to return to Toscanini. I'm positively amazed at the panegyrics with which the critics have showered him. His secret ideals, I'm inclined to think, are Puccini and Giordano and Respighi. And no man with such ideals should attempt to interpret the classics. I've heard him do Brahms and Beethoven and Mozart, and they all exuded a strong Italian aroma under his baton. But the Americans worship him. They have no sense of pure intellectual beauty, of sweeping classic lines and magistral form. They crave strongly contrasted *pianissimos* and *fortissimos*, sudden changes in tempi, leaping *accelerandos* and crawling *ritardandos*. And Toscanini gives it all to 'em... Furtwängler, Walter, Klemperer, Mengelberg, Van Hoogstraaten—any one of these conductors is, in my opinion, superior to Toscanini when it comes to the great German classics..."

"Would you mind, Vance," Markham asked irritably, "dropping these irrelevancies and outlining to me your theory of the Kyle case?"

"I'd mind terribly," was Vance's amiable reply. "After the *Bar-le-duc* and *Gervaise*, however..."

As a matter of fact it was nearly midnight before the subject of the tragedy was again broached. We had returned to Vance's apartment after a long drive through Van Cortlandt Park; and Markham and he and I had gone up to the little roof garden to seek whatever air was stirring along East Thirty-eighth Street. Currie had made a delicious champagne cup—what the Viennese call a *Bowle*—with fresh fruit in it; and we sat under the summer stars smoking and waiting. I say, "waiting," for there is no doubt that each of us expected something untoward to happen.

Vance, for all his detachment, was inwardly tense—I could tell this by his slow, restrained movements. And Markham was loath to go home: he was far from satisfied with the way the investigation had progressed, and was hoping—as a result of Vance's prognostication—that something would develop to take the case out of the hazy realm of conjecture and place it upon a sound basis where definite action could be taken.

Shortly before twelve o'clock Markham held a long conversation with Heath on the telephone. When he hung up the receiver he heaved a hopeless sigh.

"I don't like to think of what the opposition papers are going to say to-morrow," he remarked gloomily, as he cut the tip off of a fresh cigar. "We've got absolutely nowhere in this investigation…"

"Oh, yes, we have." Vance was staring up into the sultry night. "We've made amazin' progress. The case, d'ye see, is closed as far as the solution is concerned. We're merely waitin' for the murderer to get panic-stricken. The moment he does, we'll be able to take action."

"Why must you be so confounded mysterious?" Markham was in a vile humor. "You're always indulging in cabalistic rituals. The Delphic Pythia herself was no vaguer or more obscure than you. If you think you know who killed Kyle, why not come out with it?"

"I can't do it." Vance, too, was distressed. "Really, y'know, Markham, I'm not trying to be illusory. I'm strivin' to find some tangible evidence to corroborate my theory. And if we bide our time we'll secure that evidence." He looked at Markham seriously. "There's danger, of course. Something unforeseen may happen. But there's no human way to stop it. Whatever step we might take now would lead to tragedy. We have given the murderer an abundance of rope; let us hope he will hang himself…"

It was exactly twenty minutes past twelve that night when the thing that Vance had been waiting for happened. We had been sitting in silence for perhaps ten minutes when Currie stepped out into the garden carrying a portable telephone.

"I beg your pardon, sir—" he began; but before he could continue Vance had risen and walked toward him.

"Plug it in, Currie," he ordered. "I'll answer the call."

Vance took the instrument and leaned against the French door.

"Yes...yes. What has happened?" His voice was low and resonant. He listened for perhaps thirty seconds, his eyes half closed. Then he said merely: "We'll be there at once," and handed the telephone to Currie.

He was unquestionably puzzled, and stood for several moments, his head down, deep in thought.

"It's not what I expected," he said, as if to himself. "It doesn't fit."

Presently he lifted his head, like one struck sharply.

"But it *does* fit! Of course it fits! It's what I should have expected." Despite the careless pose of his body his eyes were animated. "Logic! How damnably logical!... Come, Markham. Phone Heath—have him meet us at the museum as soon as he can get there..."

Markham had risen and was glaring at Vance in ferocious alarm.

"Who was on the phone?" he demanded. "And what has happened?"

"Please be tranquil, Markham." Vance spoke quietly. "It was Doctor Bliss who spoke to me. And, accordin' to his hysterical tale, there has been an attempted murder in his house. I promised him we'd look in..."

Markham had already snatched the telephone from Currie's hands and was frantically asking for Heath's number.

CHAPTER SEVENTEEN

The Golden Dagger
(Saturday, July 14; 12.45 a.m.)

We HAD TO walk to Fifth Avenue to find a taxicab at that hour, and even then there was five minutes' wait until an unoccupied one came by. The result was that it was fully twenty minutes before we turned into Gramercy Park and drew up in front of the Bliss residence.

As we alighted another taxicab swung round the corner of Irving Place and nearly skidded into us as its brakes were suddenly thrown on. The door was flung open before the cab had come to a standstill, and the bulky figure of Sergeant Heath projected itself to the sidewalk. Heath lived in East Eleventh Street and had managed to dress and reach the museum almost simultaneously with our arrival.

"My word, Sergeant!" Vance hailed him. "We synchronize, don't y'know. We arrive at the same destination at the same time, but from opposite directions. Jolly idea."

Heath acknowledged the somewhat enigmatical pleas-antry with a grunt.

"What's all the excitement anyway?" he asked Markham. "You didn't give me much of an earful over the phone."

"An attempt has been made on Doctor Bliss's life," Markham told him.

Heath whistled softly.

"I certainly didn't expect that, sir."

"Neither did Mr. Vance." The rejoinder was intended as a taunt.

We went up the stone steps to the vestibule, but before we could ring the bell Brush opened the door. He placed his forefinger to his lips and, leaning forward mysteriously, said in a stage whisper:

"Doctor Bliss requests that you gentlemen be very quiet so as not to disturb the other members of the household... He's in his bedchamber waiting for you."

Brush was clad in a flannel robe and carpet slippers, but despite the hot sultriness of the night he was visibly shivering. His face, always pale, now appeared positively ghastly in the dim light.

We stepped into the hall, and Brush closed the door cautiously with trembling hands. Suddenly Vance wheeled about and caught him by the arm, spinning him round.

"What do you know about the occurrence here to-night?" he demanded in a low tone.

The butler's eyes bulged and his jaw sagged.

"Nothing—nothing," he managed to stammer.

"Really, now! Then why are you so frightened?" Vance did not relax his hold.

"I'm afraid of this place," came the plaintive answer. "I want to leave here. Strange things are going on—"

"So they are. But don't fret; you'll be able to look for another berth before long."

"I'm glad of that, sir." The man seemed greatly relieved. "But what *has* happened to-night, sir?"

"If you're ignorant of what has taken place," returned Vance, "how do you happen to be here at this hour awaiting our arrival and acting like a villain in a melodrama?"

"I was told to wait for you, sir. Doctor Bliss came down-stairs to my room—"

"Where is your room, Brush?"

"In the basement, at the rear, just off the kitchen."

"Very good. Go on."

"Well, sir, Doctor Bliss came to my room about half an hour ago. He seemed very much upset, and frightened—if you know what I mean. He told me to wait at the front door for you gentlemen—that you'd arrive any minute. And he instructed me to make no noise and also to warn you—"

"Then he went up-stairs?"

"At once, sir."

"Where is Doctor Bliss's room?"

"It's the rear door on the second floor, just at the head of the stairs. The forward door is the mistress's bedchamber."

Vance released the man's arm.

"Did you hear any disturbance to-night?"

"None, sir. Everything has been quiet. Every one retired early, and I myself went to bed before eleven."

"You may go back to bed now," Vance told him.

"Yes, sir." And Brush went quickly away and disap-peared through the door at the rear of the hall. Vance made a gesture for us to follow him and led the way up-stairs. A small electric bulb was burning in the upper hall, but we did not need it to find Doctor Bliss's room, for his door was a few inches ajar and a shaft of light fell diagonally across the floor outside.

Vance, without knocking, pushed the door inward and stepped into the room. Bliss was sitting rigidly in a straight chair in the far corner, leaning slightly forward, his eyes riveted on the door. In his hand was a brutal-looking army revolver. At our entrance he leapt to his feet, and brought the gun up simultaneously.

"Tut, tut, doctor!" Vance smiled whimsically. "Put the firearms away and chant us the distressin' rune."

Bliss drew an audible sigh of relief, and placed the weapon on a small table at his side.

"Thank you for coming, Mr. Vance," he said in a strained tone. "And you, Mr. Markham." He acknowledged Heath's and my presence with a slight, jerky bow. "The thing you predicted has happened... There's a murderer in this house!"

"Well, well! That would hardly come under the head of news." (I could not understand Vance's attitude.) "We've known that fact since eleven this morning."

Bliss, too, was perplexed and, I imagine, somewhat piqued by Vance's negligent manner, for he stepped stiffly to the bed and, pointing at the headboard, remarked irritably:

"And there's the proof!"

The bed was an old Colonial piece, of polished mahogany, with a great curving headboard rising at least four feet above the mattress. It stood against the left-hand wall at a right angle to the door.

The object at which Bliss pointed with a quivering finger was an antique Egyptian dagger, about eleven inches long, whose blade was driven into the headboard just above the pillow. The direction of penetration was on a line with the door.

We all moved forward and stood for several seconds staring at the sinister sight. The dagger had undoubtedly been thrown with great force to have entered the hard mahogany wood so firmly; and it was obvious that if any one had been lying on the pillow at the time it was hurled, he would have received the full brunt of it somewhere in the throat.

Vance studied the position of the dagger, gauging its alignment and angulation with the door, and then he reached out his hand to grasp it. But Heath intercepted the movement.

"Use your handkerchief, Mr. Vance," he admonished. "There'll be finger-prints—"

"Oh, no, there won't, Sergeant." Vance spoke with an impressive air of knowledge. "Whoever threw that dagger was

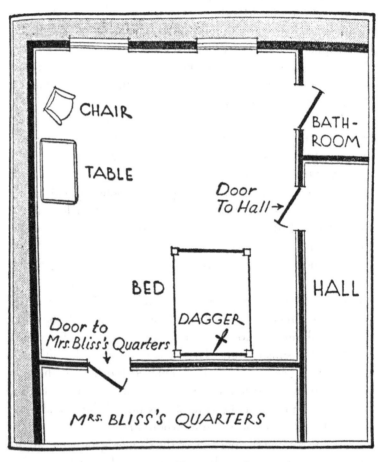

DOCTOR BLISS'S BEDROOM

careful to avoid any such incriminatin' tokens…" Whereupon he drew the blade, with considerable difficulty, from the headboard, and took it to the table-lamp.

It was a beautiful and interesting piece of workmanship. Its handle was ornamented with decorations of granulated gold and with strips of cloisonné and semi-precious stones—amethysts, turquoises, garnets, carnelians, and tiny cuttings of obsidian, chalcedony and felspar. The haft was surmounted with a lotiform knob of rock crystal, and at the hilt was a chain-scroll design in gold wire. The blade was of hardened gold adorned with shallow central grooves ending in an engraved palmette decoration.*

"Late Eighteenth Dynasty," murmured Vance, fingering the dagger and studying its designs. "Pretty, but decadent. The rugged simplicity of early Egyptian art went frightfully to pot during the opulent renaissance following the Hyksos invasion… I say, Doctor Bliss; how did you come by this flamboyant gewgaw?"

Bliss was ill at ease, and when he answered his tone was apologetic and embarrassed.

"The fact is, Mr. Vance, I smuggled that dagger out of Egypt. It was an unusual and unexpected find, and purely accidental. It's a most valuable relic, and I was afraid the Egyptian Government would claim it."

"I can well imagine they'd want to keep it in their own country." Vance tossed the dagger to the table. "And where did you ordinarily keep it?"

"Under some papers in one of my desk drawers in the study," he replied presently. "It was a rather personal item, and I thought it best not to list it in the museum."

"Most discreet… Who besides yourself knew of its existence?"

---

* *A similar dagger was found on the royal mummy in the tomb of Tut-ankh-Amûn by the late Earl of Carnarvon and Howard Carter, and is now in the Cairo Museum.*

"My wife, of course, and—" He broke off suddenly, and a peculiar light came in his eyes.

"Come, come, doctor." Vance spoke with annoyance. "This won't do. Finish your sentence."

"It is finished. My wife was the only person I confided in."

Vance accepted the statement without further argument.

"Still," he said, "any one might have discovered it, what?"

Bliss nodded slowly.

"Provided he had been snooping through my desk."

"Exactly. When did you last see the dagger in your desk drawer?"

"This morning. I was searching for some foolscap paper on which to check my report for poor Kyle…"

"And who, to your knowledge, has been in your study since we left the house this afternoon?"

Bliss pondered, and shortly a startled expression came over his face.

"I'd rather not say."

"We can't do anything to help you, doctor, if you take that attitude," Vance said severely. "Was it Mr. Salveter who was in the study?"

Bliss paused for several seconds. Then he set his jaw.

"Yes!" The word fairly burst from his lips. "I sent him to the study after dinner to-night to get me a memorandum book…"

"And where did you keep the book?"

"In the desk." This information was given reluctantly. "But any attempt to connect Salveter—"

"We're not attemptin' just now to connect anyone with this episode," Vance interrupted. "We're merely tryin' to accumulate all the information possible… However, you must admit, doctor," Vance added, "that young Mr. Salveter is—how shall I put it?—rather interested in Mrs. Bliss—"

"What's that?" Bliss stiffened and glared at Vance ferociously. "How dare you intimate such a thing? My wife, sir—"

"No one has criticised Mrs. Bliss," Vance said mildly. "And one a.m. is hardly the time for indignant pyrotechnics."

Bliss sank into his chair and covered his face with his hands.

"It may be true," he conceded in a despairing voice. "I'm too old for her—too much absorbed in my work... But that doesn't mean that the boy would attempt to kill me."

"Perhaps not." Vance spoke indifferently. "But who, then, do you suspect of endeavorin' to sever your carotid?"

"I don't know—I don't know." The man's voice rose pitifully.

At this moment the door leading into the front apartment opened, and Mrs. Bliss stood on the threshold, a long flowing robe of Oriental pattern draped about her. She was perfectly calm, and her eyes were steady, if a bit brilliant, as they took in the scene before her.

"Why have you gentlemen returned at this hour?" she inquired imperiously.

"An attempt has been made on your husband's life, madam," Markham answered sombrely; "and he telephoned to us—"

"An attempt on his life? Impossible!" She spoke with over-emphasis, and her face turned perceptibly pale. Then she went to Bliss and put her arms about him in an attitude of affectionate protection. Her eyes were blazing as she lifted them to Vance. "What absurdity is this? Who would want to take my husband's life?"

"Who, indeed?" Vance met her gaze calmly. "If we knew, we could at least arrest the person for assault with a deadly weapon—I believe that's the phrase."

"A deadly weapon?" She frowned with obvious distress. "Oh, tell me what happened!"

Vance indicated the dagger on the table.

"All we know thus far is that yon golden dagger was projectin' from the head of the bed when we arrived. We were on the point of asking your husband for a full account of the affair when you appeared—a charming Nefret-îti—at the door... Perhaps," he went on, turning to Bliss, "the doctor will recount the entire episode for us now."

"There's really little to tell." Bliss sat up and began nervously to make creases in the folds of his dressing-gown. "I came here to my room shortly after dinner, and went to bed. But I couldn't sleep, and got up. Just then Salveter passed my door on his way up-stairs and I asked him to fetch the memorandum book from the study,—I thought I might take my mind off the dreadful events of the day—"

"One moment, doctor," Vance interposed. "Was your door open?"

"Yes. I had opened it when I arose, in order to get a little more air in the room,—the atmosphere was stifling... Then I went over a few old notes and entries relating to last winter's excavations. But I couldn't keep my mind on them, and finally I closed the door, switched off the lights, and lay down again on the bed."

"That would have been about what time?"

"Between half past ten and eleven, I should say... I dozed intermittently till midnight—I could see the time by that clock with the luminous dial—and then became unaccountably restless. I got to thinking about poor Kyle, and all inclination to sleep left me. However, I was dog-tired physically, and lay quite still... About a quarter past twelve—the house was very quiet, you understand —I thought I could hear footsteps on the stairs—"

"Which stairs, doctor?"

"I couldn't determine. The footsteps might have been coming down from the third floor, or they might have been ascending from the first floor. They were very quiet, and if I had not been wide awake and keyed up I wouldn't have noticed them. As it was, I couldn't be sure, though at one time I imagined I heard a slight creak as if a board were a little loose under the carpet."

"And then?"

"I lay speculating on who it might be, for I knew the other members of the house had retired early. I did not exactly worry about the sounds until I heard them approach my own door and suddenly halt. Then your warning, Mr. Vance, swept over me with full force, and I felt that some terrible unknown danger was lurking on the threshold. I was, I admit, temporarily paralyzed with fright: I could feel the roots of my hair tingle, and my body broke out in cold perspiration."

He took a deep breath, as if to rid himself of a haunting memory.

"Just then the door began to open slowly and softly. The light in the hall had been turned out and the room here was in almost pitch darkness, so I was unable to see anything. But I could hear the gentle swish of the door as it swung open, and I could feel the mild current of air that came in from the hall..."

A tremor ran over his body, and his eyes glowed unnaturally.

"I would have called out, but my throat seemed constricted, and I did not want to imperil Mrs. Bliss, who might have answered my call and run unwittingly into something dangerous and deadly... And then the blinding ray of a flash-light was thrown directly into my eyes, and I instinctively lurched to the far side of the bed. At that moment I heard a swift, brushing sound followed by a dull wooden detonation near my head. And immediately I became conscious of footsteps retreating—"

"In which direction?" Vance again interrupted.

"I'm not sure—they were very faint. I was aware only of their stealthy retreat..."

"What did you do after that, doctor?"

"I waited several minutes. Then I cautiously closed the door and switched on the lights. It was at that moment I realized what had made the noise at the head of the bed, for the first thing I saw was the dagger. And I knew that I had been the object of a murderous attack."

Vance nodded and, picking up the dagger, weighed it on the palm of his hand.

"Yes," he mused; "it's blade-heavy and could easily have been thrown accurately even by an amateur... A peculiar form of assassination, though," he went on, almost to himself. "Much simpler and surer for the wielder to have sneaked to the bed and thrust it into his intended victim's ribs... Most peculiar! Unless, of course—" He stopped and glanced thoughtfully at the bed. Presently he shrugged his shoulders, and looked at Bliss. "After discovering the dagger, I opine, you telephoned to me."

"Within five minutes. I listened at the door a while and then went down to the study and called your number. After that I roused Brush and told him to watch for you at the front door. I came back up-stairs,—I'd armed myself with my revolver while in the study,—and awaited your arrival."

Mrs. Bliss had been watching her husband with a look of deep anxiety during his recital.

"I heard the sound of the dagger striking the headboard," she said in a low, fearful voice. "My bed is against the other side of the wall. It startled me and woke me up, but I didn't give it a second thought, and went to sleep again." She threw her head back and glared at Vance. "This is shameful and outrageous! You insist upon my husband staying in this house that harbors a murderer—a murderer who is plotting against him—and you do nothing to protect him."

"But nothing has happened to him, Mrs. Bliss," Vance replied with gentle sternness. "He has lost an hour's sleep, but really, y'know, that's not a serious catastrophe. And I can assure you that no further danger will beset him." He looked straight into the woman's eyes, and I was conscious that some understanding passed between them in that moment of mutual scrutiny.

"I do hope you find the guilty person," she said with slow, tragic emphasis. "I can bear the truth—now."

"You are very courageous, madam," Vance murmured. "And in the meantime you can best help us by retiring to your room and waiting there until you hear from us. You can trust me."

"Oh, I know I can!" There was a catch in her voice. Then she bent impulsively, touched her lips to Bliss's forehead, and returned to her room.

Vance's eyes followed her with a curious expression: I could not determine if it was one of regret or sorrow or admiration. When the door had closed after her he strolled to the table and replaced the dagger on it.

"I was just wonderin', doctor," he said. "Don't you lock or bolt your door at night?"

"Always," was the immediate reply. "It makes me nervous to sleep with an unlocked door."

"But what about to-night?"

"That is what puzzles me." Bliss's forehead was knit in perplexity. "I'm sure I locked it when I first came to my room. But, as I told you, I got up later and opened the door to get some air. The only explanation I can think of is that when I went back to bed I forgot to relock the door. It's possible of course, for I was very much upset..."

"It couldn't have been unlocked from the outside?"

"No, I'm sure it couldn't. The key was in the lock, just as you see it now."

"What about finger-prints on the outside knob?" Heath queried. "That cut glass would take 'em easy."

"My word, Sergeant!" Vance shook his head despairingly. "The concocter of this plot knows better than to leave his visitin' card wherever he goes..."

Bliss sprang to his feet.

"An idea has just struck me," he exclaimed. "There was a gold-and-cloisonné sheath to that dagger; and if the sheath should not be in my desk drawer now, perhaps—perhaps—"

"Yes, yes. Quite." Vance nodded. "I see your point. The sheath might still be in the frustrated assassin's possession. An excellent clew... Sergeant, would you mind going with Doctor Bliss to the study to ascertain if the sheath was taken with the dagger? No use worryin' ourselves about it if it's still in the drawer."

Heath went promptly to the hall, followed by Bliss. We could hear them descending to the first floor.

"What do you make of this, Vance?" Markham asked, when we were alone. "It looks pretty serious to me."

"I make a great deal of it," Vance returned sombrely. "And it *is* pretty serious. But, thank Heaven, the *coup* was not very brilliant. The whole thing was frightfully botched."

"Yes, I can see that," Markham agreed. "Imagine any one hurling a knife six feet or more when he could have dealt a single thrust in a vital spot."

"Oh, that?" Vance lifted his eyebrows. "I wasn't thinking of the technic of the knife-thrower. There were other points about the affair still less intelligent. I can't understand it altogether. Perhaps too much panic. Anyway we may get a definite key to the plot through the doctor's suggestion about the sheath."

Bliss and Heath were heard returning up the stairs.

"Well, it's gone," the Sergeant informed us, as the two stepped into the room.

"No doubt taken with the dagger," Bliss supplemented.

"Suppose I send for a couple of the boys and give the house the once-over," Heath suggested.

"That's not necess'ry, Sergeant," Vance told him. "I've a feelin' it won't be hard to find."

Markham was becoming annoyed at Vance's vagueness.

"I suppose," he said, with a tinge of sarcasm, "you can tell us exactly where we can find the sheath."

"Yes, I rather think so." Vance spoke with thoughtful seriousness. "However, I'll verify my theory later... In the meantime"—he addressed himself to Bliss—"I'd be greatly obliged if you'd remain in your room until we finish our investigation."

Bliss bowed in acquiescence.

"We're going to the drawing-room for a while," Vance continued. "There's a little work to be done there."

He moved toward the hall, then stopped as if on sudden impulse and, going to the table, slipped the dagger into his pocket. Bliss closed the door after us, and we could hear the key turn in the lock. Markham and Heath and I started down the stairs, Vance bringing up the rear.

We had descended but a few steps when a calm, flat voice from the upper hall arrested us.

"Can I be of any assistance, *effendi*?"

The unexpected sound in that dim quiet house startled us, and we instinctively turned. At the head of the stairs leading to the third floor stood the shadowy figure of Hani, his flowing kaftan a dark mass against the palely lighted wall beyond.

"Oh, rather!" Vance answered cheerfully. "We were just repairin' to the drawing-room to hold a little conversational *séance*. Do join us, Hani."

CHAPTER EIGHTEEN

A Light in the Museum
(*Saturday, July 14; 1.15 a.m.*)

Hani JOINED US in the drawing-room. He was very calm and dignified, and his inscrutable eyes rested impassively on Vance like those of an ancient Egyptian priest meditating before the shrine of Osiris.

"How do you happen to be up and about at this hour?" Vance asked casually. "Another attack of gastritis?"

"No, *effendi*." Hani spoke in slow, measured tones. "I rose when I heard you talking to Brush. I sleep with my door open always."

"Perhaps, then, you heard Sakhmet when she returned to the house to-night."

"Did Sakhmet return?" The Egyptian lifted his head slightly in mild interest.

"In a manner of speaking... But she's a most inefficient deity. She bungled everything again."

"Are you sure she did not intentionally bungle things?" Despite the droning quality of Hani's voice, there was a significant note in it.

Vance regarded him for a moment. Then:

"Did you hear footsteps on the stairs or along the second-floor corridor shortly after midnight?"

The man shook his head slowly.

"I heard nothing. But I was asleep for at least an hour before you arrived; and the soft tread of footsteps on the deep carpet would scarcely have been sufficient to rouse me."

"Doctor Bliss himself," Vance explained, "came downstairs and telephoned to me. You did not hear him either?"

"The first sound I perceived was when you gentlemen came into the front hall and talked to Brush. Your voices, or perhaps the door opening, awakened me. Later I could hear your muffled tones in Doctor Bliss's bedroom, which is just below mine; but I could not distinguish anything that was said."

"And of course you were not aware that any one turned off the light in the second-story hall round midnight."

"Had I not been asleep I would certainly have noticed it, as the light shines dimly up the stairs into my room. But when I awoke the light was on as usual." Hani frowned slightly. "Who would have turned the hall light off at that hour?"

"I wonder..." Vance did not take his eyes from the Egyptian. "Doctor Bliss has just told us that it was some one who had designs on his life."

"Ah!" The exclamation was like a sigh of relief. "But the attempt, I gather, was not successful."

"No. It was quite a fiasco. The technic, I might say, was both stupid and hazardous."

"It was not Sakhmet." Hani's pronouncement was almost sepulchral.

"Really, now!" Vance smiled slightly. "She is still reclinin', then, by the side of the great west wind of heaven.*... I'm jolly glad to be able to rule her out. And since no occult force was at work, perhaps you can suggest who would have had a motive to cut the doctor's throat."

"There are many who would not weep if he were to quit this life; but I know of none who would take it upon himself to precipitate that departure."

Vance lighted a *Régie* and sat down.

"Why, Hani, did you imagine you might be of service to us?"

"Like you, *effendi*," came the soft reply, "I expected that something distressing, and perhaps violent, would happen in this house to-night. And when I heard you enter and go to Doctor Bliss's room, it occurred to me that the looked-for event had come to pass. So I waited on the upper landing until you came out."

"Most considerate and thoughtful of you," Vance murmured, and took several puffs on his cigarette. After a moment he asked: "If Mr. Salveter had emerged from his room to-night after you had gone to bed, would you have known of the fact?"

The Egyptian hesitated, and his eyes contracted.

"I think I would. His room is directly opposite mine—"

"I'm familiar with the arrangement."

"It does not seem probable that Mr. Salveter could have unlocked his door and come out without my being cognizant of it."

"It's possible though, is it not?" Vance was insistent. "If you were asleep, and Mr. Salveter had good reason for not disturbing you, he might have emerged so cautiously that you would have slept on in complete ignorance of his act."

"It is barely possible," Hani admitted unwillingly. "But I am quite sure that he did not leave his room after retiring."

---

*   *Vance was referring jocularly to the declaration of Sakhmet in the Chapter of Opening the Mouth of the Osiris Ani in the Egyptian Book of the Dead:* ☐𝓍☐🜚☐☐🜚𓃭𓏏𓎡☐☐☐☐☐☐☐☐☐ *"I am the Goddess Sakhmet, and I take my seat upon the side of the great west (wind?) of the skies."*

"Your wish, I fear, is father to your assurance," Vance sighed. "However, we sha'n't belabor the point."

Hani was watching Vance with lowering concern.

"Did Doctor Bliss suggest that Mr. Salveter left his room to-night?"

"Oh, to the contr'ry," Vance assured him. "The doctor said quite emphatically that any attempt to connect Mr. Salveter with the stealthy steps outside of his door at midnight, would be a grave error."

"Doctor Bliss is wholly correct," the Egyptian declared.

"And yet, Hani, the doctor insisted that a would-be assassin was prowlin' about the house. Who else could it have been?"

"I cannot imagine." Hani appeared almost indifferent.

"You do not think that it could have been Mrs. Bliss?"

"Never!" The man's tone had become quickly animated. "Meryt-Amen would have had no reason to go into the hall. She has access to her husband's room through a communicating door—"

"So I observed a while ago,—she joined our *pour-parler* in the doctor's room. And I must say, Hani, that she was most anxious for us to find the person who had made the attempt on her husband's life."

"Anxious—and sad, *effendi*." A new note crept into Hani's voice. "She does not yet understand the things that have happened to-day. But when she does—"

"We won't speculate along those lines now," Vance cut in brusquely. He reached in his pocket and drew out the golden dagger. "Did you ever see that?" he asked, holding the weapon toward the Egyptian.

The man's eyes opened wide as he stared at the glittering, jewelled object. At first he appeared fascinated, but the next moment his face clouded, and the muscles of his jowls worked spasmodically. A smouldering anger had invaded him.

"Where did that Pharaonic dagger come from?" he asked, striving to control his emotion.

"It was brought from Egypt by Doctor Bliss," Vance told him.

Hani took the dagger and held it reverently under the table-lamp.

"It could only have come from the tomb of Ai. Here on the crystal knob is faintly engraved the king's cartouche. Behold: Kheper-kheperu-Rê Iry-Maët—"

"Yes, yes. The last Pharaoh of the Eighteenth Dynasty. The doctor found the dagger during his excavations in the Valley of the Tombs of the Kings." Vance was watching the other intently. "You are quite positive you have never seen it before?"

Hani drew himself up proudly.

"Had I seen it, I would have reported it to my Government. It would no longer be in the possession of an alien desecrator, but in the country where it belongs, cared for by loving hands at Cairo... Doctor Bliss did well to keep it hidden."

There was a bitter hatred in his words, but suddenly his manner changed.

"May I be permitted to ask when you first saw this royal dagger?"

"A few minutes ago," Vance answered. "It was projectin' from the headboard of the doctor's bed—just behind the place where his head had lain a second earlier."

Hani's gaze travelled past Vance to some distant point, and his eyes became shrewdly thoughtful.

"Was there no sheath to this dagger?" he asked.

"Oh, yes." There was a flicker in the corners of Vance's eyes. "Gold and cloisonné—though I haven't seen it. The fact is, Hani, we're deuced interested in the sheath. It's disappeared—lying *perdu* somewhere hereabouts. We're going to make a bit of a search for it ere long."

Hani nodded his head understandingly.

"And if you find it, are you sure you'll know more than you do now?"

"It may at least verify my suspicions."

"The sheath would be an easy object to hide securely," Hani reminded him.

"I really don't anticipate any difficulty in putting my hands on it." Vance rose and confronted the man. "Could you perhaps suggest where we might best start our search?"

"No, *effendi*," Hani returned, after a perceptible hesitation. "Not at this moment. I would need time to think about it."

"Very well. Suppose you go to your room and indulge in some lamaic concentration. You're anything but helpful."

Hani handed the dagger back, and turned toward the hall.

"And be so good," Vance requested, "as to knock on Mr. Salveter's door and tell him we would like to see him here at once."

Hani bowed, and disappeared.

"I don't like that bird," Heath grumbled, when the Egyptian was out of hearing. "He's too slippery. And he knows something he's not telling. I'd like to turn my boys loose on him with a piece of rubber hose—they'd make him come across... I wouldn't be surprised, Mr. Vance, if he threw the dagger himself. Did you notice the way he held it, laying out flat in the palm of his hand with the point toward the fingers?—just like those knife-throwers in vaudeville."

"Oh, he might have been thinkin' caressingly of Doctor Bliss's trachea," Vance conceded. "However, the dagger episode doesn't worry me half as much as something that *didn't* happen to-night."

"Well, it looks to me like plenty happened," retorted Heath.

Markham regarded Vance inquisitively.

"What's in your mind?" he asked.

"The picture presented to us to-night, d'ye see, wasn't finished. I could still detect some of the under-painting. And there was no *vernissage*. The canvas needed another form— the generating line wasn't complete..."

Just then we could hear footsteps on the stairs. Salveter, with a wrinkled Shantung dressing-gown wrapped about his pyjamas, blinked as he faced the lights in the drawing-room. He appeared only half awake, but when his pupils had become adjusted to the glare, he ran his eyes sharply over the four of us and then shot a glance at the bronze clock on the mantel.

"What now?" he asked. "What has happened?" He seemed both bewildered and anxious.

"Doctor Bliss phoned me that some one had tried to kill him," Vance explained. "So we hobbled over... Know anything about it?"

"Good God, no!" Salveter sat down heavily in a chair by the door. "Some one tried to kill the doctor? When?... How?" He fumbled in his dressing-gown pockets, and Vance, reading his movements correctly, held out his cigarette-case. Salveter lighted a *Régie* nervously, and drew several deep inhalations on it.

"Shortly after midnight," Vance answered. "But the attempt failed dismally." He tossed the dagger in Salveter's lap: "Familiar with that knick-knack?"

The other studied the weapon a few seconds without touching it. A growing astonishment crept into his expression, and he carefully picked up the dagger and inspected it.

"I never saw it in my life," he said in an awed tone. "It's a very valuable archæological specimen—a rare museum piece. Where, in Heaven's name, did you unearth it? It certainly doesn't belong to the Bliss collection."

"Ah, but it does," Vance assured him. "A private item, so to speak. Always kept secluded from pryin' vulgar eyes."

"I'm amazed. I'll bet the Egyptian Government doesn't know about it." Salveter looked up abruptly. "Has this dagger anything to do with the attempt on the doctor's life?"

"Everything apparently," Vance replied negligently. "We found it lodged in the headboard of the doctor's bed, evidently thrown with great force at the spot where his throat should have been."

Salveter contracted his brow and set his lips.

"See here, Mr. Vance," he declared at length; "we haven't any Malayan jugglers in this house... Unless," he added, as a startled afterthought, "Hani knows the art. Those Orientals are full of unexpected lore and practices."

"The performance to-night was not, according to all accounts, what one would unqualifiedly call artistic. It was, in fact, somewhat amateurish. I'm sure a Malay could have done much better with his kris. In the first place, the intruder's footsteps and the opening of the door were plainly heard by Doctor Bliss; and, in the second place, there was sufficient delay between the projection of the flash-light and the actual hurling of the dagger to give the doctor time to remove his head from the line of propulsion..."

At this moment Hani appeared at the door holding a small object in his hand. Walking forward he laid it on the centre-table.

"Here, *effendi*," he said in a low voice, "is the sheath of the royal dagger. I found it lying against the baseboard of the second-story hall, near the head of the stairs."

Vance scarcely glanced at it.

"Thanks awfully," he drawled. "I rather thought you'd find it. But of course it wasn't in the hall."

"I assure you—"

"Oh, quite." Vance looked straight into Hani's eyes, and presently a faint, gentle smile crept into his gaze. "Isn't it true, Hani," he asked pointedly, "that you found the sheath exactly where you and I believed it to be hidden?"

The Egyptian did not answer at once. Presently he said:

"I have told my story, *effendi*. You may draw your own conclusion."

Vance appeared satisfied and waved his hand toward the door.

"And now, Hani, go to bed. We sha'n't need you any more to-night. *Leiltak sa'îda.*"

"*Leiltak sa'îda wemubâraka.*" The man bowed and departed.

Vance picked up the sheath and, taking the dagger from Salveter, fitted the blade into its holder, looking at the gold embossing critically.

"Ægean influence," he murmured. "Pretty, but too fussy. These ornate floral devices of the Eighteenth Dynasty bear the same relation to early Egyptian art that the Byzantine gingerbread does to the simple Greek orders." He held the sheath closer to his monocle. "And, by the by, here's a decoration that may interest you, Mr. Salveter. The formal scrolls terminate in a jackal's head."

"Anûpu, eh? Hani's given name. That's curious." Salveter rose and looked at the design. "And another point might be considered, Mr. Vance," he went on, after a pause. "These lower-class Copts are, for all their superficial Christian veneer, highly superstitious. Their minds run along one traditional groove: they like to fit everything to a pre-conceived symbolism. There have been nine more or less coincidental deaths of late among those connected with the excavations in Egypt,* and the natives ridiculously imagine that the afrîts of their ancestors lay in ambush in the various tombs to mow down the western intruders, as a kind of punitive measure. They actually believe in such malefic forces… And here is Hani, at bottom a superstitious Egyptian, who resents the work of Doctor Bliss:—is it not possible he might consider the death of the doctor by a dagger once worn by a Pharaoh as a sort of mystical retribution in line with all these other irrational ghost stories? And Hani might even regard the jackal's head on that sheath as a sign that he— named after the jackal-headed god, Anûbis—had been divinely appointed the agent in this act of vengeance."

"A charmin' theory," was Vance's somewhat uninterested comment. "But a bit too specious, I fear. I'm comin' to the opinion that Hani is not nearly so stupid and superstitious as he

---

* *Salveter was here referring to the Earl of Carnarvon, Colonel the Honorable Aubrey Herbert, General Sir Lee Stack, George J. Gould, Woolf Joel, Sir Archibald Douglas Reid, Professor Lafleur, H. G. Evelyn-White, and Professor Georges-Aaron Bénédite. Since that time two more names have been added to the fatal list—those of the Honorable Richard Bethell, secretary to Howard Carter, and Lord Westbury.*

would have us think. He's a kind of modern Theogonius, who has found it the part of wisdom to simulate mental inferiority."*

Salveter slowly nodded agreement.

"I've felt that same quality in him at times... But who else—?"

"Ah! Who else?" Vance sighed. "I say, Mr. Salveter; what time did you go to bed to-night?"

"At ten-thirty," the man returned aggressively. "And I didn't wake up until Hani called me just now."

"You retired, then, immediately after you had fetched the memorandum-book from the study for Doctor Bliss."

"Oh, he told you about that, did he?... Yes, I handed him the book and went on up to my room."

"The book, I understand, was in his desk."

"That's right.—But why this cross-examination about a memorandum-book?"

"That dagger," Vance explained, "was also kept in one of the drawers of the doctor's desk."

Salveter leapt to his feet.

"I see!" His face was livid.

"Oh, but you don't," Vance mildly assured him. "And I'd appreciate it immensely if you'd try to be calm. Your vitality positively exhausts me.—Tell me, did you lock your bedroom door to-night?"

"I always lock it at night."

"And during the day?"

"I leave it open—to air the room."

"And you heard nothing to-night after retiring?"

"Nothing at all. I went to sleep quickly—the reaction, I suppose."

Vance rose.

"One other thing: where did the family have dinner to-night?"

---

* Theogonius was a friend of Simon Magus, who, because of his fear of the Emperor Caligula, pretended imbecility in order to hide his wisdom. Suetonius refers to him as Theogonius, but Scaliger, Casaubon and other historians give "Telegenius" as the correct spelling.

"In the breakfast-room. It could hardly be called dinner, though. No one was hungry. It was more like a light supper. So we ate down-stairs. Less bother."

"And what did the various members of the household do after dinner?"

"Hani went up-stairs at once, I believe. The doctor and Mrs. Bliss and I sat here in the drawing-room for an hour or so, when the doctor excused himself and went to his room. A little later Meryt-Amen went up-stairs, and I sat here until about half past ten trying to read."

"Thank you, Mr. Salveter. That will be all." Vance moved toward the hall. "Only, I wish you'd tell Mrs. Bliss and the doctor that we sha'n't disturb them any more to-night. We'll probably communicate with them to-morrow... Let's go, Markham. There's really nothing more we can do here."

"I could do a whole lot more," Heath objected with surly antagonism. "But this case is being handled like a pink tea. Somebody in this house threw that dagger, and if I had my way I'd steam the truth out of him."

Markham endeavored diplomatically to soothe the Sergeant's ruffled feelings, but without any marked success.

We were now standing just inside of the front door preparatory to departing, and Vance paused to light a cigarette. He was facing the great steel door leading into the museum, and I saw his frame suddenly go taut.

"Oh, just a moment, Mr. Salveter," he called; and the man, who was now nearly at the head of the first flight of stairs, turned and retraced his steps. "What are the lights doing on in the museum?"

I glanced toward the bottom of the steel door where Vance's gaze was resting, and for the first time saw a tiny illuminated line. Salveter, too, glanced at the floor, and frowned.

"I'm sure I don't know," he said in a puzzled voice. "The last person in the museum is supposed to turn off the switch. But no one to my knowledge has been in there to-night... I'll see." He stepped toward the door, but Vance moved in front of him.

"Don't trouble yourself," he said peremptorily. "I'll attend to it… Good-night."

Salveter took the dismissal uneasily, but without another word he went up-stairs.

When he had disappeared round the banisters on the second floor, Vance gently turned the knob, and pushed the museum door open. Below us, on the opposite side of the room, seated at the desk-table near the obelisk, and surrounded by filing-boxes, photographs, and cardboard folders, was Scarlett. His coat and waistcoat were hanging over the back of his chair; a green celluloid shade covered his eyes; and a pen was in his hand, poised above a large note-book.

He looked up as the door opened.

"Oh, hallo!" he called cheerily. "Thought you were through with the Bliss ménage for to-day."

"It's to-morrow now," returned Vance, going down the stairs and crossing the museum.

"What!" Scarlett reached behind him and took out his watch. "Great Scott! So it is. Had no idea of the hour. Been working here since eight o'clock—"

"Amazin'." Vance glanced over a few of the upturned photographs. "Very interestin'… Who let you in, by the by?"

"Brush, of course." Scarlett seemed rather astonished at the question. "Said the family were having dinner in the breakfast-room. I told him not to disturb 'em—that I had a bit of work to finish…"

"He didn't mention your arrival to us." Vance was apparently engrossed in a photograph of four amuletic bracelets.

"But why should he, Vance?" Scarlett had risen and was getting into his coat. "It's a commonplace thing for me to come here and work in the evenings. I'm drifting in and out of the house constantly. When I work at night I always shut off the light on going and see that the front door is fastened. Nothing unusual about my coming here after dinner."

"That probably accounts for Brush's not telling us, don't y'know." Vance tossed the photographs back on the table. "But something out of the ordin'ry did happen here to-night." He laid the sheathed dagger before Scarlett. "What do you know about that bizarre parazonium?"

"Oh, much." The other grinned, and shot Vance an interrogatory look. "How did you happen on it? It's one of the doctor's dark secrets."

"Really?" Vance lifted his eyebrows in simulated surprise. "Then you're familiar with it?"

"Rather. I saw the old scalawag slip it into his khaki shirt when he found it. I kept mum—none of my business. Later, when we were here in New York, he told me he'd smuggled it out of Egypt, and confided to me that he was keeping it sequestered in his study. He was in constant fear that Hani would unearth it, and swore me to secrecy. I agreed. What's one dagger, more or less? The Cairo Museum has the cream of all the excavated items anyway."

"He kept it ensconced under some papers in one of his desk drawers."

"Yes, I know. Safe hiding-place. Hani rarely goes in the study... But I'm curious—"

"We're all curious. Distressin' state, what?" Vance gave him no time to speculate. "Who else knew of the dagger's existence?"

"No one, as far as I know. The doctor certainly didn't disclose the fact to Hani; and I doubt seriously if he informed Mrs. Bliss. She has peculiar loyalties in regard to her native country, and the doctor respects them. No telling how she'd react to the theft of such a valuable treasure."

"What about Salveter?"

"I'd say no." Scarlett made an unpleasant grimace. "He'd be sure to confide in Meryt-Amen. Impulsive young cub."

"Well, some one knew of its whereabouts," Vance remarked. "Doctor Bliss phoned me shortly after midnight that he had escaped assassination by the proverbial hair's-breadth; so we sped hither and found the point of that poniard infixed in the head of his bed."

"By Jove! You don't say!" Scarlett seemed shocked and perplexed. "Some one must have discovered the dagger…and yet—" He stopped suddenly and shot Vance a quick look. "How do you account for it?"

"I'm not accountin' for it. Most mysterious… Hani, by the by, found the sheath in the hall near the doctor's door."

"That's odd…" Scarlett paused as if considering. Then he began arranging his papers and photographs in neat piles and stacking his filing-boxes under the table. "Couldn't you get any suggestions out of the rest of the household?" he asked.

"Any number of suggestions. All of 'em conflictin', and most of 'em silly. So we're toddlin' along home. Happened to see the light under the door and was overcome with curiosity… Quitting now?"

"Yes." Scarlett took up his hat. "I'd have knocked off long ago but didn't realize how late it was."

We all left the house together. A heavy silence had fallen over us, and it was not until Scarlett paused in front of his quarters that any one of us spoke. Then Vance said:

"Good-night. Don't let the dagger disturb your slumbers."

Scarlett waved an abstracted adieu.

"Thanks, old man," he rejoined. "I'll try to follow your advice."

Vance had taken several steps when he turned suddenly.

"And I say, Scarlett; if I were you I'd keep away from the Bliss house for the time being."

CHAPTER NINETEEN

A Broken Appointment
(Saturday, July 14; 2 a.m.–10 p.m.)

HEATH LEFT US at Nineteenth Street and Fourth Avenue; and Vance, Markham and I took a taxicab back to Vance's apartment. It was nearly two o'clock, but Markham showed no indication of going home. He followed Vance up-stairs to the library, and throwing open the French windows gazed out into the heavy, mist-laden night. The events of the day had not gone to his liking; and yet I realized that his quandary was so deep that he felt disinclined to make any decisive move until the conflicting factors of the situation became more clarified.

The case at the outset had appeared simple, and the number of possible suspects was certainly limited. But, despite these two facts, there was a subtle and mysterious intangibility about the affair that rendered a drastic step impossible. The elements were too fluid, the cross-currents of motives too contradictory. Vance had been the first to sense the elusory complications, the first to indicate the invisible paradoxes; and so surely had he put his finger upon the vital points of the plot—so accurately had he foretold certain phases of the plot's development—that Markham had, both figuratively and literally, stepped into the background and permitted him to deal with the case in his own way.

Withal, Markham was dissatisfied and impatient. Nothing definitely leading to the actual culprit had, so far as could be seen, been brought to light by Vance's unprofessional and almost casual process of investigation.

"We're not making headway, Vance," Markham complained with gloomy concern, turning from the window. "I've stood aside all day and permitted you to deal with these people as you saw fit, because I felt your knowledge of them and your familiarity with things Egyptological gave you an advantage over impersonal official cross-questioning. And I also felt that you had a plausible theory about the whole matter, which you were striving to verify. But Kyle's murder is as far from a solution as it was when we first entered the museum."

"You're an incorrigible pessimist, Markham," Vance returned, getting into a printed foulard dressing-gown. "It has been just fifteen hours since we found Sakhmet athwart Kyle's skull; and you must admit, painful as it may be to a District Attorney, that the average murder investigation has scarcely begun in so brief a time…"

"In the average murder case, however," Markham retorted acidly, "we'd at least have found a lead or two and outlined a workable routine. If Heath had been handling the matter he'd have made an arrest by now—the field of possibilities is not an extensive one."

"I dare say he would. He'd no doubt have had every one in jail, including Brush and Dingle and the Curators of the Metropolitan Museum. Typical tactics: butcher innocent persons to make a journalistic holiday. I'm not entranced with that technic, though. I'm far too humane—I've retained too many of my early illusions. Sentimentality, alas! will probably be my downfall."

Markham snorted, and seated himself at the end of the table. For several moments he beat the devil's tattoo on a large, vellum-bound copy of "Malleus Maleficarum."

"You told me quite emphatically," he said, "that when this second episode happened—the attempt on Bliss's life—you'd understand all the phases of the plot and perhaps be able to adduce some tangible evidence against Kyle's murderer. It appears to me, however, that to-night's affair has simply plunged us more deeply into uncertainty."

Vance shook his head seriously in disagreement.

"The throwing of that dagger and the hiding and finding of the sheath have illuminated the one moot point in the plot."

Markham looked up sharply.

"You think you know now what the plot is?"

Vance carefully fitted a *Régie* into a long jet holder and gazed at a small Picasso still-life beside the mantel.

"Yes, Markham," he returned slowly; "I think I know what the plot is. And if the thing that I expect to happen to-night occurs, I can, I believe, convince you that I am right in my diagnosis. Unfortunately the throwing of the dagger was only part of the pre-arranged episode. As I said to you a while ago, the tableau was not completed. Something intervened. And the final touch—the rounding-out of the episode—is yet to come."

He spoke with impressive solemnity, and Markham, I could see, was strongly influenced by his manner.

"Have you any definite notion," he inquired, "what that final touch will prove to be?"

"Oh, quite. But just what shape it will take I can't say. The plotter himself probably doesn't know, for he must wait for a propitious opportunity. But it will centre about one specific object, or, rather, clew—a planted clew, Markham. That clew has been carefully prepared, and the placing of it is the only indefinite factor left... Yes, I am waiting for a specific item to appear; and when it does, I can convince you of the whole devilish truth."

"When do you figure this final clew will turn up?" Markham asked uneasily.

"At almost any moment." Vance spoke in low, level and quiet tones. "Something prevented its taking shape to-night, for it is an intimate corollary of the dagger-throwing. And by refusing to take that episode too seriously, and by letting Hani find the sheath, I made the immediate planting of the final clew necess'ry. Once again we refused to fall into the murderer's trap—though, as I say, the trap was not fully baited."

"I'm glad to have some kind of explanation for your casual attitude to-night." Despite the note of sarcasm in Markham's voice, it was obvious that at bottom he was not indulging in strictures upon Vance's conduct. He was at sea and inclined, therefore, to be irritable. "You apparently had no interest in determining who hurled the dagger at Bliss's pillow."

"But, Markham old dear, I knew who hurled the bejewelled bodkin." Vance made a slight gesture of impatience. "My only concern was with what the reporters call the events leading up to the crime."

Markham realized it was of no use to ask, at this time, who had thrown the dagger; so he pursued his comments on Vance's recent activities at the Bliss house.

"You might have got some helpful suggestions from Scarlett—he evidently was in the museum during the entire time..."

"Even so, Markham," Vance countered, "don't forget there is a thick double wall between the museum and the Bliss domicile, and that those steel doors are practically sound-proof. Bombs might have been exploded in the doctor's room without any one in the museum hearing them."

"Perhaps you're right." Markham rose and stood contemplating Vance appraisingly. "I'm putting a lot of trust in you—you confounded æsthete. And I'm going against all my principles and stultifying the whole official procedure of my office because I believe in you. But God help you if you fail me... What's the programme for to-morrow?"

Vance shot him a grateful, affectionate look. Then, at once, a cynical smile overspread his face.

"I'm the unofficial straw, so to speak, at which the drowning District Attorney clutches—eh, what? Not an overwhelmin' compliment."

It was always the case with these two old friends that when one uttered a generous remark the other immediately scotched it, lest there be some outward show of sentiment.

"The programme for to-morrow?" Vance took up Markham's question. "Really, y'know, I hadn't given it any Cartesian consideration... There's an exhibition of Gauguins at Wildenstein's. I might stagger in and bask in the color harmonics of the great Pont-Avenois. Then there's a performance of the Beethoven *Septet* at Carnegie Hall; and a preview of Egyptian wall paintings from the tombs of Nakhte and Menena and Rekh-mi-Rê—"

"And there's an orchid show at the Grand Central Palace," Markham suggested with vicious irony. "But see here, Vance: if we let this thing run on another day without taking some kind of action, there may be danger ahead for some one else, just as there was danger for Bliss to-night. If the murderer of Kyle is as ruthless as you say and his job hasn't been completed—"

"No, I don't think so." Vance's face clouded again. "The plot doesn't include another act of violence. I believe it has now entered upon a quiescent and subtle—and more deadly— stage." He smoked a moment speculatively. "And yet...there may be a remote chance. Things haven't gone according to the murderer's calculations. We've blocked his two most ambitious moves. But he has one more combination left, and I'm countin' on his trying it..."

His voice faltered, and rising he walked slowly to the French window and back.

"Anyway, I'll take care of the situation in the morning," he said. "I'll guard against any dangerous possibility. And at the same time I'll hasten the planting of that last clew."

"How long is this rigmarole going to take?" Markham was troubled and nervous. "I can't go on indefinitely waiting for apocalyptic events to happen."

"Give me twenty-four hours. Then, if we haven't received further guidance from the gentleman who is pullin' the strings, you may turn Heath loose on the family."

It was less than twenty-four hours when the culminating event occurred. The fourteenth of July will always remain in my memory as one of the most terrible and exciting days of my life; and as I set down this record of the case, years later, I can hardly refrain from a shudder. I do not dare think of what might have happened—of what soul-stirring injustice might have been perpetrated in good faith—had not Vance seen the inner machinations of the diabolical plot underlying Kyle's murder, and persisted in his refusal to permit Markham and Heath taking the obvious course of arresting Bliss.

Vance told me months later that never in his career had he been confronted by so delicate a task as that of placating Markham and convincing him that an impassive delay was the only possible means of reaching the truth. Almost from the moment Vance entered the museum in answer to Scarlett's summons, he realized the tremendous difficulties ahead; for everything had been planned in order to force Markham and the police into making the very move against which he had so consistently fought.

Though Markham did not take his departure from Vance's apartment on the night of the dagger episode until half past two, Vance rose the next morning before eight o'clock. Another sweltering day was promised, and he had his coffee in the roof-garden. He sent Currie to fetch all the morning newspapers, and spent a half hour or so reading the accounts of Kyle's murder.

Heath had been highly discreet about giving out the facts, and only the barest skeleton of the story was available to the press. But the prominence of Kyle and the distinguished reputation of Doctor Bliss resulted in the murder creating a tremendous furore. It was emblazoned across the front page of every metropolitan journal, and there were long reviews of Bliss's Egyptological work and the financial interest taken in it by the dead philanthropist. The general theory seemed to be—and I recognized the Sergeant's shrewd hand in it—that some one from the street had entered the museum, and, as an act of vengeance or enmity, had killed Kyle with the first available weapon.

Heath had told the reporters of the finding of the scarab beside the body, but had given no further information about it. Because of this small object, which was the one evidential detail that had been vouchsafed, the papers, always on the lookout for identifying titles, named the tragedy the Scarab murder case; and that appellation has clung to it to the present day. Even those persons who have forgotten the name of Benjamin H. Kyle still remember the sensation caused by his murder, as a result of that ancient piece of lapis-lazuli carved with the name of an Egyptian Pharaoh of the year 1650 B.C.

Vance read the accounts with a cynical smile.

"Poor Markham!" he murmured. "Unless something definite happens very soon, the anti-administration critics will descend on him like a host of trolls. I see that Heath has announced to the world that the District Attorney's office has taken full charge of the case..."

He smoked meditatively for a time. Then he telephoned to Salveter and asked him to come at once to his apartment.

"I'm hopin' to remove every possibility of disaster," he explained to me as he hung up the receiver; "though I'm quite certain another attempt to hoodwink us will be made before any desperate measures are taken."

For the next fifteen minutes he stretched out lazily and closed his eyes. I thought he had fallen asleep, but when Currie softly opened the door to announce Salveter, Vance bade him show the visitor up before the old man could speak.

Salveter entered a minute later looking anxious and puzzled.

"Sit down, Mr. Salveter." Vance waved him indolently to a chair. "I've been thinkin' about Queen Hetep-hir-es and the Boston Museum. Have you any business that might reasonably take you to Boston to-night?"

Salveter appeared even more puzzled.

"I always have work that I can do there," he replied, frowning. "Especially in view of the excavations of the Harvard-Boston Expedition at the Gîzeh pyramids. It was in connection with these excavations that I had to go to the Metropolitan yesterday morning for Doctor Bliss... Does that answer your question satisfactorily?"

"Quite... And these reproductions of the tomb furniture of Hetep-hir-es: couldn't you arrange for them more easily if you saw Doctor Reisner personally?"

"Certainly. The fact is, I'll have to go north anyway in order to close up the business. I was merely on the trail of preliminary information yesterday."

"Would the fact that to-morrow is Sunday handicap you in any way?"

"To the contrary. I could probably see Doctor Reisner away from his office, and go into the matter at leisure with him."

"That being the case, suppose you hop a train to-night after dinner. Come back, let us say, to-morrow night. Any objection?"

Salveter's puzzlement gave way to astonishment.

"Why—no," he stammered. "No particular objection. But—"

"Would Doctor Bliss think it strange if you jumped out on such sudden notice?"

"I couldn't say. Probably not. The museum isn't a particularly pleasant place just now..."

"Well, I want you to go, Mr. Salveter." Vance abandoned his lounging demeanor and sat up. "And I want you to go without question or argument... There's no possibility of Doctor Bliss's forbidding you to go, is there?"

"Oh, nothing like that," Salveter assured him. "He may think it's queer, my running off at just this time; but he never meddles in the way I choose to do my work."

Vance rose.

"That's all. There's a train to Boston from the Grand Central at half past nine to-night. See that you take it... And," he added, "you might phone me from the station, by way of verification. I'll be here between nine and nine-thirty... You may return to New York any time you desire after to-morrow noon."

Salveter gave Vance an abashed grin.

"I suppose those are orders."

"Serious and important orders, Mr. Salveter," Vance returned with quiet impressiveness. "And you needn't worry about Mrs. Bliss. Hani, I'm sure, will take good care of her."

Salveter started to make a reply, changed his mind, and, turning abruptly, strode rapidly away.

Vance yawned and rose languorously.

"And now I think I'll take two more hours' sleep."

After lunch at Marguéry's, Vance went to the Gauguin exhibition, and later walked to Carnegie Hall to hear the Beethoven *Septet*. It was too late when the concert was over to see the Egyptian wall paintings at the Metropolitan Museum of Art. Instead, he called for Markham in his car, and the three of us drove to the Claremont for dinner.

Vance explained briefly what steps he had taken in regard to Salveter. Markham made scant comment. He looked tired and discouraged, but there was a distracted tensity about his manner that made me realize how greatly he was counting on Vance's prediction that something tangible would soon happen in connection with the Kyle case.

After dinner we returned to Vance's roof-garden. The enervating mid-summer heat still held, and there was scarcely a breath of air stirring.

"I told Heath I'd phone him—" Markham began, sinking into a large peacock wicker chair.

"I was about to suggest getting in touch with the Sergeant," Vance chimed in. "I'd rather like to have him on hand, don't y'know. He's so comfortin'."

He rang for Currie and ordered the telephone. Then he called Heath and asked him to join us.

"I have a psychic feelin'," he said to Markham, with an air of forced levity, "that we are going to be summoned anon to witness the irrefutable proof of some one's guilt. And if that proof is what I think it is..."

Markham suddenly leaned forward in his chair.

"It has just come to me what you've been hinting about so mysteriously!" he exclaimed. "It has to do with that hieroglyphic letter you found in the study."

Vance hesitated but momentarily.

"Yes, Markham," he nodded. "That torn letter hasn't been explained yet. And I have a theory about it that I can't shake off—it fits too perfectly with the whole fiendish scheme."

"But you have the letter," Markham argued, in an effort to draw Vance out.

"Oh, yes. And I'm prizin' it."

"You believe it's the letter Salveter said he wrote?"

"Undoubtedly."

"And you believe he is ignorant of its having been torn up and put in the doctor's waste-basket?"

"Oh, quite. He's still wonderin' what became of it—and worryin', too."

Markham studied Vance with baffled curiosity. "You spoke of some purpose to which the letter might have been put before it was thrown away."

"That's what I'm waiting to verify. The fact is, Markham, I expected that the letter would enter into the mystery of the dagger throwing last night. And I'll admit I was frightfully downcast when we'd got the whole family snugly back to bed without having run upon a single hieroglyph." He reached for a cigarette. "There was a reason for it, and I think I know the explanation. That's why I'm pinnin' my childlike faith on what may happen at any moment now..."

The telephone rang, and Vance himself answered it at once. It was Salveter calling from the Grand Central Station; and after a brief verbal interchange, Vance replaced the instrument on the table with an air of satisfaction.

"The doctor," he said, "was evidently quite willin' to endure to-night and to-morrow without his assistant curator. So that bit of strategy was achieved without difficulty..."

Half an hour later Heath was ushered into the roof-garden. He was glum and depressed, and his greeting was little more than a guttural rumble.

"Lift up your heart, Sergeant," Vance exhorted him cheerfully. "This is Bastille Day.* It may have a symbolic meaning. It's not beyond the realm of possibility that you will be able to incarcerate the murderer of Kyle before midnight."

"Yeah?" Heath was utterly sceptical. "Is he coming here to give himself up, bringing all the necessary proof with him? A nice, accommodating fella."

"Not exactly, Sergeant. But I'm expecting him to send for us; and I think he may be so generous as to point out the principal clew himself."

"Cuckoo, is he? Well, Mr. Vance, if he does that, no jury'll convict him. He'll get a bill of insanity with free lodging and medical care for the rest of his life." He looked at his watch. "It's ten o'clock. What time does the tip-off come?"

"Ten?" Vance verified the hour. "My word! It's later than I thought...." A look of anxiety passed over his set features. "I wonder if I could have miscalculated this whole affair."

He put out his cigarette and began pacing back and forth. Presently he stopped before Markham, who was watching him uneasily.

---

*   *Vance of course was referring to the French* Fête Nationale *which falls on July 14th.*

"When I sent Salveter away," he began slowly, "I was confident that the expected event would happen forthwith. But I'm afraid something has gone wrong. Therefore I think I had better outline the case to you now."

He paused and frowned.

"However," he added, "it would be advisable to have Scarlett present. I'm sure he could fill in a few of the gaps."

Markham looked surprised.

"What does Scarlett know about it?"

"Oh, much," was Vance's brief reply. Then he turned to the telephone and hesitated. "He hasn't a private phone, and I don't know the number of the house exchange..."

"That's easy." Heath picked up the receiver and asked for a certain night official of the company. After a few words of explanation, he clicked the hook and called a number. There was considerable delay, but at length some one answered at the other end.

From the Sergeant's questions it was evident Scarlett was not at home.

"That was his landlady," Heath explained disgustedly, when he had replaced the receiver. "Scarlett went out at eight o'clock—said he was going to the museum for a while and would be back at nine. Had an appointment at nine with a guy at his apartment, and the guy's still waiting for him..."

"We can reach him at the museum, then." Vance rang up the Bliss number and asked Brush to call Scarlett to the phone. After several minutes he pushed the instrument from him.

"Scarlett isn't at the museum either," he said. "He came, so Brush says, at about eight, and must have departed unobserved. He's probably on his way back to his quarters. We'll wait a while and phone him there again."

"Is it necessary to have Scarlett here?" Markham asked impatiently.

"Not precisely necess'ry," Vance returned evasively; "but most desirable. You remember he admitted quite frankly he could tell me a great deal about the murderer—"

He broke off abruptly, and with tense deliberation selected and lighted another cigarette. His lids drooped, and he stared fixedly at the floor.

"Sergeant," he said in a repressed tone, "I believe you said Mr. Scarlett had an appointment with some one at nine and had informed his landlady he would return at that hour."

"That's what the dame told me over the phone."

"Please see if he has reached home yet."

Without a word Heath again lifted the receiver and called Scarlett's number. A minute later he turned to Vance.

"He hasn't shown up."

"Deuced queer," Vance muttered. "I don't at all like this, Markham..."

His mind drifted off in speculation, and it seemed to me that his face paled slightly.

"I'm becoming frightened," he went on in a hushed voice. "We should have heard about that letter by now... I'm afraid there's trouble ahead."

He gave Markham a look of grave and urgent concern.

"We can't afford to delay any longer. It may even be too late as it is. We've got to act at once." He moved toward the door. "Come on, Markham. And you, Sergeant. We're overdue at the museum. If we hurry we may be in time."

Both Markham and Heath had risen as Vance spoke. There was a strange insistence in his tone, and a foreboding of terrible things in his eyes. He disappeared swiftly into the house; and the rest of us, urged by the suppressed excitement of his manner, followed in silence. His car was outside, and a few moments later we were swinging dangerously round the corner of Thirty-eighth Street and Park Avenue, headed for the Bliss Museum.

CHAPTER TWENTY

The Granite Sarcophagus
(Saturday, July 14; 10.10 p.m.)

WE ARRIVED AT the museum in less than ten minutes. Vance ran up the stone steps, Markham and Heath and I at his heels. Not only was there a light burning in the vestibule, but through the frosted glass panels of the front door we could see a bright light in the hall. Vance pressed the bell vigorously, but it was some time before Brush answered our summons.

"Napping?" Vance asked. He was in a tense, sensitive mood.

"No, sir." Brush shrank from him. "I was in the kitchen—"

"Tell Doctor Bliss we're here, and want to see him at once."

"Yes, sir." The butler went down the hall and knocked on the study door. There was no answer, and he knocked again. After a moment he turned the knob and looked in the room. Then he came back to us.

"The doctor is not in his study. Perhaps he has gone to his bedroom... I'll see."

He moved toward the stairs and was about to ascend when a calm, even voice halted him.

"Bliss *effendi* is not up-stairs." Hani came slowly down to the front hall. "It is possible he is in the museum."

"Well, well!" Vance regarded the man reflectively. "Amazin' how you always turn up... So you think he may be potterin' among his treasures—eh, what?" He pushed open the great steel door of the museum. "If the doctor is in here, he's whiling away his time in the dark." Stepping to the stair-landing inside the museum door, he switched on the lights and looked about the great room. "You're apparently in error, Hani, regarding the doctor's whereabouts. To all appearances the museum is empty."

The Egyptian was unruffled.

"Perhaps Doctor Bliss has gone out for a breath of air."

There was a troubled frown on Vance's face. "That's possible," he murmured. "However, I wish you'd make sure he is not up-stairs."

"I would have seen him had he come up-stairs after dinner," the Egyptian replied softly. "But I will follow your instructions nevertheless." And he went to search for Bliss.

Vance stepped up to Brush and asked in a low voice:

"At what time did Mr. Scarlett leave here to-night?"

"I don't know, sir." The man was mystified by Vance's manner. "I really don't know. He came at about eight—I let him in. He may have gone out with Doctor Bliss. They often take a walk together at night."

"Did Mr. Scarlett go into the museum when he arrived at eight?"

"No, sir. He asked for Doctor Bliss..."

"Ah! And did he see the doctor?"

"Yes, sir... That is,"—Brush corrected himself—"I suppose he did. I told him Doctor Bliss was in the study, and he at once went down the hall. I returned to the kitchen."

"Did you notice anything unusual in Mr. Scarlett's manner?"

The butler thought a moment.

"Well, sir, since you mention it, I might say that Mr. Scarlett was rather stiff and distant, like there was something on his mind—if you know what I mean."

"And the last you saw of him was when he was approaching the study door?"

"Yes, sir."

Vance nodded a dismissal.

"Remain in the drawing-room for the time being," he said.

As Brush disappeared through the folding door Hani came slowly down the stairs.

"It is as I said," he responded indifferently. "Doctor Bliss is not up-stairs."

Vance scrutinized him sternly.

"Do you know that Mr. Scarlett called here to-night?"

"Yes, I know." A curious light came into the man's eyes. "I was in the drawing-room when Brush admitted him."

"He came to see Doctor Bliss," said Vance.

"Yes. I heard him ask Brush—"

"Did Mr. Scarlett see the doctor?"

The Egyptian did not answer at once. He met Vance's gaze steadily as if trying to read the other's thoughts. At length, reaching a decision, he said:

"They were together—to my knowledge—for at least half an hour. When Mr. Scarlett entered the study he left the door open by the merest crack, and I was able to hear them talking together. But I could not distinguish anything that was said. Their voices were subdued."

"How long did you listen?"

"For half an hour. Then I went up-stairs."

"You have not seen either Doctor Bliss or Mr. Scarlett since?"

"No, *effendi*."

"Where was Mr. Salveter during the conference in the study?" Vance was striving hard to control his anxiety.

"Was he here in the house?" Hani asked evasively. "He told me at dinner that he was going to Boston."

"Yes, yes—on the nine-thirty train. He needn't have left the house until nine.—Where was he between eight and nine?"

Hani shrugged his shoulders.

"I did not see him. He went out before Mr. Scarlett arrived. He was certainly not here after eight—"

"You're lying." Vance's tone was icy.

"*Wahyât en-nabi*—"

"Don't try to impress me—I'm not in the humor."

Vance's eyes were like steel. "What do you think happened here to-night?"

"I think perhaps Sakhmet returned."

A pallor seemed to overspread Vance's face: it may, however, have been only the reflection of the hall light.

"Go to your room and wait there," he said curtly.

Hani bowed.

"You do not need my help now, *effendi*. You understand many things." And the Egyptian walked away with much dignity.

Vance stood tensely until he had disappeared. Then, with a motion to us, he hurried down the hall to the study. Throwing open the door he switched on the lights.

There was anxiety and haste in all his movements, and the electric atmosphere of his demeanor was transmitted to the rest of us. We realized that something tragic and terrible was leading him on.

He went to the two windows and leaned out. By the pale reflected light he could see the asphalt tiles on the ground below. He looked under the desk, and measured with his eyes the four-inch clearance beneath the divan. Then he went to the door leading into the museum.

"I hardly thought we'd find anything in the study; but there was a chance..."

He was now swinging down the spiral stairs.

"It will be here in the museum," he called to us. "Come along, Sergeant. There's work to do. A fiend has been loose to-night…"

He walked past the state chair and the shelves of *shawabtis*, and stood beside the long glass table case, his hands deep in his coat pockets, his eyes moving rapidly about the room. Markham and Heath and I waited at the foot of the stairs.

"What's this all about?" Markham asked huskily. "What has taken place? And what, incidentally, are you looking for?"

"I don't know what has taken place." Something in Vance's tone sent a chill through me. "And I'm looking for something damnable. If it isn't here…"

He did not finish the sentence. Going swiftly to the great replica of Kha-ef-Rê he walked round it. Then he went to the statue of Ramses II and inspected its base. After that he moved to Teti-shiret and tapped the pedestal with his knuckles.

"They're all solid," he muttered. "We must try the mummy cases." He recrossed the museum. "Start at that end, Sergeant. The covers should come off easily. If you have any difficulty, tear them off." He himself went to the anthropoid case beside Kha-ef-Rê and, inserting his hand beneath the upstanding lid, lifted it off and laid it on the floor.

Heath, apparently animated by an urgent desire for physical action, had already begun his search at the other end of the line. He was by no means gentle about it. He tore the lids off viciously, throwing them to the floor with unnecessary clatter.

Vance, absorbed in his own task, paid scant attention except to glance up as each lid was separated from the case. Markham, however, had begun to grow uneasy. He watched the Sergeant disapprovingly for several minutes, his face clouding over. Then he stepped forward.

"I can't let this go on, Vance," he remarked. "These are valuable treasures, and we have no right—"

Vance stood up and looked straight at Markham.

"And if there is a dead man in one of them?" he asked with a cold precision that caused Markham to stiffen.

"A dead man?"

"Placed here to-night—between eight and nine."

Vance's words had an ominous and impressive quality, and Markham said no more. He stood by, his features strained and set, watching the feverish inspection of the remaining mummy cases.

But no grisly discovery was made. Heath removed the lid of the last case in obvious disappointment.

"I guess something's gone wrong with your ideas, Mr. Vance," he commented without animus: indeed, there was a kindly note in his voice.

Vance, distraught and with a far-away look in his eyes, now stood by the glass case. His distress was so apparent that Markham went to him and touched him on the arm.

"Perhaps if we could re-calculate this affair along other lines—" he began; but Vance interrupted.

"No; it can't be re-calculated. It's too logical. There's been a tragedy here to-night—and we were too late to intercept it."

"We should have taken precautions." Markham's tone was bitter.

"Precautions! Every possible precaution was taken. A new element was introduced into the situation to-night—an element that couldn't possibly have been foreseen. To-night's tragedy was not part of the plot..." Vance turned and walked away. "I must think this thing out. I must trace the murderer's reasoning..." He made an entire circuit of the museum without taking his eyes from the floor.

Heath was puffing moodily on his cigar. He had not moved from in front of the mummy cases, and was pretending to be interested in their crudely colored hieroglyphs. Ever since the "Canary" murder case, when Tony Skeel had failed to keep his appointment in the District Attorney's office, he had, for all his protests, believed in Vance's prognostications; and now he was deeply troubled at the other's failure. I was watching him, a bit dazed myself, when I saw a frown of puzzled curiosity wrinkle his forehead. Taking his cigar from his mouth he bent over one of the fallen mummy cases and lifted out a slender metal object.

"That's a hell of a place to keep an automobile jack," he observed. (His interest in the jack was obviously the result of an unconscious attempt to distract his thoughts from the tense situation.)

He threw the jack back into the case and sat down on the base of Kha-ef-Rê's statue. Neither Vance nor Markham had apparently paid the slightest attention to his irrelevant discovery.

Vance continued pacing round the museum. For the first time since our arrival at the house he took out a cigarette and lighted it.

"Every line of reasoning leads here, Markham." He spoke in a low, hopeless tone. "There was no necessity for the evidence to have been taken away. In the first place, it would have been too hazardous; and, in the second place, we were not supposed to have suspected anything for a day or two..."

His voice faltered and his body went suddenly taut. He wheeled toward Heath.

"An automobile jack!" A dynamic change had come over him. "Oh, my aunt! I wonder... I wonder..."

He hurried toward the black sarcophagus beneath the front windows, and scrutinized it anxiously. "Too high," he murmured. "Three feet from the floor! It couldn't have been done... But it had to be done—somehow..." He looked about him. "That taboret!" He pointed to a small solid oak stand, about twenty inches high, against the wall near the Asiatic wooden statue. "It was not there last night; it was beside the desk-table by the obelisk—Scarlett was using it." As he spoke he went to the taboret and picked it up. "And the top is scratched—there's an indentation..." He placed the stand against the head of the sarcophagus. "Quick, Sergeant! Bring me that jack."

Heath obeyed with swiftness; and Vance placed the jack on the taboret, fitting its base over the scars in the wood.

The lifting-head came within an inch of the under-side of the sarcophagus's lid where it extended a few inches over the end elevation between the two projecting lion-legged supports at the corners.

We had gathered about Vance in tense silence, not knowing what to expect but feeling that we were on the threshold of some appalling revelation.

Vance inserted the elevating lever, which Heath handed him, into the socket, and moved it carefully up and down. The jack worked perfectly. At each downward thrust of the lever there was a metallic click as the detent slipped into the groove of the rack. Inch by inch the end of the ponderous granite lid—which must have weighed over half a ton*—rose.

Heath suddenly stepped back in alarm.

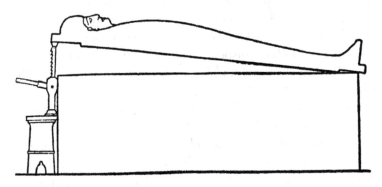

"Ain't you afraid, Mr. Vance, that the lid'll slide off the other end of the coffin?"

"No, Sergeant," Vance assured him. "The friction alone of so heavy a mass would hold it at a much greater angle than this jack could tilt it."

---

*   *This was my guess during Vance's operation. Later I calculated the weight of the lid. It was ten feet long, four feet wide, and was surmounted by a large carved figure. A conservative estimate would give us ten cubic feet for the lid; and as the density of granite is approximately 2.70 grams per cubic centimeter, or 170 pounds per cubic foot, the lid would have weighed at least 1,700 pounds.*

The head of the cover was now eight inches in the clear, and Vance was using both hands on the lever. He had to work with great care lest the jack slip from the smooth under-surface of the granite. Nine inches...ten inches...eleven...twelve... The rack had almost reached its limit of elevation. With one final thrust downward, Vance released the lever and tested the solidity of the extended jack.

"It's safe, I think..."

Heath had already taken out his pocket-light and flashed it into the dark recesses of the sarcophagus.

"Mother o' God!" he gasped.

I was standing just behind him, leaning over his broad shoulders; and simultaneously with the flare of his light I saw the horrifying thing that had made him call out. In the end of the sarcophagus was a dark, huddled human body, the back hunched upward and the legs hideously cramped, as if some one had hastily shoved it through the aperture, head first.

Markham stood bending forward like a person paralyzed in the midst of an action.

Vance's quiet but insistent voice broke the tension of our horror.

"Hold your light steady, Sergeant. And you, Markham, lend me a hand. But be careful. Don't touch the jack..."

With great caution they reached into the sarcophagus and turned the body until the head was toward the widest point of the opening. A chill ran up my spine as I watched them, for I knew that the slightest jar, or the merest touch on the jack, would bring the massive granite lid down upon them. Heath, too, realized this—I could see the glistening beads of sweat on his forehead as he watched the dangerous operation with fearful eyes.

Slowly the body emerged through the small opening, and when the feet had passed over the edge of the sarcophagus and clattered to the floor, the flash-light went out, and Heath sprawled back on his haunches with a convulsive gasp.

"Hell! I musta stumbled, Mr. Vance," he muttered. (I liked the Sergeant even more after that episode.)

Markham stood looking down at the inert body in stupefaction.

"*Scarlett!*" he exclaimed in a voice of complete incredulity.

Vance merely nodded, and bent over the prostrate figure. Scarlett's face was cyanosed, due to insufficient oxygenation of the blood; his eyes were set in a fixed bulging stare; and there was a crust formation of blood at his nostrils. Vance put his ear on the man's chest and took his wrist in one hand to feel the pulse. Then he drew out his gold cigarette-case and held it before Scarlett's lips. After a glance at the case he turned excitedly to Heath.

"The ambulance, Sergeant! Hurry! Scarlett's still alive..."

Heath dashed up the stairs and disappeared into the front hall.

Markham regarded Vance intently.

"I don't understand this," he said huskily.

"Nor do I—entirely." Vance's eyes were on Scarlett. "I advised him to keep away from here. He, too, knew the danger, and yet... You remember Rider Haggard's dedication of 'Allan Quartermain' to his son, wherein he spoke of the highest rank to which one can attain—the state and dignity of an English gentleman?*... Scarlett was an English gentleman. Knowing the peril, he came here to-night. He thought he might end the tragedy."

Markham was stunned and puzzled.

"We've got to take some sort of action—now."

"Yes..." Vance was deeply concerned. "But the difficulties! There's no evidence. We're helpless... Unless—" He stopped short.

---

* *The actual dedication reads: "I inscribe this book of adventure to my son, Arthur John Rider Haggard, in the hope that in days to come he, and many other boys whom I shall never know, may in the acts and thoughts of Allan Quartermain and his companions, as herein recorded, find something to help him and them to reach to what, with Sir Henry Curtis, I hold to be the highest rank whereto we can obtain—the state and dignity of English gentlemen."*

"That hieroglyphic letter! Maybe it's here somewhere. To-night was the time; but Scarlett came unexpectedly. I wonder if he knew about that, too…" Vance's eyes drifted thoughtfully into space, and for several moments he stood rigid. Then he suddenly went to the sarcophagus and, striking a match, looked inside.

"Nothing." There was dire disappointment in his tone. "And yet, it should be here…" He straightened up. "Perhaps… yes! That, too, would be logical."

He knelt down beside the unconscious man and began going through his pockets. Scarlett's coat was buttoned, and it was not until Vance had reached into the inner breast pocket that his search was rewarded. He drew out a crumpled sheet of yellow scratch paper of the kind on which Salveter's Egyptian exercise had been written, and after one glance at it thrust it into his own pocket.

Heath appeared at the door.

"O.K.," he called down, "I told 'em to rush it."

"How long will it take?" Vance asked.

"Not more'n ten minutes. I called Headquarters; and they'll relay it to the local station. They generally pick up the cop on the beat—but that don't delay things. I'll wait here at the door for 'em."

"Just a moment." Vance wrote something on the back of an envelope and handed it up to Heath. "Call Western Union and get this telegram off."

Heath took the message, read it, whistled softly, and went out into the hall.

"I'm wiring Salveter at New Haven to leave the train at New London and return to New York," Vance explained to Markham. "He'll be able to catch the Night Express at New London, and will get here early to-morrow morning."

Markham looked at him shrewdly.

"You think he'll come?"

"Oh, yes."

When the ambulance arrived, Heath escorted the interne, the blue-uniformed driver and the police officer into the museum. The interne, a pink-faced youth with a serious brow, bowed to Markham and knelt beside Scarlett. After a superficial examination, he beckoned to the driver.

"Go easy with his head."

The man, assisted by the officer, lifted Scarlett to the stretcher.

"How bad is he, doctor?" Markham asked anxiously.

"Pretty bad, sir." The interne shook his head pompously. "A messy fracture at the base of the skull. Cheyne-Stokes breathing. If he lives, he's luckier than I'll ever be." And with a shrug he followed the stretcher out of the house.

"I'll phone the hospital later," Markham said to Vance. "If Scarlett recovers, he can supply us with evidence."

"Don't count on it," Vance discouraged him. "To-night's episode was isolated." He went to the sarcophagus and reversed the jack. Slowly the lid descended to its original position. "A bit dangerous, don't y'know, to leave it up."

Markham stood by frowning.

"Vance, what paper was that you found in Scarlett's pocket?"

"I imagine it was an incriminatin' document written in Egyptian hieroglyphs. We'll see."

He spread the paper out smoothly on the top of the sarcophagus. It was almost exactly like the letter Vance had pieced together in Bliss's study. The color of the paper was the same, and it contained four rows of hieroglyphs drawn in green ink.

Vance studied it while Markham and Heath, who had returned to the museum, and I looked on.

"Let me see how well I remember my Egyptian," he murmured. "It's been years since I did any transliterating…"

He placed his monocle in his eye and bent forward.

"*Meryet-Amûn, aha-y o er yu son maut-y en merya-y men seshem pen dya-y em yeb-y era-y en marwet mar-en yu, rekha-t khet nibet hir-sa hetpa-t na-y kheft shewa-n em debat nefra-n entot hena-y…* This is done very accurately, Markham.

The nouns and adjectives agree as to gender, and the verb endings—"

"Never mind those matters," Markham interrupted impatiently. "What does that paper say?"

"I beg of you, Markham old dear!" Vance protested. "Middle-Kingdom Egyptian is a most difficult language. Coptic and Assyrian and Greek and Sanskrit are abecedarian beside it. However, I can give you a literal translation." He began reading slowly: "'Beloved of Amûn, I stop here until comes the brother of my mother. Not do I wish that should-endure this situation. I have-placed in my heart that I should-act for the sake of our well-being. Thou shalt-know every-thing later. Thou shalt-be satisfied toward me when we are-free from what-blocks-the-way, happy-are we, thou together-with me...' Not what you'd call Harvardian. But such were the verbal idiosyncrasies of the ancient Egyptians."

"Well, it don't make sense to me," Heath commented sourly.

"But properly paraphrased it makes fiendish sense, Sergeant. Put into everyday English, it says: 'Meryt-Amen: I am waiting here for my uncle. I cannot endure this situation any longer; and I have decided to take drastic action for the sake of our happiness. You will understand everything later, and you will forgive me when we are free from all obstacles and can be happy together.' ... I say, Sergeant; does that make sense?"

"I'll tell the world!" Heath looked at Vance with an air of contemptuous criticism. "And you sent that bird Salveter to Boston!"

"He'll be back to-morrow," Vance assured him.

"But see here";—Markham's eyes were fixed on the incriminating paper—"what about that other letter you pieced together? And how did this letter get in Scarlett's pocket?"

Vance folded the paper carefully and placed it in his wallet.

"The time has come," he said slowly, "to tell you everything. It may be, when you have the facts in hand, you can

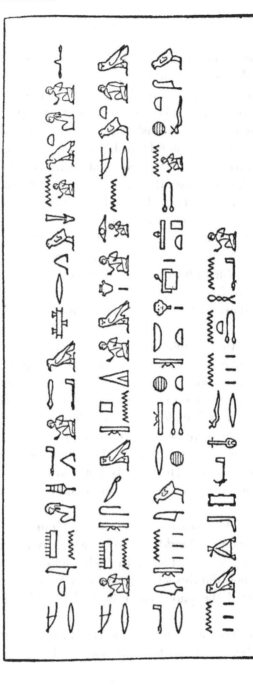

THE HIEROGLYPHIC LETTER

figure out some course of procedure. I can see legal difficulties ahead; but I now have all the evidence we can ever hope for." He was uneasy and troubled. "Scarlett's intrusion in to-night's happenings changed the murderer's plans. Anyway, I can now convince you of the incredible and abominable truth."

Markham studied him for several moments, and a startled light came in his eyes.

"*God Almighty!*" he breathed. "I see what you mean." He clicked his teeth together. "But first I must phone the hospital. There's a chance that Scarlett can help us—if he lives."

He went to the rear of the museum and mounted the spiral stairs to the study. A few minutes later he reappeared, his face dark and hopeless.

"I spoke to the doctor," he said. "There's not one chance in a thousand for Scarlett. Concussion of the brain—and suffocation. They've got the pulmotor on him now. Even if he does pull through he'll be unconscious for a week or two."

"I was afraid of that." I had rarely seen Vance so distressed. "We were too late. But—dash it all!— I couldn't have foreseen his quixotism. And I warned him…"

"Come, old man." Markham spoke with paternal kindliness. "It's not your fault. There was nothing you could have done. And you were right in keeping the truth to yourself—"

"Excuse *me*!" Heath was exasperated. "I myself ain't exactly an enemy of truth. Why can't I get in on this?"

"You can, Sergeant." Vance placed his hand on the other's shoulder. "Let's go to the drawing-room. 'And every mountain and hill shall be made low; and the crooked shall be made straight, and the rough places plain.'"

He moved toward the stairs; and we followed him.

CHAPTER TWENTY-ONE

The Murderer
(Saturday, July 14; 10.40 p.m.)

As WE ENTERED the drawing-room Brush rose. He was pale and palpably frightened.

"Why are you worried?" Vance asked.

"Suppose, sir, I should be blamed!" the man blurted. "It was I who left the front door open yesterday morning— I wanted to get some fresh air. And then you came and said something had happened to Mr. Kyle. I know I shouldn't have unlatched the door." (I realized then why he had acted in so terrified a manner.)

"You may cheer up," Vance told him. "We know who killed Mr. Kyle, and I can assure you, Brush, that the murderer didn't come in the front door."

"Thank you, sir." The words were like a sigh of relief.

"And now tell Hani to come here. Then you may go to your room."

Brush had scarcely left us when there was the sound of a key being inserted in the front door. A moment later Doctor Bliss appeared at the entrance to the drawing-room.

"Good-evening, doctor," Vance greeted him. "I hope we're not intrudin'. But there are several questions we wish to ask Hani during Mr. Salveter's absence."

"I understand," Bliss returned, with a sad nod.

"You know, then, of Salveter's excursion to Boston."

"He phoned me and asked if he might go."

Bliss looked at Vance with heavy, inquisitive eyes. "His wanting to go north at this time was most unusual," he said; "but I did not raise any objection. The atmosphere here is very depressing, and I sympathized with his desire to escape from it."

"What time did he leave the house?" Vance put the question carelessly.

"About nine. I offered to drive him to the station…"

"At nine, what? And where was he between eight and nine?"

Bliss looked unhappy.

"He was with me in the study. We were going over details regarding the reproductions of Hotepheres' tomb furniture."

"Was he with you when Mr. Scarlett arrived?"

"Yes." Bliss frowned. "Very peculiar, Scarlett's visit. He evidently wanted to talk to Salveter alone. He acted most mysteriously—treated Salveter with a sort of resentful coldness. But I continued to discuss the object of Salveter's trip north—"

"Mr. Scarlett waited?"

"Yes. He watched Salveter like a hawk. Then, when Salveter went out, Scarlett went with him."

"Ah! And you, doctor?" Vance was apparently absorbed in selecting a cigarette from his case.

"I stayed in the study."

"And that's the last you saw of either Scarlett or Salveter?"

"Yes…I went for a walk about half past nine. I looked in the museum on my way out, thinking possibly Scarlett had remained and would join me; but the room was dark. So I strolled down the avenue to Washington Square…"

"Thank you, doctor." Vance had lighted his cigarette and was smoking moodily. "We sha'n't trouble you any more to-night."

Hani entered the room.

"You wish to see me?" His manner was detached and, I thought, a trifle bored.

"Yes." Vance indicated a chair facing the table. Then he turned quickly to Bliss who was on the point of going out.

"On second thought, doctor, it may be advisable for us to question you again regarding Mr. Salveter.—Would you mind waiting in the study?"

"Not at all." Bliss shot him a comprehending glance, and went down the hall. A few moments later we heard the study door close.

Vance gave Hani a curious look, which I did not understand.

"I have something I wish to tell to Mr. Markham," he said. "Will you be good enough to stand in the hall and see that no one disturbs us?"

Hani rose.

"With pleasure, *effendi*." And he took his post outside.

Vance closed the folding doors, and coming back to the centre-table, settled himself comfortably.

"You, Markham—and you, Sergeant—were both right yesterday morning when you concluded that Doctor Bliss was guilty of murdering Kyle—"

"Say, listen!" Heath leapt to his feet. "What the hell—!"

"Oh, quite, Sergeant. Please sit down and control yourself."

"I said he killed him! And you said—"

"My word! Can't you be tranquil? You're so upsettin', Sergeant." Vance made an exasperated gesture. "I'm aware you remarked inelegantly that Bliss had 'croaked' Mr. Kyle. And I trust you have not forgotten that I said to you last night that we often arrive at the same destination at the same time—but from opposite directions."

"That was what you meant, was it?" Heath resumed his seat surlily. "Then why didn't you let me arrest him?"

"Because that's what he wanted you to do."

"I'm floundering," Heath wailed. "The world has gone nuts."

"Just a moment, Sergeant." Markham spoke peremptorily. "I'm beginning to understand this affair. It's not insane in the least.—Let Mr. Vance continue."

Heath started to expostulate, but instead made a grimace of resignation, and began chewing on his cigar.

Vance regarded him sympathetically.

"I knew, Sergeant—or at least I strongly suspected—within five minutes after entering the museum yesterday morning, that Bliss was guilty. Scarlett's story about the appointment gave me the first clew. Bliss's telephone call in the presence of every one and his remarks about the new shipment struck me as fitting in perfectly with a preconceived plan. Then, when I saw the various clews, I felt positive they had been planted by Bliss himself. With him it was not only a matter of pointing suspicion to himself, but—on second view—of throwing suspicion on another. Fortunately he overstepped the grounds of plausibility; for had some one else committed the crime, the planted clews would have been less numerous and less obvious. Consequently, I leapt to the conclusion that Bliss had murdered Kyle and had, at the same time, striven to lead us to think that he was the victim of a plot—"

"But, Mr. Vance," interrupted Heath, "you said—"

"*I did not say one word to give you the definite impression that I exonerated Bliss. Not once did I say he was innocent...* Think back. You'll remember I said only that the clews did not ring true—that things were not what they seemed. I knew the clews were traps, set by Bliss to deceive us. And I also knew—as Mr. Markham knew—that if we arrested Bliss on the outward evidence, it would be impossible to convict him."

Markham nodded thoughtfully.

"Yes, Sergeant. Mr. Vance is quite correct. I can't recall a single remark of his inconsistent with his belief in Bliss's guilt."

"Although I knew Bliss was guilty," Vance continued, "I didn't know what his ultimate object was or whom he was trying to involve. I suspected it was Salveter—though it might have been either Scarlett or Hani or Mrs. Bliss. I at once saw the necessity of determining the real victim of his plot. So I pretended to fall in with the obvious situation. I couldn't let Bliss think that I suspected him,—my only hope lay in pretending that I believed some one else was guilty. But I did avoid the traps set for us. I wanted Bliss to plant other clews against his victim and perhaps give us some workable evidence. That was why I begged you to play a waiting game with me."

"But what was Bliss's idea in having himself arrested?" Markham asked. "There was danger in that."

"Very little. He probably believed that even before an indictment he or his lawyer could persuade you of his innocence and of Salveter's guilt. Or, if he had been held for trial, he was almost sure of an acquittal, and would then be entirely safe on the caressin' principle of double jeopardy, or *autrefois acquit*... No, he was running no great risk. And remember, too, he was playing a big game. Once he had been arrested, he would have felt justified in pointing openly to Salveter as the murderer and plotter. Hence I fought against your arresting him, for *it was the very thing he wanted*. As long as he thought he was free from suspicion, there was no point in his defending himself at Salveter's expense. And, in order to involve Salveter, he was forced to plant more evidence, to concoct other schemes. And it was on these schemes that I counted for evidence."

"I'm sunk!" The ashes of Heath's cigar toppled off and fell over his waistcoat, but he didn't notice them.

"But, Sergeant, I gave you many warnings. And there was the motive. I'm convinced that Bliss knew there was no more financial help coming from Kyle; and there's nothing he wouldn't have done to insure a continuation of his researches. Furthermore, he was intensely jealous of Salveter: he knew Mrs. Bliss loved the young cub."

"But why," put in Markham, "did he not merely kill Salveter?"

"Oh, I say! The money was a cardinal factor,—he wanted Meryt-Amen to inherit Kyle's wealth. His second'ry object was to eliminate Salveter from Meryt-Amen's heart: he had no reason for killing him. Therefore he planned subtly to disqualify him by making it appear that Salveter not only had murdered his uncle but had tried to send another to the chair for it."

Vance slowly lighted a fresh cigarette.

"Bliss was killing three birds with one stone. He was making himself a martyr in Meryt-Amen's eyes; he was eliminating Salveter; he was insuring his wife a fortune with which he could continue his excavations. Few murders have had so powerful a triple motive... And one of the tragic things is that Mrs. Bliss more than half believed in Salveter's guilt. She suffered abominably. You recall how she took the attitude that she wanted the murderer brought to justice. And she feared all the time that it was Salveter..."

"Still and all," said Heath, "Bliss didn't seem very anxious to get Salveter mixed up in the affair."

"Ah, but he was, Sergeant. He was constantly involving Salveter while pretending not to. A feigned reluctance, as it were. He couldn't be too obvious about it—that would have given his game away... You remember my question of who had charge of the medical supplies. Bliss stuttered, as if trying to shield some one. Very clever, don't y'know."

"But if you knew this—," Heath began.

"I didn't know *all* of it, Sergeant. I knew only that Bliss was guilty. I was not sure that Salveter was the object of his plot. Therefore I had to investigate and learn the truth."

"Anyhow, I was right in the first place when I said Bliss was guilty," Heath declared doggedly.

"Of course you were, Sergeant." Vance spoke almost affectionately. "And I felt deuced bad to have to appear to contradict you." He rose and, going to Heath, held out his hand. "Will you forgive me?"

"Well...maybe." Heath's eyes belied his gruff tone as he grasped Vance's hand. "Anyhow, I was right!"

Vance grinned and sat down.

"The plot itself was simple," he continued after a moment. "Bliss phoned Kyle in the presence of every one and made the appointment for eleven. He specifically mentioned the new shipment, and suggested that Kyle should come early. You see, he had decided on the murder—and on the whole plot, in fact—when he made the fatal rendezvous. And he deliberately left the scarab pin on the study desk. After killing Kyle he placed the pin and the financial report near the body. And note, Markham, that Salveter had access to both objects. Moreover, Bliss knew that Salveter was in the habit of going to the museum after breakfast; and he timed Kyle's appointment so that Salveter and his uncle would probably meet. He sent Salveter to the Metropolitan to get him out of the house while he himself killed Kyle. And he also fixed the statue of Sakhmet so that it would look like a trap. The murderer could easily have come back at any time before we arrived and planted the pin and the report and made the foot-prints—provided of course Bliss had been asleep with the opium..."

Heath sat upright and squinted at Vance.

"That trap was only a stall?" he asked indignantly.

"Nothing else, Sergeant. It was set up after the murder, so that even if Salveter had had an alibi, he still could have been guilty. Furthermore, the possibility of Kyle's having been killed by an absent person was another point in favor of Bliss. Why should Bliss have made a death-trap when he had every opportunity to kill Kyle by direct contact? The trap was merely another counter-clew."

"But the pencil used in the trap," interposed Markham. "It was not the kind Salveter used."

"My dear Markham! Bliss used one of his own pencils for the 'upright' in order to create another clew against himself. A man actually planning a death-trap is not going to use his own pencil,—he would use the pencil of the man he was trying to involve. The doctor therefore used his own pencil—*in order to throw suspicion elsewhere*. But the trap did not fool me. It was too fortuitous. A murderer would not have taken such a chance. The falling statue might not have fallen exactly on Kyle's head. And another thing: a man struck in that fashion is not likely to fall in the position we found Kyle, with his head just beneath the place where the statue struck him, and with his arms stretched out. When I made my experiment, and the statue fell exactly where Kyle's head had been, I realized how unlikely it was that he had actually been killed by the statue falling." Vance's eyes twinkled. "I did not raise the point at the time, for I wanted you to believe in the death-trap."

"Right again!" Heath slapped his forehead dramatically with his palm. "And I never thought of it!... Sure, I'll forgive you, Mr. Vance!"

"The truth is, Sergeant, I did everything I could to make you overlook the inconsistency of it. And Mr. Markham didn't see it either.* As a matter of fact, Kyle was killed while he was looking into the cabinet, by a blow from some one behind him. I have an idea, too, that one of those heavy flint or porphyry maces was used. His body was arranged in the position we found it, and the statue of Sakhmet was then dropped on his skull, obliterating the evidence of the first blow."

"But suppose," objected Markham, "you hadn't seen the loose ring on the curtain?"

"The trap was arranged so that we would discover it. If we had overlooked it, Bliss would have called our attention to it."

"But the finger-prints—" began Heath, in a kind of daze.

---

*   *Nor did I. But while this record of mine was running serially in the* American Magazine *several readers wrote to me pointing out the inconsistency.*

"They were purposely left on the statue. More evidence, d'ye see, against Bliss. But he had an alibi in reserve. His first explanation was so simple and so specious:—he had moved Sakhmet because it wasn't quite straight. But the second explanation why there were no other finger-prints on Sakhmet was to come later, after his arrest—to wit, no one had actually wielded the statue: it was a death-trap set by Salveter!"

Vance made an open-handed gesture.

"Bliss covered every clew against himself with a stronger clew pointing to Salveter... Regard, for instance, the evidence of the foot-prints. Superficially these pointed to Bliss. But there was the omnipresent counter-clew—namely: he was wearing bedroom slippers yesterday morning, and only one tennis shoe was to be found in the study. The other tennis shoe was in his room, *exactly where he said he had left it the night before.* Bliss simply brought one shoe down-stairs, made the foot-prints in the blood, and placed the shoe in the waste-basket. He wanted us to find the prints and to discover the shoe. And we did— that is, the Sergeant did. His answer to the foot-prints, after his arrest, would merely have been that some one who had access to his room had taken one tennis shoe down-stairs and made the tracks to involve him."

Markham nodded.

"Yes," he said; "I'd have been inclined to exonerate him, especially after the discovery of opium in his coffee cup."

"Ah, that opium! The perfect alibi! What jury would have convicted him after the evidence of the opium in his coffee? They would have regarded him as the victim of a plot. And the District Attorney's office would have come in for much severe criticism... And how simple the opium episode was! Bliss took the can from the cabinet, extracted what he needed for the ruse, and placed the powder in the bottom of his coffee cup."

"You didn't think he had been narcotized?"

"No. I knew he hadn't. A narcotic contracts the pupils; and Bliss's were distended with excitement. I knew he was pretending, and that made me suspect I'd find a drug in his coffee."

"But what about the can?" Heath put the question. "I never did get that can business straight. You sent Hani—"

"Now, Sergeant!" Vance spoke good-naturedly. "I knew where the can was, and I merely wanted to ascertain how much Hani knew."

"But I see the Sergeant's point," Markham put in. "We don't know that the opium can was in Salveter's room."

"Oh, don't we, now?" Vance turned toward the hall. "Hani!"

The Egyptian opened the sliding door.

"I say;"—Vance looked straight into the man's eyes—"I'm dashed admirin' of your deceptive attitude, but we could bear some facts for a change.—Where did you find the opium tin?"

"*Effendi*, there is no longer any need for dissimulation. You are a man of profound wisdom, and I trust you. The tin was hidden in Mr. Salveter's room."

"Thanks awfully." Vance was almost brusque. "And now return to the hall."

Hani went out and softly closed the door.

"And by not going down to breakfast yesterday morning," Vance continued, "Bliss knew that his wife and Salveter would be in the breakfast-room alone, and that Salveter might easily have put the opium in the coffee..."

"But," asked Markham, "if you knew Bliss put the opium in his own coffee, why all the interest in the samovar?"

"I had to be sure who it was Bliss's plot was aimed at. He was trying to make it appear that *he* was the victim of the plot; and since his object was to involve some one else, I knew the real victim would have had to have access to the coffee yesterday morning."

Heath nodded ponderously.

"That's easy enough. The old boy was pretending some one had fed him knock-out drops, but if the bird he was aiming at couldn't have fed him the drops, his plot would have gone blooey... But look here, Mr. Vance;"—he suddenly remembered something—"what was the idea of the doc's trying to escape?"

"It was a perfectly logical result of what had gone before," Vance explained. "After we had refused to arrest him, he began to worry. Y'see, he yearned to be arrested; and we disappointed him frightfully. Sittin' in his room, he got to planning. How could he make us re-order his arrest and thus give him the chance to point out all the evidences of Salveter's heinous plot against him? He decided to attempt an escape. That gesture, he figured, would surely revive suspicion against him. So he simply went out, drew his money openly from the bank, taxied to the Grand Central Station, asked loudly about trains to Montreal, and then stood conspicuously by the gate waiting for the train... He knew that Guilfoyle was following him; for, had he really intended making his escape, you may rest assured Guilfoyle would never have traced him. You, Sergeant, accepted Bliss's action at its face value; and I was afraid that his silly disappearance would produce the very result he intended—namely, his re-arrest. That was why I argued against it so passionately."

Vance leaned back but did not relax. There was a rigid alertness in his attitude.

"And because you did not manacle him, Sergeant," he continued, "he was forced to take a further step. He had to build up a case against Salveter. So he staged the drama with the dagger. He deliberately sent Salveter to the study to get a memorandum-book in the desk—where the dagger was kept..."

"And the sheath!" exclaimed Markham.

"Oh, quite. That was the real clew against Salveter. Having put the sheath in Salveter's room, Bliss suggested to us that we might find the would-be assassin by locating the sheath. I knew where it was the moment he so helpfully mentioned it; so I gave Hani a chance to lie about it..."

"You mean Hani didn't find the sheath in the hall?"

"Of course not."

Vance again called Hani from the hall.

"Where did you find the sheath of the royal dagger?" he asked.

Hani answered without a moment's hesitation.

"In Mr. Salveter's room, *effendi*—as you well know."

Vance nodded.

"And by the by, Hani, has any one approached this door to-night?"

"No, *effendi*. The doctor is still in his study."

Vance dismissed him with a gesture, and went on:

"Y'see, Markham, Bliss put the sheath in Salveter's room, and then threw the dagger into the headboard of his bed. He phoned me and, when we arrived, told an elaborate but plausible tale of having been assaulted by an *inconnu*."

"He was a damn good actor," Heath commented.

"Yes—in the main. But there was one psychological point he overlooked. If he had actually been the victim of a murderous attack he would not have gone down-stairs alone in the dark to phone me. He would have first roused the house."*

"That's reasonable." Markham had become impatient. "But you said something about the picture not being complete—"

"The letter!" Vance sat up and threw away his cigarette. "That was the missing factor. I couldn't understand why the forged hieroglyphic letter didn't show up last night,—it was the perfect opportunity. But it was nowhere in evidence; and that's what troubled me... However, when I found Scarlett working in the museum, I understood. The doctor, I'm convinced, intended to plant the forged letter—which he had placed temporarily in the desk-table drawer—in Meryt-Amen's room or some place where we'd find it. But when he looked into the museum through the study door he saw Scarlett at work at the desk-table. So he let the letter go, reserving it for future use— in case we didn't arrest Salveter after the dagger episode. And when I deliberately avoided the clews he had prepared against

---

* *It will be recalled that in the Greene murder case the murderer, pretending to be frightened at the sinister danger lurking in the dim corridors of the old Greene mansion, made a similar error in psychological judgment by descending to the pantry in the middle of the night for no other reason than to gratify a mild appetite for food.*

Salveter, I knew the letter would appear very soon. I was afraid Scarlett might in some way block Bliss's scheme, so I warned him to keep away from the house. I don't know what more I could have done."

"Nor I." Markham's tone was consoling. "Scarlett should have followed your advice."

"But he didn't." Vance sighed regretfully.

"You think, then, that Scarlett suspected the truth?"

"Undoubtedly. And he suspected it early in the game. But he wasn't sure enough to speak out. He was afraid he might be doing the doctor an injustice; and, being an English gentleman, he kept silent. My belief is, he got to worrying about the situation and finally went to Bliss—"

"But something must have convinced him."

"The dagger, Markham. Bliss made a grave error in that regard. Scarlett and Bliss were the only two persons who knew about that smuggled weapon. And when I showed it to Scarlett and informed him it had been used in an attempt on Bliss's life, he knew pretty conclusively that Bliss had concocted the whole tale."

"And he came here to-night to confront Bliss...?"

"Exactly. He realized that Bliss was trying to involve Salveter; and he wanted to let Bliss know that his monstrous scheme was seen through. He came here to protect an innocent man—despite the fact that Salveter was his rival, as it were, for the affections of Meryt-Amen. That would be like Scarlett..." Vance looked sad. "When I sent Salveter to Boston I believed I had eliminated every possibility of danger. But Scarlett felt he had to take matters in his own hands. His action was fine, but ill-advised. The whole trouble was, it gave Bliss the opportunity he'd been waiting for. When he couldn't get the forged letter from the museum last night, and when we declined his invitation to find the sheath in Salveter's room, it was necessary for him to play his ace—the forged letter."

"Yes, yes. I see that. But just where did Scarlett fit?"

"When Scarlett came here to-night Bliss no doubt listened to his accusation diplomatically, and then on some pretext or other got him into the museum. When Scarlett was off guard Bliss struck him on the head—probably with one of those maces in the end cabinet—and put him in the sarcophagus. It was a simple matter for him to get the jack from his car, which he keeps parked in the street outside,—you recall that he offered to drive Salveter to the station..."

"But the letter?"

"Can't you see how everything fitted? The attack on Scarlett took place between eight and eight-thirty. Salveter was probably up-stairs bidding adieu to Mrs. Bliss. At any rate, he was in the house, and therefore could have been Scarlett's murderer. In order to make it appear that Salveter *was actually the murderer of Scarlett* Bliss crumpled up the forged telltale letter and stuck it in Scarlett's pocket. He wanted to make it appear that Scarlett had come to the house to-night to confront Salveter, had mentioned the letter he'd found in the desk-table drawer, and had been killed by Salveter."

"But why wouldn't Salveter have taken the letter?"

"The assumption would have been that Salveter didn't know that Scarlett had the letter in his pocket."

"What I want to know," put in Heath, "is how Bliss found out about Salveter's original letter."

"That point is easily explained, Sergeant." Vance drew out his cigarette-case. "Salveter undoubtedly returned to the museum yesterday morning, as he told us, and was working on his letter when Kyle entered. He then put the letter in the table-drawer, and went to the Metropolitan Museum on his errand. Bliss, who was probably watching him through a crack in the study door, saw him put the paper away, and later took it out to see what it was. Being an indiscreet letter to Meryt-Amen, it gave Bliss an idea. He took it to his study and rewrote it, making it directly incriminating; and then tore up the original. When I learned that the letter had disappeared I was worried, for I suspected that Bliss had taken it. And when

I saw it had been destroyed and thrown away, I was convinced we would find another letter. But since I had the original, I believed that the forged letter would, when it appeared, give us evidence against Bliss."

"So that's why you were so interested in those three words?"

"Yes, Sergeant. I hardly thought Bliss would use *tem* and *was* and *ankh* in rewriting the letter, for he couldn't have known that Salveter had told us about the letter and specifically mentioned these three words. And not one of the three words was in the forgery."

"But a handwriting expert—"

"Oh, I say, Sergeant! Don't be so *naïf*. A handwriting expert is a romantic scientist even when the writing is English script and familiar to him. And all his rules are based on chirographic idiosyncrasies. No art expert can tell with surety who drew a picture—and Egyptian writing is mostly pictures. Forged Michelangelo drawings, for instance, are being sold by clever dealers constantly. The only approach in such matters is an æsthetic one—and there is no æsthetics in Egyptian hieroglyphs."

Heath made a wry face.

"Well, if the forged letter couldn't be admitted as evidence, what was the doctor's idea?"

"Don't you see, Sergeant, that even if the letter couldn't be absolutely identified with Salveter, it would have made every one believe that Salveter was guilty and had escaped a conviction on a legal technicality. Certainly Meryt-Amen would have believed that Salveter wrote the letter; and that was what Bliss wanted."

Vance turned to Markham.

"It's a legal point which really doesn't matter. Salveter might not have been convicted; but Bliss's plot would none the less have succeeded. With Kyle dead, Bliss would have had access to one-half of Kyle's fortune—in his wife's name, to be sure—and Meryt-Amen would have repudiated Salveter. Thus

Bliss would have won every trick. And even legally Salveter might have been convicted had it not been for Hani's removal of two direct clews from Salveter's room—the opium can and the sheath. Furthermore, there was the letter in Scarlett's pocket."

"But, Vance, how would the letter have been found?" Markham asked. "If you had not suspected the plot and looked for Scarlett's body, it might have remained in the sarcophagus almost indefinitely."

"No." Vance shook his head. "Scarlett was to have remained in the sarcophagus only for a couple of days. When it was discovered to-morrow that he was missing Bliss would probably have found the body for us, along with the letter."

He looked questioningly at Markham.

"How are we going to connect Bliss with the crime, since Salveter was in the house at the time of the attack?"

"If Scarlett should get well—"

"If!... Just so. But suppose he shouldn't—and the chances are against him. Then what? Scarlett at most could only testify that Bliss had made an abortive and unsuccessful attack on him. True, you might convict him for felonious assault, but it would leave Kyle's murder still unsolved. And if Bliss said that Scarlett attacked him and that he struck Scarlett in self-defense, you'd have a difficult time convicting him even for assault."

Markham rose and walked up and down the room. Then Heath asked a question.

"How does this Ali Baba fit into the picture, Mr. Vance?"

"Hani knew from the first what had happened; and he was shrewd enough to see the plot that Bliss had built up about Salveter. He loved Salveter and Meryt-Amen, and he wanted them to be happy. What could he do except lend his every energy to protecting them? And he has certainly done this, Sergeant. Egyptians are not like Occidentals. It was against his nature to come out frankly and tell us what he suspected. Hani played a clever game—the only game he could have played. He never believed in the vengeance of Sakhmet. He used his superstitious logomachy to cover up the truth. He fought with words for Salveter's safety."

Markham halted in front of Vance.

"The thing is incredible! I have never known a murderer like Bliss."

"Oh, don't give him too much credit." Vance lighted the cigarette he had been holding for the past five minutes. "He frightfully overdid the clews: he made them too glaring. Therein lay his weakness."

"Still," said Markham, "if you hadn't come into the case I'd have brought a murder charge against him."

"And you would have played into his hands. Because I didn't want you to, I appeared to argue against his guilt."

"A palimpsest!" Markham commented after a pause.

Vance took a deep draw on his cigarette.

"Exactly. *Palimpsestos*—'again rub smooth.' First came the true story of the crime, carefully indicated. Then it was erased, and the story of the murder, with Salveter as the villain, was written over it. This, too, was erased, and the original story—in grotesque outline and filled with inconsistencies and loopholes—was again written. We were supposed to read the third version, become sceptical about it, and find the evidences of Salveter's guilt between the lines. My task was to push through to the first and original version—the twice written-over truth."

"And you did it, Mr. Vance!" Heath had risen and gone toward the door. "The doc is in the study, Chief. I'll take him to Headquarters myself."

CHAPTER TWENTY-TWO

The Judgment of Anûbis
(Saturday, July 14; 11 p.m.)

"**I** SAY, SERGEANT! Don't be rash." Despite the drawling quality of Vance's tone Heath halted abruptly. "If I were you I'd take a bit of legal advice from Mr. Markham before arresting the doctor."

"Legal advice be damned!"

"Oh, quite. In principle I agree with you. But there's no need to be temerarious about these little matters. Caution is always good."

Markham, who was standing beside Vance, lifted his head.

"Sit down, Sergeant," he ordered. "We can't arrest a man on theory." He walked to the fireplace and back. "This thing has to be thought out. There's no evidence against Bliss. We couldn't hold him an hour if a clever lawyer got busy on the case."

"And Bliss knows it," said Vance.

"But he killed Kyle!" Heath expostulated.

"Granted." Markham sat down beside the table and rested his chin in his hands. "But I've nothing tangible to present to a grand jury. And, as Mr. Vance says, even if Scarlett should recover I'd have only an assault charge against Bliss."

"What wallops me, sir," moaned Heath, "is how a guy can commit murder almost before our very eyes, and get away with it. It ain't reasonable."

"Ah, but there's little that's reasonable in this fantastic and ironical world, Sergeant," remarked Vance.

"Well, anyhow," returned Heath, "I'd arrest that bird in a minute and take my chances at making the charge stick."

"I feel the same way," Markham said. "But no matter how convinced we are of the truth, we must be able to produce conclusive evidence. And this fiend has covered all the evidence so cleverly that any jury in the country would acquit him, even if we could hold him for trial—which is highly dubious."

Vance sighed and stood up.

"The law!" He spoke with unusual fervor. "And the rooms in which this law is put on public exhibition are called courts of justice. *Justice!*—oh, my precious aunt! *Summum jus, summa injuria.* How can there be justice, or even intelligence, in echolalia?... Here we three are—a District Attorney; a Sergeant of the Homicide Bureau; and a lover of Brahms' B-flat piano concerto—with a known murderer within fifty feet of us; and we're helpless! Why? Because this elaborate invention of imbeciles, called the law, has failed to provide for the extermination of a dangerous and despicable criminal, who not only murdered his benefactor in cold blood, but attempted to kill another decent man, and then endeavored to saddle an innocent third man with both crimes so that he could continue digging up ancient and venerated corpses!... No wonder Hani detests him. At heart Bliss is a ghoul; and Hani is an honorable and intelligent man."

"I admit the law is imperfect," Markham interrupted tartly. "But your dissertation is hardly helpful. We're confronted with a terrible problem, and a way must be found to handle it."

Vance still stood before the table, his eyes fixed on the door.

"But your law will never solve it," he said. "You can't convict Bliss; you don't even dare arrest him. He could make you the laughing-stock of the country if you tried it. And furthermore, he'd become a sort of persecuted hero who had been hounded by an incompetent and befuddled police, who had unjustly pounced on him in a moment of groggy desperation in order to save their more or less classic features."

Vance took a deep draw on his cigarette.

"Markham old dear, I'm inclined to think the gods of ancient Egypt were more intelligent than Solon, Justinian, and all the other law-givers combined. Hani was spoofing about the vengeance of Sakhmet; but, after all, that solar-disked lady would be just as effective as your silly statutes. Mythological ideas are largely nonsense; but are they more nonsensical than the absurdities of present-day law?...."

"For God's sake, be still." Markham was irritable.

Vance looked at him in troubled concern.

"Your hands are tied by the technicalities of a legalistic system; and, as a result, a creature like Bliss is to be turned loose on the world. Moreover, a harmless chap like Salveter is to be put under suspicion and ruined. Also, Meryt-Amen—a courageous lady—"

"I realize all that." Markham raised himself, an agonized look on his face. "And yet, Vance, there's not one piece of convincing evidence against Bliss."

"Most distressin'. Your only hope seems to be that the eminent doctor will meet with a sudden and fatal accident. Such things do happen, don't y'know."

Vance smoked for a moment.

"If only Hani's gods had the supernatural power attributed to them!" he sighed. "How deuced simple! And really, Anûbis hasn't shown up at all well in this affair. He's been excruciatingly lazy. As the god of the underworld—"

"That's enough!" Markham rose. "Have a little sense of propriety. Being an æsthete without responsibilities is no doubt delightful, but the world's work must go on…"

"Oh, by all means." Vance seemed wholly indifferent to the other's outburst. "I say, you might draw up a new law altering the existing rules of evidence, and present it to the legislature. The only difficulty would be that, by the time those intellectual Sandows got through debating and appointing committees, you and I and the Sergeant and Bliss would have passed forever down the dim corridors of time."

Markham slowly turned toward Vance. His eyes were mere slits.

"What's behind this childish garrulity?" he demanded. "You've got something on your mind."

Vance seated himself on the edge of the table and, putting out his cigarette, thrust his hands deep into his pockets.

"Markham," he said, with serious deliberation, "you know, as well as I, that Bliss is outside the law, and that there's no human way to convict him. The only means by which he can be brought to book is trickery."

"Trickery?" Markham was momentarily indignant.

"Oh, nothing reprehensible," Vance answered lightly, taking out another cigarette. "Consider, Markham…" And he launched out into a detailed recapitulation of the case. I could not understand the object of his wordy repetitions, for they seemed to have little bearing on the crucial point at issue. And Markham, also, was puzzled. Several times he attempted to interrupt, but Vance held up his hand imperatively and continued with his résumé.

After ten minutes Markham refused to be silenced.

"Come to the point, Vance," he said somewhat angrily. "You've gone over all this before. Have you—or haven't you— any suggestion?"

"Yes, I have a suggestion." Vance spoke earnestly. "It's a psychological experiment; and there is a chance that it'll prove effective. I believe that if Bliss were confronted suddenly with what we know, and if a little forceful chicanery were used on him, he might be surprised into an admission that would give you a hold on him. He doesn't know we found Scarlett in the sarcophagus, and we might pretend that we have got an incriminatin' statement from the poor chap. We might go so far as to tell him that Mrs. Bliss is thoroughly convinced of the truth; for if he believes that his plot has failed and that there is no hope of his continuing his excavations, he may even confess everything. Bliss is a colossal egoist, and, if cornered, might blurt out the truth and boast of his cleverness. And you must admit that your one chance of shipping the old codger to the executioner lies in a confession."

"Chief, couldn't we arrest the guy on the evidence he planted against himself?" Heath asked irritably. "There was that scarab pin, and the bloody foot-marks and the finger-prints—"

"No, no, Sergeant." Markham was impatient. "He has covered himself at every point. And the moment we arrested him he'd turn on Salveter. All we'd achieve would be the ruination of an innocent man and the unhappiness of Mrs. Bliss."

Heath capitulated.

"Yeah, I can see that," he said sourly, after a moment. "But this situation slays me. I've known some clever crooks in my day; but this bird Bliss has 'em all beat... Why not take Mr. Vance's suggestion?"

Markham halted in his nervous pacing, and set his jaw.

"I guess we'll have to." He fixed his gaze on Vance. "But don't handle him with silk gloves."

"Really, now, I never wear 'em. Chamois, yes—on certain occasions. And in winter I'm partial to pigskin and reindeer. But silk! Oh, my word!..."

He went to the folding door and threw it open. Hani stood just outside in the hall, with folded arms, a silent, watchful sentinel.

"Has the doctor left the study?" Vance asked.

"No, *effendi*." Hani's eyes looked straight ahead.

"Good!" Vance started down the hall. "Come, Markham. Let's see what a bit of extra-legal persuasion will do."

Markham and Heath and I followed him. He did not knock on the study door, but threw it open unceremoniously.

"Oh, I say! Something's amiss." Vance's comment came simultaneously with our realization that the study was empty. "Dashed queer." He went to the steel door leading to the spiral stairs, and opened it. "No doubt the doctor is communin' with his treasures." He passed through the door and descended the steps, the rest of us trailing along.

Vance drew up at the foot of the stairs and put his hand to his forehead.

"We'll never interview Bliss again in this world," he said in a low voice.

There was no need for him to explain. In the corner opposite, in almost the exact place where we had found Kyle's body the preceding day, Bliss lay sprawled face downward in a pool of blood. Across the back of his crushed skull stretched the life-sized statue of Anûbis. The heavy figure of the underworld god had apparently fallen on him as he leaned over his precious items in the cabinet before which he had murdered Kyle. The coincidence was so staggering that none of us was able to speak for several moments. We stood, in a kind of paralyzed awe, looking down on the body of the great Egyptologist.

Markham was the first to break the silence.

"It's incredible!" His voice was strained and unnatural. "There's a divine retribution in this."

"Oh, doubtless." Vance moved to the feet of the statue and bent over. "However, I don't go in for mysticism myself. I'm an empiricist—same like Weininger said the English are."* He

---

*   *Vance was here referring to the famous passage in the Chapter—*
"Das Judentum"—in Otto Weininger's "Geschlecht und Charakter":
"Der Engländer hat dem Deutschen als tüchtiger Empiriker, als Realpolitiker im Praktischen wie im Theoretischen, imponiert, aber damit ist seine Wichtigkeit für die Philosophie auch erschöpft. Es hat noch nie einen tieferen Denker gegeben, der beim Empirismus stehen geblieben ist; und noch nie einen Engländer, der über ihn selbstständig hinausgekommen wäre."

adjusted his monocle. "Ah!... Sorry to disappoint you, and all that. But there's nothing supernatural about the demise of the doctor. Behold, Markham, the broken ankles of Anûbis... The situation is quite obvious. While the doctor was leaning over his treasures, he jarred the statue in some way, and it toppled over on him."

We all bent forward. The heavy base of the statue of Anûbis stood where it had been when we first saw it; but the figure, from the ankles up, had broken off.

"You see," Vance was saying, pointing to the base, "the ankles are very slender, and the statue is made of limestone— a rather fragile substance. The ankles no doubt were cracked in shipping, and the tremendous weight of the body weakened the flaw."

Heath inspected the statue closely.

"That's what happened, all right," he remarked, straightening up... "I ain't had many breaks in my life, Chief," he added to Markham with feigned jauntiness; "but I never want a better one than this: Mr. Vance mighta lured the doc into a confession—and he mighta failed. Now we got nothing to worry about."

"Quite true." Markham nodded vaguely. He was still under the influence of the astounding change in the situation. "I'm leaving you in charge, Sergeant. You'd better call the local ambulance and get the Medical Examiner. Phone me at home as soon as the routine work is finished. I'll take care of the reporters in the morning... The case is on the shelf, thank God!"

He stood for some time, his eyes fixed on the body. He looked almost haggard, but I knew a great weight had been taken off of his mind by Bliss's unexpected death.

"I'll attend to everything, sir," Heath assured him. "But what about breaking the news to Mrs. Bliss?"

"Hani will do that," said Vance. He put his hand on Markham's arm. "Come along, old friend. You need sleep... Let's stagger round to my humble abode, and I'll give you a brandy-and-soda. I still have some *Napoléon*-'48 left."

"Thanks." Markham drew a deep sigh.

As we emerged into the front hall Vance beckoned to Hani.

"Very touchin', but your beloved employer has gone to Amentet to join the shades of the Pharaohs."

"He is dead?" The Egyptian lifted his eyebrows slightly.

"Oh, quite, Hani. Anûbis fell on him as he leaned over the end cabinet. A most effective death. But there was a certain justice in it. Doctor Bliss was guilty of Mr. Kyle's murder."

"You and I knew that all along, *effendi*." The man smiled wistfully at Vance. "But I fear that the doctor's death may have been my fault. When I unpacked the statue of Anûbis and set it in the corner, I noticed that the ankles were cracked. I did not tell the doctor, for I was afraid he might accuse me of having been careless, or of having deliberately injured his treasure."

"No one is going to blame you for Doctor Bliss's death," Vance said casually. "We're leaving you to inform Mrs. Bliss of the tragedy. And Mr. Salveter will be returning early to-morrow morning... *Es-salâmu alei-kum.*"

"*Ma es-salâm, effendi.*"

Vance and Markham and I passed out into the heavy night air.

"Let's walk," Vance said. "It's only a little over a mile to my apartment, and I feel the need of exercise."

Markham fell in with the suggestion, and we strolled toward Fifth Avenue in silence. When we had crossed Madison Square and passed the Stuyvesant Club, Markham spoke.

"It's almost unbelievable, Vance. It's the sort of thing that makes one superstitious. Here we were, confronted by an insoluble problem. We knew Bliss was guilty, and yet there was no way to reach him. And while we were debating the case he stepped into the museum and was accidentally killed by a falling statue on practically the same spot where he murdered Kyle... Damn it! Such things don't happen in the orderly course of the world's events. And what makes it even more fantastic is that you suggested that he might meet with an accident."

"Yes, yes. Interestin' coincidence." Vance seemed disinclined to discuss the matter.

"And that Egyptian," Markham rumbled on. "He wasn't in the least astonished when you informed him of Bliss's death. He acted almost as if he expected some such news—"

He suddenly drew up short. Vance and I stopped, too, and looked at him. His eyes were blazing.

"*Hani killed Bliss!*"

Vance sighed and shrugged.

"Of course he did, Markham. My word! I thought you understood the situation."

"Understood?" Markham was spluttering. "What do you mean?"

"It was all so obvious, don't y'know," Vance said mildly. "I realized, just as you did, that there was no chance of convicting Bliss; so I suggested to Hani how he could terminate the whole silly affair—"

"You suggested to Hani?"

"During our conversation in the drawing-room. Really, Markham old dear, I'm not in the habit of indulgin' in weird conversations about mythology unless I have a reason. I simply let Hani know there was no legal way of bringing Bliss to justice, and intimated how he could overcome the difficulty and incidentally save you from a most embarrassin' predicament…"

"But Hani was in the hall, with the door closed." Markham's indignation was rising.

"Quite so. I told him to stand outside the door. I knew very well he'd listen to us…"

"You deliberately—"

"Oh, most deliberately." Vance spread his hands in a gesture of surrender. "While I babbled to you and appeared foolish no doubt, I was really talking to Hani. Of course, I didn't know if he would grasp the opportunity or not. But he did. He equipped himself with a mace from the museum—I do hope it was the same mace that Bliss used on Kyle—and struck Bliss over the head. Then he dragged the body down the spiral stairs and laid it at the feet of Anûbis. With the mace he broke the statue's sandstone ankles, and dropped the figure over Bliss's skull. Very simple."

"And all that rambling chatter of yours in the drawing-room—"

"Was merely to keep you and Heath away in case Hani had decided to act."

Markham's eyes narrowed.

"You can't get away with that sort of thing, Vance. I'll send Hani up for murder. There'll be finger-prints—"

"Oh, no, there won't, Markham. Didn't you notice the gloves on the hat-rack? Hani is no fool. He put on the gloves before he went to the study. You'd have a harder time convicting him than you'd have had convicting Bliss. Personally, I rather admire Hani. Stout fella!"

For a time Markham was too angry to speak. Finally, however, he gave voice to an ejaculation.

"It's outrageous!"

"Of course it is," Vance agreed amiably. "So was the murder of Kyle." He lighted a cigarette and puffed on it cheerfully. "The trouble with you lawyers is, you're jealous and blood-thirsty. You wanted to send Bliss to the electric chair yourself, and couldn't; and Hani simplified everything for you. As I see it, you're merely disappointed because some one else took Bliss's life before you could get round to it... Really, y'know, Markham, you're frightfully selfish."

I feel that a short postscript will not be amiss. Markham had no difficulty, as you will no doubt remember, in convincing the press that Bliss had been guilty of the murder of Benjamin H. Kyle, and that his tragic "accidental" death had in it much of what is commonly called divine justice.

Scarlett, contrary to the doctor's prediction, recovered; but it was many weeks before he could talk rationally. Vance and I visited him in the hospital late in August, and he corroborated Vance's theory about what had happened on that fatal night in the museum. Scarlett went to England early in September,—his father had died, leaving him an involved estate in Bedfordshire.

Mrs. Bliss and Salveter were married in Nice late the following spring; and the excavations of Intef's tomb, I see from the bulletins of the Archæological Institute, are continuing. Salveter is in charge of the work, and I am rather happy to note that Scarlett is the technical expert of the expedition.

Hani, according to a recent letter from Salveter to Vance, has become reconciled to the "desecration of the tombs of his ancestors." He is still with Meryt-Amen and Salveter, and I'm inclined to think that his personal love for these two young people is stronger than his national prejudices.